# The Secret Mantra

**Other titles by David Michie**

**Fiction**

**The Dalai Lama's Cat series**

*The Dalai Lama's Cat*

*The Art of Purring*

*The Power of Meow*

*The Four Paws of Spiritual Success*

**Matt Lester Spiritual Thrillers**

*The Magician of Lhasa*

*The Secret Mantra*

**Other Fiction**

*The Queen's Corgi*

*The Astral Traveler's Handbook & Other Tales*

**Nonfiction**

*Buddhism for Busy People: Finding Happiness in an Uncertain World*

*Buddhism for Pet Lovers: Supporting our Closest Companions through Life and Death*

*Hurry Up and Meditate: Your Starter Kit for Inner Peace and Better Health*

*Enlightenment to Go: Shantideva and the Power of Compassion to Transform Your Life*

*Mindfulness is Better than Chocolate*

♦♦♦

# The Secret Mantra

A MATT LESTER SPIRITUAL THRILLER

David Michie

Conch Books

First published in 2020

CONCH

Conch Books, an imprint of Mosaic Reputation Management (Pty) Ltd
Cover and book design: Sue Campbell Book Design
Author photo: Susan Cameron

Cataloguing-in-Publication details are available from the National Library of Australia www.trove.nla.gov.au
ISBN 978-0-6488665-2-7 (print)
ISBN 978-0-6488665-3-4 (e-book)

*DEDICATION*

*With heartfelt gratitude to my precious gurus:*
*Les Sheehy, extraordinary source of inspiration and wisdom;*
*Geshe Acharya Thubten Loden, peerless master and*
*embodiment of the Dharma;*
*Zasep Tulku Rinpoche, precious Vajra Acharya and yogi.*

*Guru is Buddha, Guru is Dharma, Guru is Sangha,*
*Guru is the source of all happiness.*
*To all gurus I prostrate, make offerings and go for refuge.*

*May this book carry waves of inspiration from my own gurus*
*To the hearts and minds of countless living beings.*

*May all beings have happiness and the true causes of happiness.*
*May all beings be free from suffering and*
*the true causes of suffering;*
*May all beings never be parted from the happiness that is*
*without suffering, the great joy of nirvana liberation;*
*May all beings abide in peace and equanimity, their minds free*
*from attachment and aversion, and free from indifference.*

# Author Note

Dear Reader,

You can read *The Secret Mantra*, without having read the first book in the series, *The Magician of Lhasa*.

If you haven't yet read *The Magician of Lhasa*, or if it's been a while since you did, you'll find the following summary helpful. And just so you know, it contains no spoilers!

Warm wishes,

David

www.davidmichie.com

# The Magician of Lhasa: Summary

Tibet. March 1959. Novice monk Tenzin Dorje is summoned by his teacher, Lama Tsering, and told that the long-feared Red Army invasion of Lhasa has begun. Monasteries are being ransacked and monks brutally killed. Tenzin and his brother and fellow novice, Paldon Wangpo, have just minutes to decide if they wish to go home to their parents, or join their elderly teacher on a perilous journey through the mountains—and to freedom in India.

The fleeing monks are poorly clothed, dependent on villagers for food, and must walk at night to avoid Red Army soldiers. Things go from bad to worse—at one point they are only moments from capture. Lama Tsering leads his novices to a cave, one used as a place of retreat by the 8th century master Padmasambhava, famous for his prophecies. Here he reveals that their special purpose is to carry a precious scroll, or *terma* (meaning treasure), to freedom. The scroll, sealed in a metal tube for over 1,200 years, may be opened only under auspicious circumstances by the right person. Motivated by the importance of their mission, the novice monks are devastated when, soon after leaving the cave, Lama Tsering is trapped beneath a snow avalanche and can't move. Further disaster strikes the escaping monks, who face overwhelming odds if they are to complete their mission.

•••

The focus of the present-day story, running in parallel, is Matt Lester, a brilliant, good-looking, thirty-something scientist with a vivacious girlfriend, Isabella. He faces a dilemma. His boss at the Imperial Science Institute in London, the insightful but chaotic Harry Saddler, tells him that his brainchild Nanobot research program, a potential game-changer for cancer treatment, has been snapped up by U.S. biotech investor Bill Blakely. Blakely loves Nanobot, plans massive investment to accelerate it, and wants Matt to lead the program. But Matt will have to relocate to Los Angeles. Will Isabella be willing to leave her senior marketing job and London behind—especially with her dad having just been diagnosed with Alzheimer's?

Matt and Isabella move to L.A. Despite the money, smart car and sunshine, problems pile up from the start. Work pressure for Matt is relentless and Isabella can't get a job. With tensions between them escalating, the most positive thing in Matt's life is a meditation center next door. He feels drawn to Geshe-la, the founding lama of the center, who singles him out for special teachings, and Alice Weisenstein, a calm and beautiful meditation teacher, whose day job is doing mind-body research. Matt visits Alice at her laboratory where the two discover shared research interests. The meditation center becomes a refuge when Isabella decides to go on a wine-making course in Napa Valley, a seven hours' drive away.

Matt's situation at work becomes intolerable and there's a massive showdown. His relationship with Isabella is on a knife-edge.

At the moment that Matt seems at risk of losing everything, Geshe-la reveals a story about a secret, 8th century scroll smuggled out of Tibet in 1959. He explains why all Matt's scientific training and growing meditation experience have qualified him for an extraordinary purpose. Matt also discovers a connection to this mission that is more intensely personal than he could have imagined. The real reason he moved to L.A.—though he didn't know it at the time.

Humbled to be the person chosen to undertake a task envisioned over 1,200 years before, Matt sets out for the Himalayas with a burning sense of purpose.

# Chapter One

*Approach to Tiger's Nest Monastery*
Bhutan, The Himalayas

Dusk was already falling—and the last part of our journey was still to come. I knew about the dangers of nightfall on the mountains. How it was better to stop and wait out the darkness than risk a single, false step on sheer cliff tracks. But I didn't want to stop—I'd been working towards this moment for too long.

'Return on the full moon in May,' Lama Tsering had told me, his expression bright with significance. 'Then it will be time.'

When we'd set out from the valley floor earlier, our objective had looked like nothing more than a white speck on a distant rock face. Following the goat track that picked its way through the foothills, jack-knifing around increasingly precipitous crevices, many hours later we approached a place where the mountain curved sharply away revealing an altogether different view of our destination.

A few steps ahead, my guide Sangay reached the bend. And despite his familiarity with the scene, even he felt compelled to stop, gazing directly ahead as I scrambled up beside him. For there, only a hundred yards away, was Tiger's Nest Monastery, magnificent and other-worldly, built on an impossibly narrow ledge jutting from a sheer rock face that plunged three miles to the valley floor. A series of high-towered buildings with elaborate wooden shutters, the monastery's gold pagoda roofs glowed in the long, slanting rays of the sun, like a vision from some other realm of consciousness.

Between the buildings and where we stood was a chasm, giving the monastery an even more illusory appearance, like a mirage that might, at any moment, evaporate into mist. All that connected us were ribbons of multi-colored prayer flags crossing the gulf to the most remote monastery in the Himalayas.

Despite my aching legs, I felt an involuntary welling up of emotion—the powerful tug of homecoming. I had first come here five years ago in my early thirties, a Londoner and research scientist who knew little about the mysteries of the Himalayas. Five years later I was in no doubt that the most transformative experiences of my life had occurred in this special place. It was also the home of one of the most revered masters in the Tibetan Buddhist tradition—my kind and much-loved teacher, Lama Tsering.

After the briefest pause, Sangay gestured that we should continue. Lengthening fingers of darkness were already stretching towards the final approach to Tiger's Nest, a narrow ledge cut into the dramatic zigzag cliff. Sangay was vigilant, directing me along the rock-strewn path. There was no margin for error. Legs shaking, I battled to place one foot in front of the other as the pathway tapered sharply and footholds were swallowed up in the deepening shadows.

Sangay pulled out a torch from his tunic and used it to point the way to safety. Concentrating so completely, step by step, when we reached the solid, stone walls of the fortified gatehouse it was almost by surprise. Suddenly the path widened to a much broader ledge, lush with grass.

I sank to the ground, stretching gratefully on the softness of the lawn. Sangay tugged on a brass chain hanging outside the massive, locked gates. Inside, a duty monk would alert Lama Tsering to our arrival.

'Just in time,' said Sangay, looking up at where the clear, May sky rapidly darkened.

•••

I remembered my first visit, how I'd arrived bright with expectation and busyness. Excited about my purpose, I had expected Lama Tsering to be equally eager for me to fulfill my mission. Even though we had never met, I felt I had come to know him through Geshe-la, who was his student. I was in no doubt that my visit was significant. In his mid-nineties, I believed that Lama Tsering had been biding his time for much of the second half of his life to meet me.

Which only showed how much I had to learn! To begin with, it had been a full day before I was admitted to his presence. We might be in the most isolated monastery in the Himalayas but there were protocols. Finally ushered into his room at sunset on the day after I'd arrived, that first encounter had been unlike anything I had expected. I had already played out this scene in anticipation many, many times—Lama Tsering as the wizened, rheumy-eyed old monk greatly relieved at the appearance of me, the youthful Westerner, the Chosen One, to whom he could pass on the torch of some very specific wisdom.

Instead, the door opened onto a small room in which the monk, sitting in meditation, didn't seem to be of any particular age. Greeting me with a smile, he gestured I should sit in front of him, before lowering his gaze. Several minutes had passed before he spoke, leaving me plenty of time to observe him. He had a longer face than the traditional rounded features of Tibetans, with prominent cheekbones and a high forehead. His hair, shaven close to the head, was dark, with only traces of grey. There was a gentle suppleness about his features and his arms, which were folded in meditative posture in front of him. His face and neck barely lined, there was an astonishing agelessness about him.

This being the first time I'd ever been in his presence, after scrutinizing his appearance, I took in the low table in front of him on which were placed several books, the small window behind him to the left, and the incense burner from which a steady blue-grey ribbon of smoke curled elegantly upwards. It was only then that I became aware of my own mental agitation. Here I was, in the presence of one of the tradition's most revered masters, and where was my mind? Not settled in a state of ease—expansive, relaxed, and open to the wisdom of a guru. But instead looking around at his room, his books, the incense.

It was as if, without saying a word, Lama Tsering invited me into a different state of being. Lowering my gaze, I tried to meditate the way I had been shown by Geshe-la in recent months, focusing on being simply here and now, in the present moment. I felt my mind settle, to an extent that had eluded me in the past. Instead of constant thoughts and distracting chatter I felt myself slip into an awareness that was peaceful and benevolent. I had experienced some enjoyable meditation sessions in the past, but the sense of profound wellbeing I felt even that first time in Lama Tsering's presence was so absorbing, so oceanic that I didn't want it to end.

Eventually I sensed a movement and, looking up, I met his eyes.

'I am very happy to see you,' he folded his hands together at his heart and bowed towards me.

Unsure what to do, I reciprocated. Then feeling awkward in the unfamiliar stillness, I felt compelled to tell him how I'd met Geshe-la, and the sequence of events which had led to my coming here, as well as my eagerness to undertake the specific purpose for which I was visiting.

After I finished speaking, the silence that followed seemed to underline how unnecessary it had been. 'Before starting on our important work,' his expression was warm with compassion. 'It is necessary to cultivate some meditative concentration.'

'Yes, Lama.'

'Knowledge is very good. But experience is better. A little practice and then we will be ready.'

I had guessed, from the way he said it, that his definition of 'a little' practice went beyond a couple of sessions.

I found myself engaged in an intensive study and meditation program that had started out at weeks, then stretched into months. More and more as I understood the magnitude of the truths I was being trained to reveal, my sense of purpose only grew stronger. Months had turned to years.

Lama Tsering had personally supervised my preparation, the culmination being the three-month solitary retreat which I had just completed.

"Return on the full moon in May. Then it will be time." Time to pass on the very special knowledge of which he'd been custodian for the previous half-century but which, he had once told me, was much older than that. It had been kept secret for over a millennium, in exactly what form I could only guess, but secured in a hidden repository in the Himalayas for the time of its revelation—a time when it would be of maximum benefit to the world.

And I was the person chosen to reveal it.

Quite how it turned out to be me was something that still left me humbled. And tonight, in particular, filled with a sense of greater awe and anticipation than I had ever experienced. I could hardly believe that the time had finally come. The moment of transmission. The event, I realized now, to which my whole life had been leading me. And in accordance with the Buddhist view of rebirth, not only this lifetime, but many lives before it.

◆◆◆

THE MONASTERY GATES FINALLY OPENED TO REVEAL KELSANG, ASSISTANT to Abbot Lhamo. His usual cheerful features were drawn. 'Welcome back, Matt,' he inclined his head politely. Before saying, 'The abbot will see you now.'

'The abbot?' I raised my eyebrows.

'He has something to tell you,' he frowned.

Sangay followed us into the monastery and returned to his quarters as Kelsang set an unusually brisk pace through the maze of corridors. Why wasn't I being taken directly to Lama Tsering? Where was Dorje, Lama Tsering's attendant, who I had expected to greet us? Was the abbot also to be present for the revelation?

Abbot Lhamo was standing alone on the worn, embroidered carpet in the middle of his office, his gaze calm and unwavering when I was ushered in. Tall, ascetic, highly regarded for his scholarship, he was considered remote by some, but this evening his expression was full of compassion.

'Lama Tsering has been looking forward to your return today,' he told me after Kelsang left the room, closing the door behind him. 'Several times in the past few weeks he has spoken to me about it. A few minutes ago, when you arrived, Dorje went looking for him.' He stepped closer towards me. 'He found him in the main temple.'

The abbot took my left hand and held it between his. As he made that simple gesture, I felt my heart thundering. I suddenly knew exactly what he was going to tell me before he said it.

'Matt, I am very sorry to have to tell you this sad news. Lama Tsering is dead.'

# Chapter Two

It seemed impossible to believe: my kind guru dead? As I stood facing the abbot, an eternity passed. What he'd said made no sense at all. I felt so numb, for a while I could do nothing except stand in shock.

Lama Tsering had been the center of my world for the past five years. Everything in both our lives, it seemed, had been propelled by a special purpose, leading to this particular time and place, here and now. How could this be happening?

A short while later I was following Kelsang and the abbot. We passed through dimly lit corridors and up flights of stairs. What if Dorje had been mistaken? What if Lama wasn't dead at all, but in a state of deep, meditative Samadhi? It wouldn't be the first time such an error had been made.

The main temple at Tiger's Nest was surprisingly small—not much larger than the dining room of an average home and far less regularly proportioned, being built around a cliff face. Its walls bulged around protruding boulders, the ceiling curved in a dramatic warp.

As we arrived, Jangbu, the monastery First Aid attendant, was on his knees. Dorje was standing next to him, holding a hissing gas lamp. On the floor, Lama Tsering looked small and frail, a bundle of bones in red robes.

I knelt down immediately, studying those familiar features, wanting so much to find a sign that this wasn't what I'd been told. But the moment my knees touched the stone floor, I knew. Eyes closed and features expressionless, Lama's face was a pale reminder of what had once been. The consciousness that had defined him with such immense benevolence in life was no more.

Jangbu gently rolled the body so he was lying on his back. The left side of his head was dark, the skin of his cheek grazed. The movement of his body caused Lama's wooden mala beads to rattle from his robes onto the stone. The abbot quickly swooped to collect them, handing them to me in a fluid gesture. 'I am sure Lama Tsering would have wanted you to have this.'

Wordlessly I accepted the rosary with both hands, pressing them in prayer mudra to my heart. Even in my numbed state, the significance of the abbot's gesture wasn't lost on me.

As Jangbu studied the left side of Lama's head, concentrating on the graze to his face, Dorje murmured something. Placing Lama's head back on the floor with infinite care, Jangbu quickly rose, seizing the gas lamp and holding it to where Dorje was gesturing towards the wall. The abbot and I both stepped forward, staring at the same spot.

It was evident that Lama's head had struck the wall with some force. This was not the mark of an elderly man falling to his side in the throes of a seizure.

The abbot stepped away, his eyes meetings Dorje's with an expression I had never seen before. A look of such darkness, such deep foreboding, I felt a chill pass through my body.

'Were there visitors today?' he asked.

'Only two this afternoon, Abbot. They were Khampas.'

The Khampas! Massive, fearless men from the Kham province of Tibet, it was said that Khampas had been the fiercest warriors in Genghis Khan's Mongol army. Sangay and I had passed by two of them, less than an hour from the monastery, dark shadows moving with unusual haste. I explained how we'd seen them, clambering across a precipitous ledge. We had thought they were descending quickly on account of the failing light. Now I realized the true reason for their furtive maneuvers.

Looking down at my lama's diminished form, I wondered about his last moments of consciousness. Was it possible that he'd been alone and defenseless against two such formidable assailants? But why would they treat a frail, old monk like this?

In the spluttering sepia light, I looked towards the altar. On arriving at Tiger's Nest, over sixty years before, Lama Tsering had presented the abbot a statue of a Buddha called Sangye Menla, which he had brought all the way through the Himalayas on his back. The statue, which had once occupied pride of place on the altar of his own monastery, was no more than eighteen inches tall, but was both ancient and exquisite, dating back to the ninth century. Before the Chinese invasion, despite the many temples and countless beautiful images of Sangye Menla throughout Tibet, this particular statue, belonging to the temple of Zheng-po monastery, was revered as the most auspicious. Sacred and beautiful in ways which went beyond words, the mere sight of him would bring tears to the eyes of some devout Buddhists encountering Sangye Menla for the first time.

Even more fascinating were the stories told of those who had meditated in his presence. It was said that people who sat with strong concentration in front of Zheng-po's Sangye Menla would be sure to receive visions of him in their sleep and rapidly develop in their practice, acquiring special powers, especially the gift of healing. For Sangye Menla, translated from Tibetan means Supreme Healer, or Medicine Buddha, sometimes also King of the Lapis Lazuli Light.

Sangye Menla had been among the greatest treasures to leave Tibet. Which is why the abbot of Tiger's Nest, receiving this peerless statue, had decided that it should occupy the main temple, for the benefit of resident monks as well as visitors who made the difficult pilgrimage up the mountain. There he had remained, the jewel in the crown of the world's most famous Buddhist monastery.

Until now.

Because as I stared at the place he usually occupied, to the left of the altar, there was only an empty space. The reason for Lama Tsering's death became instantly clear. And as the others followed my gaze, they understood too.

•••

At the abbot's request, I followed him. Leaving Jangbu and Dorje to deal with Lama's body, we returned to the abbot's office where he dispatched monks with urgent messages. A vigil for Lama Tsering was to be held, with mantras chanted through the night. At dawn, the whole monastery was to attend a fire puja, or purification ceremony.

The abbot arranged for Sangay to set out at first light with a letter for the police station in Thimphu, reporting the crimes of murder and theft.

As the last messenger left his office, Abbot Lhamo got up from his desk and, pushing aside a curtain, stepped into a concealed room that led off his office. I heard him move around for some time, the opening of drawers and rustle of papers, before he reappeared with an envelope in his hands. It was fashioned from a thick, fibrous paper I'd never seen before, and both longer and wider than standard.

'This is a duty I'd hoped never to have to carry out,' the abbot said. 'Lama Tsering lodged this with me the day he arrived at Tiger's Nest. He left the instruction that if he died before revealing certain information, this was to be passed onto the chosen recipient.'

I glanced at the ancient envelope before our eyes met, and he responded to my unspoken thoughts, 'What's happened to Lama Tsering is a personal tragedy. Now, of all times, when he was about to fulfill the responsibility he had been waiting all these years to accomplish.'

'The May full moon,' I murmured.

'He told me about the significance of your return. Try not to grieve for Lama Tsering. He was one of our most realized practitioners. Rest assured he is no longer limited by the constraints of an old, human body. He abides in the boundless radiance of the *dharmakaya*.

'What is of the utmost importance now is to achieve the purpose for which Lama Tsering was preparing you—not just for your own sake, but for the sake of countless living beings. This is now your responsibility, your special privilege. The lamp is handed on.'

For some moments the abbot stood, eyes closed, softly reciting a mantra. Then with all due solemnity, and with both hands, he handed the envelope to me.

With my head bowed, I accepted it with both hands, and as he looked on, I turned it over. The aging sealed flap on the reverse side was desiccated and peeled away easily. Inside was a single page, also a thick parchment of a kind I'd never seen, folded twice. A letter from a different age. I immediately recognized Lama Tsering's handwriting. Written in English and printed carefully, while the ink had faded, the short note was still clearly legible.

> *In 1959 a sealed scroll was brought from Tibet to safety. The scroll was one of the most precious texts, not only of our lineage, but of the entire Tibetan Buddhist tradition. Discovered in a Tibetan cave in which the glorious Padmasambhava was known to meditate in the 8th century, it is believed to be a terma, composed by Guru Rinpoche himself.*

As I read Lama's words, I felt overwhelmed. While I had an inkling of the origins of the secret I was to reveal, it was quite another thing to have written confirmation. Padmasambhava. He was one of the central historical figures in Tibetan Buddhism! Nearly every temple in Bhutan had him as their central Buddha statue. He was more famous in these parts than any other yogi for the prophecies, many of which he had stored in *termas*, or hidden scrolls. The most famous of all Tibetan Buddhist prophecies had been composed by him:

> *In the time that the iron bird flies,*
> *And horses run on wheels,*
> *The Tibetan people will be scattered*
> *across the face of the earth like ants,*
> *And the Dharma will come to*
> *the land of the red-faced people.*

Written almost a thousand years before cars or airplanes were invented, Padmasambhava had foreseen both tragedy for Tibet and the benefit to Westerners—the red-faced people.

During the years I was at Zheng-po I had heard the story that Lama Tsering had found a sacred scroll in a hidden cave in the mountains—a highly auspicious discovery. I'd asked him about it only once. With typical modesty he'd just shrugged his shoulders and said "yapping dogs"—his short-hand way of dismissing all forms of speculation.

*The Office of His Holiness, the Dalai Lama, has chosen you to open the scroll and reveal the text within, for the benefit of all living beings without exception.*

There, in a single sentence, was my purpose defined. It was an astonishing statement—almost unbelievable. Of all the people in the world, of all the many more knowledgeable and wise practitioners within Tibetan Buddhism, how was it that I, an unenlightened Westerner, had found myself in a position of such immense trust?

But exactly where was the scroll? Lama's letter had only one short paragraph left:

*Please show this letter to the abbot of Tiger's Nest Monastery.*
*By these words I grant you the authority to receive the scroll.*
*For safekeeping, I lodged it in the main temple, inside the statue of Sangye Menla.*
*May all beings have health, happiness, and long life!*
*Signed: Lama Tsering Gyatso at Tiger's Nest Monastery*
*October 1959.*

I brought my face to my hands and groaned. I had no words. I couldn't even think. As the abbot stepped towards me, I handed him the letter.

My purpose as the one to reveal Padmasambhava's *terma* had seemed wildly improbable. But the theft of the Sangye Menla statue made it impossible. The Khampas would already be on the lower slopes of the mountain. With no way of making contact with the outside world from Tiger's Nest, by the time Sangay got word to the local Police, both thieves and the statue would be long gone. I sat, hugging myself in the chair.

After a pause I heard the abbot say, 'You'll have to get moving.'

Having returned to his desk, he was opening a drawer and taking out a small box of cards.

'Moving?' I blinked.

Flicking briskly through the cards, he found the one he was looking for, took it from the box and was copying details onto a slip of paper using an ancient fountain pen.

'I don't hold out much hope from a police investigation,' he spoke evenly as he continued writing. 'So we'll have to do this on our own.'

'Do we even have a hope—'

'Self-reliance!' he shot me a glance, expression severe. 'It's your job, your purpose, on behalf of *many* living beings. This is no time to go soft! Tiger's Nest is where the statue belongs. The hermitage is where the *terma* must be revealed—*nowhere else on earth*!'

In the past, Lama Tsering had hinted that the *terma* – treasure – may be revealed in the hermitage, an extraordinary place kept secret throughout the whole of Tiger's Nest's existence. This was the first time I'd been told of the plan directly.

'I wouldn't know where to start," I shrugged. Having just emerged from a three-month retreat, the idea of chasing after the two Khampas was overwhelming.

'Kathmandu,' Abbot Lhamo was firm. 'The regional hub. Everything goes through there, especially—' he held my eyes. 'Stolen antiquities. You'll have to use your initiative. I also have one lead from a while back. A well-connected gentleman.'

He gestured me to approach.

'Go down the mountain with Sangay tomorrow at first light. There's an afternoon flight from Paro to Kathmandu.'

With a firm flourish he applied a rolling ink blotter to the paper on which he'd just been writing. He passed it to me.

Looking down, I read the name next to a phone number. 'Grayson Dalberg?!' I was incredulous.

•••

'MR. DALBERG IS, HOW CAN I SAY ... A LITTLE ECCENTRIC? Controversial. But he knows much more about the trade in Buddhist statues than anyone else in the world.' Abbot Lhamo pushed back from his desk.

'You are referring me to *him*, even though ...?' I could hardly believe what he was suggesting.

The abbot pushed the chair back from his desk, slowly stood, and drew himself up, meeting my eyes forcefully. 'If anyone can help us find and return the statue of Sangye Menla to its rightful place—' the abbot spoke with the authority of his office, '—it is he.'

# CHAPTER THREE

*Next day*

Paro Airport

THE AIRPORT WAS BUSY BY THE TIME WE ARRIVED, MID-AFTERNOON. Heavy rain had interrupted our descent from Tiger's Nest. Damp and weary, it felt like a victory just to reach the front of the line at the Druk Air booking office and get one of the last seats on the small aircraft. As I was paying, Sangay went to find a store that sold pre-paid SIM cards and got my cell phone operating again after years of disuse.

As soon as I said goodbye to Sangay and went through security, I took the phone from my pocket. I'd had plenty of time to reflect on Abbot Lhamo's instructions the night before. Waiting with the rest of the passengers at the departure gate, I had a call list of three.

First, despite my reservations, Grayson Dalberg. There were just a few rings from the other end before I was greeted by a deep voice, guarded in manner. I briefly explained what had happened and why I was calling. He said he'd send his driver, Dipesh, to collect me from Kathmandu airport when my flight arrived. Meantime, he'd start making inquiries.

The second call was one I looked forward to a lot more. Geshe Wangpo, or Geshe-la as he was affectionately known by all his students, was not only the person who more than anyone understood my purpose, having set me on it in the first place. He was also the only person I knew with connections in Patan, the statue-making district not far from the center of Kathmandu. He was currently a senior teacher at Sera Monastery in India.

'I'll see if he is available,' came a voice at the other end.

Geshe-la and I had exchanged several letters since I'd been at Tiger's Nest, but this would be the first time we had spoken. I couldn't wait to hear his voice at the other end of the phone.

Our first encounter had been seven years ago, in the middle of the night. Suffering from jet lag, on my very first night in L.A. I'd woken at 3 a.m. and, unable to sleep, had decided to go for a walk around what would be my new neighborhood. The exotic scent of frangipani coming from a nearby garden had brought my footsteps to a halt as I'd paused to study the flowers—delicate, five-petal stars that trembled in the night-time breeze.

I'd been startled to find that I was not alone. Through the monochrome shadows I'd seen a face that was foreign as well as oddly familiar. An Asian man in monk's robes.

Even in those first few moments I'd felt an inexplicable sense of connection. One which I'd resisted, as though I was aware that at some level, he already knew everything about me—or at least, everything that counted.

We'd exchanged a few words. I told him about the jet lag, and he asked me what had brought me to L.A. When I mentioned nanotechnology, a word that was usually a conversation stopper, he responded with a quote by Richard Feynman, a much-lauded quantum scientist. The very last thing I would have expected from a Buddhist monk.

When I'd asked him what he was doing in L.A., his response had been even more unexpected. 'To be here for you.'

I hadn't known how to take it. He couldn't have intended in personally, could he? Presumably he meant 'you' as in 'the western community?' It was only in the months that followed that I had come to discover just how personal his mission had actually been.

•••

'MATT?' SUDDENLY HE WAS AT THE OTHER END.

'Geshe-la! How did—'

'Westerner, they said. I knew.' It felt as though we had last spoken only last week. As if we had been in touch the whole time. In a way I suppose we had through the years, as my meditation practice had deepened.

'Lama Tsering visited me in a dream last night. He showed me what happened.'

In an instant I was reminded how there were different levels to everything that was happening. My kind lama had been in contact with Geshe-la?

'He asked me to pass on a message. To remind you of the best place to hide a thing.'

'In plain sight,' I repeated one of Lama Tsering's favorite sayings.

'And ...?' queried Geshe-la.

'Ah yes.' Lama Tsering had his own addition to the oft-used expression. 'There it can also be the greatest distraction.'

'You remember?'

'Of course.'

'Keep it front of mind,' Geshe-la was emphatic.

'I will.'

'When the moment comes,' it was as if he was communicating with more than words alone, *'and it could be at any moment,* the meaning of this message will be unmistakable.'

'Good.' I absorbed both the message as well as its importance, thinking how curious it was that I had phoned Geshe-la believing I was doing so for a particular reason, when there turned out to be a much broader purpose besides. 'Geshe-la, the abbot wants me to try to get the Sangay Menla statue back for Tiger's Nest. He thinks it will likely pass through Kathmandu. You have a relative who used to work in Patan?'

'Cousin.'

'Do you think he could help?'

'We haven't spoken for a while. I can ask.'

'It's just, I don't know where to start—'

'When doing something virtuous on a wide scale,' he responded to my anxiety. 'Like revealing this *terma*, there will always be interferences. Negativities. Not plain sailing.'

'That's for sure.'

'Karma is ripening, including your karma, Matt. But so, too, is your readiness.'

'It is?'

'Of course! Confidence is necessary!'

Perhaps I shouldn't be surprised that he and Abbot Lhamo were reading from the same page.

'I will call my cousin and let you know. In the meantime, you've spoken to Alice, yes?'

Alice Weisenstein, my dear friend from life before the Himalayas, was the third person on my call list. The one I wanted to reconnect to most of all.

'Not yet.'

'She needs your support,' he was emphatic.

'Okay.'

'You know about her program?'

'Only a bit.'

'Find out, Matt! This is important.' Geshe-la didn't often use my name. When he did, I paid attention.

'The only one who comes close to her understanding is Lobsang Mikmar. They worked together, I believe.'

Alice had never mentioned a Tibetan colleague—I would have remembered.

At that moment, two flight attendants were opening doors leading onto the apron. There was a surge of passengers towards them.

'My flight's about to go.'

'Good, good!' said Geshe-la. 'Nice to hear your voice again,' his voice softened.

'Yours too.'

'Be vigilant!' he hung up.

•••

*Kathmandu*

EVEN AT SEVEN THIRTY IN THE EVENING, THE FUME-FILLED STREETS OF old town Thamel were choked with rickshaws, bicycles, and scooters whining dangerously close.

'Sorry, sorry,' Dipesh kept muttering behind the steering wheel, each time he braked suddenly to avoid collision.

Looking around, it seemed that every car on the road bore the scars of the chaos.

'Only five minutes,' was the other phrase he'd been repeating since picking me up from Kathmandu airport one hour ago. It seemed an unlikely promise as a stray cow loomed up in the evening smog, bringing all traffic to an abrupt halt as it plodded, surreal and languid, past a neon-lit stall of cell phones.

During my retreat, I'd had plenty of time to contemplate how everything that appears to our senses is more illusion-like than real. Nevertheless, it still seemed especially illusion-like to be on my way to visit a person whose name I had only ever heard mentioned in connection with the biggest ever art heist in Bhutan.

Back in the mid-2000s the proprietor of Dalberg Antiquities had been a frequent and prominent visitor to Bhutan, friendly with the Royal Family, Government ministers, and lamas at numerous monasteries. It had been through his relationship with the King of Bhutan, that the right doors had been opened for a Boston-based photographer he described as 'a long-standing associate,' who'd spent several painstaking months photographing and cataloguing the artistic treasures of the country's many temples.

Shortly afterwards, a spate of steal-to-order thefts in those very same temples had rocked the small kingdom, which found itself stripped of over a dozen of its most valuable statues and wall hangings. The surgical precision with which the rarest treasures had been selected and the inside knowledge of temple security arrangements, immediately focused attention on Dalberg. He had denied the charges vehemently, but suspicion poisoned his relations from the Royal Family down. When his photographer associate died in mysterious circumstances weeks later, suspicions only deepened. Then reports surfaced that one of the stolen items had turned up, briefly, in an exhibition in Geneva. Despite his protestations of innocence, Dalberg had found himself banned from Bhutan for life.

Behind the wheel of the battered, blue Fiat, Dipesh finally turned off the congested main road of Thamel, into a narrow side-street, rutted with missing flagstones and lit only by a single, stark strip light in a kiosk selling everything from cigarettes to hair dryers. Sitting more noticeably upright in his seat, he brought the car to a halt in front of an anonymous, high wall in which was set a wrought iron security gate.

'We are arriving.'

A short while later he was keying a code into a security panel to the right of the gleaming black curls of the gate. An electric buzz was followed by a click, and we stepped inside.

Behind the walls of Dalberg's residence lay a tree-lined courtyard of dense, boxed hedges surrounding a formal sandstone square. At its center, an exquisitely sculpted, four-foot-high statue of Prajnaparamita, the female Buddha of Transcendent Wisdom, poised white and ethereal above a floodlit fountain. A short distance away, the front door of the house was ajar and from inside beckoned the chords of a piece of music I instantly recognized.

Although no expert on classical music, the piece playing was very familiar to me. The soprano aria from Mozart's Magic Flute had been on a compilation my ex-girlfriend, Isabella, had introduced me to, when we'd both lived in London. Every chord of the piece was seared into my consciousness. Hearing it again so unexpectedly made me feel strangely ambushed.

Dipesh ushered me inside, through a small hallway and into a large, high-ceilinged gallery. As unexpected but familiar as the Mozart, it was a temple to Tibetan Buddhist art. Down each side, wall hangings – *thangkas* – were blazing cascades of color. From each end, rows and rows of Buddha statues gazed down, their presence as powerful and ineffable as the gathering crescendo.

Dipesh gestured for me to stay as he went to find Dalberg. Looking from one *thangka* to the next, I realized that every one of them was no ordinary temple wall- hanging, but a superlative antiquity hundreds, maybe over a thousand years old. The elaborate brocade frames were faded with age. But the central representation of each Buddha, or *yidam*, a different aspect of enlightenment, was vivid beyond time. Cobalt-blue *yidams* like the Mahakala conveyed a wrathful power as palpable as the serenity of an exquisite green Tara in silk appliqué. Although there was no God or gods in Buddhism, the *yidams* of our tradition represented different facets of enlightenment. The symbols, colors and energetic impacts of these representations conveyed meaning beyond words. Portals through which our limited consciousness might approach a particular dimension of the enlightened mind, and even begin to resonate with it. And in resonating with one aspect, one resonated with the whole. It was a psychology of immense sophistication, a rapid pathway of non-duality by which we might find our way from the mud of the swamp to the transcendent lotus on its surface.

Caught up in both the images and the aria, it was a while before I became aware that I was being observed. Dalberg stood in the doorway. Tall, slim, there was an air of profound stillness about him. In a charcoal, linen jacket and white, Nehru collar shirt, his dark eyes were as watchful as a yogi's.

'Familiar with the music?' His baritone contrasted with the mellifluous soprano.

'Queen of the Night,' I nodded.

'Very few people could make the connection,' said Dalberg, coming over to where I was standing. His handshake was firm and bearing aristocratic. I noted the dark beard and moustache he wore trimmed close to his face. Was it true that facial hair denoted concealment?

'Queen of the Night is one of the most extravagant arias,' he regarded me carefully, 'part of Mozart's genius was to include symbols of enlightenment in his work.'

'I didn't know that enlightenment was present in Western culture.'

'In many guises,' he said, 'especially the art of the early Christian church. The halos of the saints,' he gestured to a *thangka* of Shakyamuni Buddha, with a cerulean aura about his head, 'the sign of the fish,' he nodded towards one of the eight auspicious symbols of Buddhism. From his pocket he drew out a cord of cascading bodhi seeds. 'The mala preceded the rosary by millennia.'

He was watching me closely, and I him. Intrigued though I was by what Dalberg was saying, I was also trying to work him out. There was something enigmatic about him, something hard to place. The abbot had said I could trust him. Few in Bhutan would agree.

Switching the subject abruptly, Dalberg asked, 'How *is* the abbot?'

Was this the same trick Lama Tsering used to play on me? While firmly denying that he possessed any telepathic powers, he would often catch me out by repeating a fragment of what I'd just been thinking. A flicker of amusement seemed to pass across Dalberg's face as he watched.

'Abbot Lhamo is well and sends his warm regards.' I was relieved when he turned away to lead me through a dimly lit passage to a paved garden.

Outside, Dipesh was pouring water into two glasses at a table setting.

'I know you've had a long trip,' said Dalberg. 'But when you told me the reason for your visit, I thought it best we meet immediately. Events can move with great speed with things like this.'

Completing his task, Dipesh bowed slightly and returned to the house. Dalberg sat forward in his chair. 'So,' he fixed me with that expression of quiet but intense scrutiny, 'two Khampas stole the jewel in the crown of Tiger's Nest monastery yesterday.'

'That's the sum of it,' I confirmed what I'd already told him from the airport. 'The abbot sent someone to the local police this morning to lodge an official report.'

Dalberg shrugged, acknowledging the futility of the gesture.

'And directed me to you,' I held his gaze. 'I, *we*, really need the statue back.'

'I'm flattered that Abbot Lhamo considers my network to be current.' Dalberg folded his hands in his lap. 'There was a time when I was one of the busiest dealers in Himalayan antiquities. I gave all that up years ago for more contemplative pursuits.'

Something about what he said didn't ring true. Contemplative pursuits, yes, I could believe. But was he really no longer connected?

'You said on the phone you had an idea who might be behind things?'

'Comrade Ziu is the usual suspect,' he was wry.

'Comrade?'

'Head of the Xizang Autonomous Region of China. Which the rest of us know as Tibet. In recent years he's been restocking Buddhist temples with as much original artwork and statuary as he can lay his hands on.'

'Even though Buddhists are still being suppressed?' It was well known that small groups of Tibetan refugees continued to flee through the mountains, each with their own harrowing tales of violence at the hands of the Chinese.

'"Persecuted" is the word I'd use,' said Dalberg. 'Inside the country. But to the outside world, China wants to appear open and benevolent. That's why they're turning parts of Lhasa into a Buddhist theme park. Red robed monks. Beautifully restored temples. Lamaland—with its very own Potala Palace.'

'Meantime they're running syndicates to steal back the treasures they once tried to destroy?'

'Exactly.'

'Why the Sangye Menla statue?'

Dalberg shot me a meaningful glance. 'It does seem coincidental.'

Sitting back in his chair, Dalberg appeared to suggest that I needed to work this out for myself. 'I was expecting an American accent when you called from the airport,' he mused. 'Why did I think you were from Los Angeles?'

'I lived in Los Angeles for several months before Bhutan,' I confirmed. 'But I was born and raised in Sussex.'

'That's right,' he nodded. 'One of the circle of our fellow Buddhists involved in the arcana of quantum science.'

After a pause I said, 'You seem to know a lot about me.'

'On the contrary.'

'I'm surprised you even knew of my existence?'

'The only Westerner at Tiger's Nest monastery?' Dalberg's tone was droll. 'The only student of the monastery's most highly realized lama? Have you any idea how many people tried to persuade Lama Tsering to accept them as students over the years?'

I'd heard stories of Lama Tsering's point blank refusals to take on even leading graduates from the pre-eminent Tibetan Buddhist colleges. But I'd never really thought about the reactions of those outside the monastery who might hear that no sooner had an ignorant Westerner climbed up the mountain to see the venerable lama, than he'd been taken on as a private pupil.

'You attracted a lot of gossip when you arrived,' said Dalberg. 'From that point on, whenever people talked about you, Lama Tsering came up in conversation and, by association, the statue of Sangye Menla. You do know that he and the Sangye Menla statue are seen as practically synonymous outside the monastery?'

I didn't, as it happened.

'He brought the statue with him from Tibet, and since then things at the monastery seemed to change.'

Another information gap. Change—in what way?

'When you came out of Tiger's Nest for your solitary retreat, talk started up again,' he nodded. 'I've heard the statue mentioned twice in the past few weeks.'

I tried not to reveal how much he was unnerving me. When Lama Tsering had suggested that three months devoted to meditation practice would be useful, *I* had been the one to suggest a solitary retreat. It would be a personal challenge to see how well I could cope, stripped of all company and contact. I had wanted to prove to him that I could do this. Show him I was capable.

I remembered how Lama Tsering had tried to talk me out of leaving the monastery. How adamantly I'd resisted, regarding my sojourn away from Tiger's Nest as an important test—almost like a badge of honor.

Meantime, far more important issues had been in play. It hadn't been all about me and what I wanted. When I thought I'd been making a bid for self-sufficiency, I had only drawn attention to myself. And by extension to him—and to the statue. For the first time I began to feel implicated.

'Where do we go from here?' I wanted to get this conversation back on track.

'Wait for the Sangye Menla Buddha to turn up,' Dalberg returned evenly. 'A few days, if it comes by road. If the end buyer is in a hurry, the statue probably arrived on the same plane as you. I've already been in touch with a few people at the airport. They're monitoring things closely.

So much for the obsolete network.

'Can we somehow get it stopped before it goes anywhere else?'

'Only if the Government of Bhutan requested. And they're hardly going to take action based on a tip-off from me.' His expression was pointed. 'But I can arrange to have it tracked.'

'Can we be sure the statue won't be sent somewhere instead of Kathmandu—like Delhi?'

'Unlikely,' he shrugged. 'Apart from anything else, the Khampas will probably want to top up their commission.'

From the way he said it, I realized he was being ironic.

'Help themselves – ' he responded to my perplexed expression, ' – to whatever might be inside it. The older the statue, the more likely they'll strike lucky.'

My heart began pounding. In the distant past, rare jewels and gold were placed inside statues as part of the consecration ceremony. If the Sangye Menla statue was asset stripped, what would become of the *terma*?

'They'll get a local craftsman to open it?'

'That's the standard procedure.' The scrutiny in those dark, brooding eyes had intensified. It seemed as though he was testing me in some way.

'Where would that happen?'

'An airport warehouse. There's about a dozen artisans from Patan who could work on a statue of this distinction without leaving behind any trace.'

Did this mean I was going to have to chase after not one object but two? Alarmed as I was by what he'd said, I had no intention of telling him about the *terma*. His knowing manner disturbed me.

'Somebody in Patan must know?' I said.

'Undoubtedly,' he nodded once. 'But no one could admit to such vandalism without ruining their reputation. Besides, trying to track down that kind of information in a place like Patan—' he flicked his fingertips outwards in a scattering gesture. 'It would be like searching for a needle in a haystack.'

# Chapter Four

*Kathmandu*

As soon as I got to my hotel in nearby Thamel a short while later, I sat on my bed, sending a message to Geshe-la. I updated him on what Dalberg had told me, explaining how it was more than likely the precious *terma* had been removed from the statue. Who could tell what would become of it?

As I looked out the third-floor window to a rooftop ashram opposite, white-clad adherents were clasping their palms together at their hearts in the universal hand mudra of devotion. A chant carried through the night, rising and falling like waves washing on a beach.

I had stayed at this hotel on my way through Kathmandu to Bhutan, five years earlier. Never would I have imagined that, all this time later, not only would I have yet to open the *terma*, but that goal would seem to have fallen further away than ever.

I requested Geshe-la to ask if his cousin was able to find out anything. I told him how Dalberg was able to monitor airport arrivals and track where the statue was being sent, but didn't seem connected inside Patan. 'Confidence is necessary,' Geshe-la had told me when we spoke earlier. As I pressed 'Send,' I recollected some of the mind-training from the monastery: appearances are illusion-like—don't be fooled. All that you perceive arises from a mind propelled by karma.

•••

A SHORT WHILE LATER, I FINALLY GOT TO PHONE THE THIRD PERSON on my call list. Alice Weisenstein had taught introduction classes at the Buddhist center next door to where I used to live in Los Angeles. I had immediately been attracted by her physical poise, her tousled blonde hair, the clarity of her blue eyes. In time I had also discovered that, like me, she was a researcher, but in the field of neuroscience. I had been going through a tough time with my girlfriend, Isabella, a relationship that had come to an end. But I'd always sensed a closeness with Alice, and since coming to Tiger's Nest, every few months we had exchanged letters.

At the other end, the number rang for a while before a male voice answered.

'Michael.' It was an Irish accent. Mature.

I paused. 'Is this the right number for Alice?'

'She's at work.'

'Okay.'

In her letters, I remembered, she'd mentioned a neighbor called Michael. Seemed he got on especially well with her son Josh, now in his teens.

'I'll call her there,' I said. Not knowing exactly why. This was the only number I had for her.

Hanging up, I looked out the window to where the meeting at the ashram was coming to a close. Men and women turned to hug, placing garlands of flowers around each other's necks. That was another aspect of basic mind-training: all sentient beings are the same in that we all wish for happiness and for connection to others, and we all wish to be free from suffering. Exhausted, I lay back on the bed, for just a moment.

•••

A SUDDEN, SHRILL RINGING JOLTED ME AWAKE. THE ROOM WAS STARK with morning light. Disorientated for those first, conscious moments, I looked down at where I was lying fully dressed, working out where I was.

The ringing sounded again. It was coming from my phone.

'My cousin has news.' It was Geshe-la. 'His friend, a renowned statue-maker called Rakesh Sharma, was taken by some bad men to the airport last night and told to open a statue. He described the Sangye Menla Buddha perfectly.'

I sat up.

'The men were interested only in jewels, of which there were several including a large sapphire. There was also an old metal tube that they believed to be worthless. Sharma kept it.'

'He still has it?'

'Yes.' I was wide awake now. 'And he is expecting you,' Geshe-la continued. My cousin has arranged.'

'There's some kind of payment—?'

'Fifty dollars to one hundred is usual.'

'He's in Patan?'

Geshe-la gave me the street address. 'Go there soon, before the thieves discover what they overlooked.'

I glanced at my disheveled appearance in a mirror. I was still in the clothes I'd travelled in yesterday. My jacket and shirt were crumpled. Hair sticking out like a scarecrow. Too bad. Reaching into my pocket, I checked my wallet and, on impulse, grabbed the backpack I had brought on the plane. 'I'm going now,' I said.

Downstairs, taxis were crammed in the narrow street outside the hotel entrance. Looking across, trying to work out if it would be quicker to walk to the main road nearby, I saw a man waving at me from further down the road. Another taxi driver touting for business? Then I spotted a scratched, blue Fiat a short distance behind him. Dipesh.

I was instantly wary. How long had he been staking me out? I strode towards him.

'You want a lift, Mr. Lester?'

'Go home, Dipesh,' I shook my head. 'I'm okay for transport.'

'Mr. Dalberg asked me to be of service.'

'You have been.'

From the opposite side of the road, I couldn't work out his expression, but there was an intensity about it. Was he angry I wasn't following his master's orders?

'I'll call if I need you.' I headed past him to the next crossing, and continued walking.

It unnerved me that Dalberg was spying on me. He was the one who supposedly had contacts at the airport. Why was it Geshe-la had been the one to find out what had happened to the statue?

I was soon in the back of a taxi, heading towards Patan. On the way, my phone rang. I looked at the screen. Dalberg. I'd call him back when I'd got the *terma*.

•••

We turned into one of Patan's streets of statue makers. Small shops lined both sides, most of them concealed behind security grilles still padlocked to the pavements. There were few people about. The only activity was around a couple of food kiosks, where vendors were already setting out their stalls for the day.

Our progress slowed as we both looked at the jumble of signs painted on windows and hanging from brackets on the walls, counting the street numbers.

'Sharma Sculptures Trading' looked no different from the stores on either side of it. The shopfront was only short, and the name painted above it was concealed beneath the patina of city grime. But it was open.

'I won't be long,' I told the taxi driver. 'You stay here?'

He nodded.

I got out, walking the short distance to the store.

Rakesh Sharma was a man of slight build, bespectacled, and bent over the counter as he filed the handle of a small brass bell.

'Mr. Sharma?'

'Good morning,' he nodded, gesturing the shelves around us, 'I have many exquisite statues—'

'I can see,' I nodded. 'I think you're expecting me. It's about a small metal tube from inside a statue of Sangye Menla.'

He stepped back from the counter, frowning.

'I know it's not the kind of work you usually do.'

Shaking his head, he reached into his trouser pocket and took out a key. 'Very bad men. Much pressure.'

'I understand,' I said. 'And I'm grateful.'

He unlocked a drawer behind the counter and pulled it open, reaching inside. After a few moments he produced what looked like a rectangular spectacle case. From this he extracted a narrow, weathered, and very ancient-looking metal tube. With some ceremony, he placed it on a square of red, velvet cloth on the counter.

I bent over, staring at it.

The scroll from inside Sangye Menla. The *terma* composed by Padmasambhava himself. I marveled at how such a small and insignificant looking object, an item most would consider to be worthless rubbish, was the receptacle of such unimaginable treasure.

'How much do you want for it?' I asked.

'For you, one hundred dollars.'

The top end of what Geshe-la had mentioned. No doubt the starting point of anticipated negotiations. But I had no interest in dragging things out. No monetary value could possibly be placed on what this metal roll contained.

I had already put a folded one hundred-dollar bill in my pocket. Taking it out, I handed it to Rakesh Sharma, who inspected it briefly, before slipping it into a tin box on a shelf behind him. Then he lifted a sheet of thin, green tissue paper onto the counter, quickly folded the scroll into a neat parcel, and handed it to me.

I was so absorbed by what he was doing that I hardly noticed the shop darkening. I wasn't aware of a presence outside the shop window. Until I turned to leave and saw them. Two huge men blocking the door.

# CHAPTER FIVE

MY REACTION WAS INSTINCTIVE.

I bolted in the opposite direction, through a door leading to the back of the store. It was a heavy, wooden door that locked from the inside. Slamming it shut, I turned the key. I was in a workshop filled with statues in varying stages of completion. Heart pounding, I looked around for an exit. But there were no doors. Not even a window.

The Khampas were throwing themselves at the door. I scrambled to some narrow, wooden steps that were the only way out. Upstairs was a storage area, filled with sheets of metal, paints, and gas cylinders. A narrow window.

I wrenched at the handle and climbed through it, finding myself on a small ledge overlooking a lane. It faced a balcony at the same level on the other side of the street. The opposite door was open. I could see a family inside eating breakfast.

I leaped onto their balcony and raced through where the family was sitting on the floor. Amid cries of shock and indignation I hurried downstairs, quickly finding the front door of the house.

Outside, I ducked into an alley parallel to the street where the taxi would be waiting. As I ran, I heard a huge crash as the Khampas broke through the door of the factory.

They were only seconds behind.

I rounded a corner and sprinted back towards Sharma's street. I had never felt such primal fear. My only thought was to get to the taxi—and out of Patan.

There was furious shouting as the Khampas followed my tracks through the family's home.

Just a few yards and I'd be at the road.

But when I arrived and looked up the street, there was no taxi. The place was as deserted as when we'd arrived.

I had no choice but to keep running. There was a furious bellow of recognition behind me. The sound of heavy, pounding footsteps. Glancing about, I was desperate for options.

There were only a few people about in the early morning. Stores were just opening up. Uniformed kids dawdled on their way to school. Up ahead of me a uniformed courier got off his purple Mahindra scooter, and was ordering food from a vendor at the roadside. Holding the scooter lightly in his left hand, he was reaching out with his right.

I used to ride a Vespa in London. Almost without thinking I jumped on his scooter and pulled the throttle down hard. I burned away, cries of fury following in my wake. A can of soft drink flew dangerously close past my left cheek. I felt a thud of pain as another missile struck my back. If I could put more distance between the Khampas and me, I'd be out of danger. That, at least, was the plan.

I had no idea where I was. Swerving into a larger street I had the single imperative to get away. To drive through Patan in what I hoped was the right direction towards Thamel.

Traffic on this street suddenly got busier. I nosed through a chaos of bicycles, heavy vehicles, and commuting scooters. Even in that moment, with all senses on high alert, part of my mind was shocked at how easily, how reflexively, I'd stolen the scooter. How fast things had spun out of control.

Despite five years' rigorous training in a monastery, cultivating a heartfelt determination to avoid the ten black karmas, I had stolen a man's scooter – maybe even his livelihood – without even thinking. Stealing came second only to killing in the list of karmic causes with the worst future consequences—loss, poverty, and ruin. But when faced with my own survival, the act of theft couldn't have come easier.

I was approaching an intersection with traffic lights. I squeezed aggressively between lanes of cars and pulled ahead of the car at the front. For the first time, as I stopped, I allowed myself to look in the side mirror.

Dalberg's blue Fiat was powering up the road behind me. Dipesh at the steering wheel. In the passenger and back seats—the two Khampas.

Horrified, I made a left turn and pulled away. I wasn't waiting for the lights to change. I needed to put clear distance behind me. But the lights turned green just moments later. Glancing in the mirror, I saw Dalberg's car weaving crazily through traffic. Headlights flashing, horn blasting, I glimpsed the huge, black-clad Khampa in the front passenger seat. His head was thrown back and he was punching his first from the window.

Traffic on this street was even more congested. Two lanes were reduced to walking speed. Dalberg's car was also jammed—but only twenty yards behind. Nosing up the edge of the traffic, I kept a clear fix on my pursuers. The front passenger door was opening and closing as the Khampa prepared to give chase on foot. I'd have to get onto a quieter street to break free. Coming up on the left was a narrow lane. A way out, perhaps?

I headed into the fastest moving, right-hand lane and saw the Fiat maneuver in the same direction. Luring them as far right as possible, at the last minute I turned sharply in the opposite direction.

It was just another backstreet so far as I could see, lined with warehouses and derelict buildings. I throttled hard. No sign of my pursuers. They had overshot the turn-off as I planned. I made rapid progress through the thin traffic, gunning down a lengthy, curving road.

I wondered if I should turn down a side street. Stop to work out where I was. I'd crossed a main intersection and the neighborhood was very different—crowds of tourists jamming the street, along with vendors, food kiosks, and taxis.

But from a side lane, Dalberg's Fiat suddenly pulled out behind me. It was less than ten yards away. And by now there was hardly anywhere to move and nowhere to run because of the crowds.

Up ahead a tourist bus was reversing. Automatically, I ducked and weaved through the swarms of tourists, tearing towards the narrowing gap between the reversing bus and a brick wall.

I had no choice but to drive directly for the gap. Hurtle forward like crazy. While I focused all my concentration on willing myself through, it was as though another part of me was observing what was happening calmly, dispassionately. I was on double time. Death-defying, split-second judgement. A panoramic sweep of lucid spaciousness.

The bus driver saw me. Realizing I was too far gone to stop, he jammed on the brakes. At last minute the bus shuddered to a pneumatic halt. There was just enough space between the bus and wall for a scooter. I tore through the gap. Screams of outrage followed in my wake. But I was on one side of the bus. The Fiat on the other.

Careening away from the chaos, I ducked and weaved through groups of tourists, making my way around a boom gate into a broad pedestrianized path. It led to a place I suddenly recognized. Durbar Square, one of Kathmandu's most visited tourist attractions.

Ancient stupas stood like dark and foreboding sentinels watching over rows and rows of garish market stalls. I pulled up at the base of one of the stupas, quickly got off the scooter and, pocketing the keys, lost myself in the crowded market.

On the far side of the square were restaurants ranged over several floors. Vantage from which to survey my tracks?

I made my way through tourists in the direction of the restaurants, choosing one that occupied an entire building over three floors. The atmosphere of genteel Middle Europe inside the Viennese Cake Box couldn't have been in more stark contrast with the rambling chaos of Kathmandu's streets. It was all cane chairs, gilt-framed mirrors and the familiar cadences of the Blue Danube emerging from behind tropical shrubs planted in giant brass tubs. As I stepped inside, I lifted my hand, pressing against my breast pocket. The presence of the metal tube against me was reassuring.

The ground floor restaurant was abuzz with diners and waiters laden with breakfast meals. All the window tables were taken, and besides, sheer curtains obscured the view across the square.

I hurried up two flights of steps to the first-floor dining room. Only one table was occupied. To my surprise, a group of half a dozen Buddhist monks were studying menus with expressions of absorbed concentration.

After my years at Tiger's Nest I bowed reflexively, hands at my heart, greeting them in Bhutanese. Evidently several of them were Bhutanese too, and returned my greeting with much bowing. Walking past, I headed to a window table directly overlooking the square. It was flanked on either side by elaborate scallops of cascading damask.

I drew back a chair and sat, surveying the scene outside. Observing the crowds of tourists and locals milling around market stalls that sold all kinds of Himalayan bric-a-brac, from bells and drums to ornate incense burners. The scooter I'd parked near the base of a stupa. Maybe, I thought now, I should have found somewhere more discreet to park it. Somewhere hidden completely from view. Or simply handed it to a local teenager.

A waiter came to the table. In the circumstances it felt incongruous to be ordering muesli and yoghurt. At the monk's table, meanwhile, the choosing of food was accompanied by gentle hilarity—it seemed that a celebratory breakfast had been funded by one of the monk's sponsors.

Down on the square there was a ripple of activity at the base of the stupa. One of the Khampas was clambering up its steps. The other was hurrying towards the market stalls. Dry mouthed, I rose from my chair. I stared as the first Khampa raised his hand to shield his eyes, scanning the area from side to side. His partner was shouting out and gesticulating wildly as he tramped towards the market stalls.

Heart thumping in my chest, there was a terrifying inevitability about what happened next. As his gaze swept across the square, the first Khampa saw the scooter parked on its own. He turned to a gang of street kids who were lounging about on the stupa steps. Bending, it looked like he was trying to engage them in conversation.

The kids were indifferent, continuing to lean against the stupa and talk among themselves, barely paying attention to the man even though he was a giant in their midst.

From his pockets he produced a handful of coins. Suddenly the dynamics changed. There was jostling for attention and outstretched palms. Jumping up and down and piping voices so loud I could hear them from where I was sitting. No sooner had he handed over money to a few of the more insistent children than small arms were pointing towards the

Viennese Cake Box. My arrival in the square had not gone unnoticed. Even from behind the window, and above the surge of Strauss, I could hear the roar as he summoned his partner while hurrying directly towards the restaurant.

I had no time to return downstairs. There was no escaping from this level. All other options closed, I pushed my chair back into the table so that it matched all the other empty tables. I stepped behind one of the heavy curtains. As I did, I exchanged a glance with one of the monks. Wizened and watchful, he was looking directly at me as I slipped from view.

# Chapter Six

I was alarmed by how quickly my plans had unraveled. Was I only compounding my foolishness by trying to hide? How would the monks react? I could only hope for their good intentions.

One of the well-known parables of the Buddha tells how, if you saw a deer racing through the forest, pursued a short while later by hunters, if the hunters asked in which direction it was headed, for the sake of saving the deer's life you were obliged not to reveal it. It was one of the few occasions in which not telling the truth was acceptable conduct, thus recognizing the moral complexity of general directives such as never to tell a lie. Would the monks remember the story too?

Loud footfall soon sounded from the staircase. It seemed that both Khampas were coming upstairs. The voices grew louder and more distinct. One of them had stepped inside the room. He was barking questions in guttural Tibetan. Furious and out of breath, I could almost feel his presence from behind the curtain.

Then came the heavy tread towards where I stood. For the longest of pauses, complete silence. The sense of inevitability. I held my breath, straining every fiber of my body not to move. He could only be a few feet away. Was he staring directly at the curtain? How could he not guess where I was hiding?

One of the monks spoke. I knew only enough Tibetan to catch the word "down."

The Khampa was retracing his steps. There were raised voices as he bellowed to his associate. Aggrieved shouts accompanying their noisy exit.

I remained in hiding for the longest time. Before the curtain was being lifted back. The elderly monk nodded at me gravely.

Meeting his eyes, I brought my palms to my heart.

•••

WHEN I LEFT THE VIENNESE CAKE BOX HALF AN HOUR LATER, IT WAS from the kitchen door and in the company of the monks. It turned out that one of them spoke English and acted as translator after I emerged from behind the curtain. As soon as I explained that I was a student of Lama Tsering's and was being pursued by those who wished to harm the Dharma, they were eager to help.

A couple of the monks went downstairs to get a taxi, arranging for it to collect the rest of us from the kitchen. Sandwiched in a car of red-robed monks, the journey to the outskirts of Kathmandu, was cramped but uneventful. Only able to shallow breathe between the bulk of two larger monks, who saw themselves as my sentries, I tried to work out what to do next.

The airport was one choice, but too obvious. If Dalberg really did have contacts monitoring it, he may decide that, having retrieved the scroll, I may be in a hurry to return to Bhutan. Kathmandu airport was chaotic at the best of times. I would be an easy target.

Instead, I had to opt for a choice that couldn't be predicted. It turned out to be one I hadn't been aware of myself until the taxi we were traveling in came to a stop near where the monks were staying, in an institutional-looking complex on a dusty street. People were milling around a dusty park, behind which was an old, colonial building on which a rickety billboard announced 'Terminus.' To the side of the building, I noticed a handful of ancient-looking buses.

Making an offering to the monks who had rescued me, I headed towards the terminus through the park. As elsewhere, stalls were selling everything from fresh produce to carved Hindu gods. A trestle-table of ritual Tibetan Buddhist ornaments included prayer wheels, bells, and other items. My attention caught by one of these in particular. I suddenly recollected the message that Lama Tsering had passed on to me through

Geshe-la: where is the best place to hide a thing? In plain sight. It can also be the greatest distraction.

Coming to a halt, I stared at the object.

And as I stared, I remembered what Geshe-la had said. Keep it front of mind. When the moment comes, *and it could be any moment,* the meaning of this message will be unmistakable.

I picked up the object to study it more closely, along with the card that came with it. I'd seen other such items for sale occasionally. But never with the relevance of this one, here and now.

'How much?' I asked the trader, a roguish-looking fellow in a red bandanna and protruding teeth.

'Five hundred rupees,' he tried bullishly.

'Two hundred,' I replied.

'Four hundred.'

I put it back on the table and made to walk away.

'Alright, sir! For you, special deal. Special, special! Three hundred.'

I handed over the cash and, a short while later, slipped the item into my pocket.

•••

WITHIN HALF AN HOUR, I WAS ON A BUS TO PATNA, DRIVING TOWARDS the border to India. It was going to be a long journey—we'd only get to Patna the following morning, and that was only the first stage of the trip I had in mind. I would be travelling far away from where the Sangye Menla statue was being held at the airport. But, I decided, staying in Kathmandu wasn't an option. I didn't know what kind of game Dalberg was playing, but the pursuit by the Khampas in his car left me in no doubt how dangerous it was for me to be anywhere within his network of influence. A network that probably stretched throughout India too. I needed to go somewhere I couldn't be found. My pursuers would stop at nothing to possess the *terma.*

•••

Which was why my long bus journey to Patna was followed by a short ride to Patna airport. I sent a text message to Abbot Lhamo, updating him on what had happened, and asking for further instructions—a message which, because there was no phone reception at Tiger's Nest, would be received by the abbot's sister in Paro and sent as a written message with Sangey, next time he came down the mountain.

•••

As the airplane door was closed with a thud, I sat back in my seat and closed my eyes. The past two days had been a challenge after being in solitary retreat for months, and I felt a powerful tug to return to the state of consciousness with which I had increasingly identified during my meditation journey at Tiger's Nest. One that wasn't about Matt Lester, but which was learning to let go of such a restricted view. One that was clear and boundless and, more than anything, deeply peaceful.

Taking a few deep and silent breaths, I let go, allowing all my preoccupations, just like the sounds of fellow passengers, to come and go without mental commentary.

Having been Lama Tsering's private pupil, whenever I sat in meditation, it was his voice that sounded in my head, gentle and timeless. The words of the yogi whose presence remained so palpable and real that I felt if I was to open my eyes, I would see him there, seated at the height of my forehead, with that expression of profound compassion.

"'As much as possible,'" he often began a meditation session. "'Try to be pure presence without a past, without a future, simply abiding in the here and now.'"

That instruction alone was enough for me to feel liberated, to allow the burden of thoughts to fall away, and return to an all-pervading, oceanic calm.

It had been Alice who had first explained to me why the words 'medication' and 'meditation' were only one letter different—because they both came from the same Latin word, *medeor*, meaning 'to heal' or 'to make whole.'

When I'd first arrived at Tiger's Nest, I had believed that healing, that tranquility, was emanating from Lama Tsering himself, and from other yogis like him who had attained special qualities arising from countless hours of meditation.

But I was being guided along the subtle and well-trod path of guru-yoga, coaxed to states of experience of which I wouldn't have thought myself capable. Believing all the time, that the focus, the tranquil peace, was coming from my guru. Which, in a way it was—but only because I imagined it to be.

This was the way of the Himalayas, and I saw it a hundred times before I recognized what was happening. Whether as monks or nuns or lay-people, there was a willingness to believe their teachers capable of the most extraordinary qualities. To sit at their feet, open and willing to be touched by their presence. To be moved by a love, overwhelming and unconditional, or liberated from the dead weight of grief, or to have their consciousness blown open to a state more panoramic than they might have dared imagine.

A devout farmer I met in Bhutan once told me simply: "If you believe your teacher is an ordinary person, you receive an ordinary person's blessings. If you believe your teacher is a Buddha, you receive a Buddha's blessings."

In the imagined presence of my enlightened teacher, after resting my focus in the present moment for a while, I reminded myself of the peerless motivation of bodhichitta he had taught me was to imbue all actions of body, speech, and mind. It was certainly the way to begin every meditation session: '*By this practice*,' I recited in my mind, '*may I quickly, quickly attain enlightenment to lead all other living beings – wherever in the universe they abide, equally and without exception – to complete and perfect enlightenment.*'

•••

INSTINCTIVELY I FOUND MYSELF BEGINNING A BREATH-BASED MEDITA-tion—the nine-round cycle. 'From the most foundational practice to the most advanced,' Lama Tsering had often reminded me. 'There is great value in this practice. It settles the mind and balances energies in the body. The breath is an ambrosial dwelling. Abide there and you will experience profound peace.'

For the next few hours, the aircraft seat was my ambrosial dwelling.

•••

BY THE TIME WE REACHED DUBAI, I FELT RE-ENERGIZED AND FOCUSED. I had deliberately avoided booking a flight to my final destination from India in case it was trackable. Wherever Dalberg or anyone else might guess I was heading, I was determined they'd be wrong. I was going to a place I'd never been before. And in doing so, I'd be following Geshe-la's instructions to the letter.

At Dubai Airport I bought a seat on a flight due to leave in three hours. Then I found a quiet spot in the airport gym where there was wi-fi. It was a stark, tile and glass place, with a few rowing and cross-trainer machines, an empty filtered water tank—and nobody in sight. Perched on a low wall, I found a plug where I could charge my phone. My objective: to find out as much as I could about what Alice was working on.

The truth was that having spent years diligently preparing for my own revelation, I had little idea about Alice's project. All I knew was that she worked for an organization with the impressive sounding name of The Institute of Information Medicine based in Dublin. In my imagination, the Institute was housed in a neo-classical building, all Doric columns and marble stairs. As Research Director, I wondered if she got a corner office upstairs?

But what was 'Information Medicine' about exactly? Searching online, it was hard to find a single entry on the subject among the many thousands of results for information *about* medicine.

I was rewarded, eventually, with an entry on some kind of online scientific Q and A noticeboard. When I looked at the contributor name I had to smile. Below a tiny head and shoulders photograph was the name Alice Weisenstein.

Alice answered the question 'What is information medicine?' with a definition: a method of healing that uses energetic methods – instead of chemical, physical, or biological intervention – to cure disease and promote wellbeing.

She gave context. Even though it was over a century since Einstein had written his famous equation $e = mc^2$, contemporary medicine was still largely based on the old physics of matter. Mainstream doctors still treated patients, first and foremost, as biological beings, healing them with material means such as surgery and drugs.

Information Medicine approached patients as both biological *and* energetic beings. Matter was also energy. A particle was also a wave. She quoted British scientist Sir Arthur Eddington, "It is a primitive form of thought that things either exist or do not exist."

What's more, far from mind and body being seen as entirely separate, the two formed a systemic whole. Horrified thoughts, for example, caused the prefrontal cortex of our brain to shut down, our amygdala to ramp up, and we were instantly primed for fight or flight. Sexual thoughts caused an altogether different chain of hormonal and physiological reactions. Every mind moment had a physiological impact, whether we were aware of it or not. Subconscious thoughts and feelings could have the most powerful impacts of all.

The interplay between energy and matter, or mind and body was increasingly accepted. No medical eyebrows would be raised by the suggestion that stress was a cause of cardiac arrest or that anxiety could lead to digestive problems. It was accepted that dis-ease of the mind could manifest in physical form.

What if *all* disease originated in the mind? What if illness wasn't random or accidental, but had come about because something in our inner state was out of kilter?

Wouldn't it be extraordinary if imbalances could be treated as soon as they arose in the mind, before they became physically manifest? If we could use non-invasive, energetic methods to manage disease after it occurred? That was the purpose of Information Medicine.

As I studied the small photo of Alice at the top of the page – exactly the same one she had used for her 'Introduction to Buddhism' classes at the West Hollywood center – I thought how typically Alice the blog was. She'd always had the gift of being able to explain complex ideas in a simple yet compelling way. And at the same time, to arouse your curiosity so that you wanted to know more. Like what were these 'non-invasive methods' of information medicine? And, the question that made me personally curious: exactly what practice had she spent the past five years researching?

As I continued searching for Alice Weisenstein and Information Medicine, I was surprised to find nothing at all. No papers in academic journals or conference presentations. Looking up 'Institute of Information Medicine,' I was taken to an 'Under Construction' notice. Most research institutes I knew, like the one I used to work for in London, were engaged in an ongoing war for funding. They were out there banging their drums, showcasing their research, doing whatever they could to emphasize the importance of their work.

Not the Institute of Information Medicine. Too early in its development? Organizational introversion? Or was something else going on? How did the Institute pay its bills if it didn't put itself out there?

Not being able to track down any information made me only the more curious. I tried plenty of different search options. Before eventually coming across an interview with Alice. Not in a high brow academic journal from the last two years. But in a staff newsletter called Synapse published by the neuroscience team at UCLA—*before* she left Los Angeles for Dublin. It was only half a page long, under the headline 'Farewell Alice!'.

'What have you been working on at UCLA?' began the Q and A style interview.

'I've been studying the impact of meditation on the brain. Specifically, how the practice affects our capacity for wellbeing.'

'And does it?'

'In many ways. The relationship is direct and can be very powerful. What's especially interesting is how different types of meditation have different impacts. 'Meditation' is like the word 'sport'—there are so many different meditation types. One of the most exciting findings has been discovering how different types of meditation have a variety of corresponding states of wellbeing.'

'Is that what you'll be studying further when you leave?'

'It follows from it. There are a range of biological markers affected by meditation, apart from brain activity, which go to the heart of physiological wellbeing. I'll be studying those in more detail.'

'What sort of markers are you talking about?'

'We haven't scoped them yet.'

'Sounds very mysterious?'

'Other factors will help us determine them. We're also looking at how the brain directs changes in the body. The assumed model of neural communication doesn't seem like a complete explanation when we watch what happens via fMRI. Perhaps it points to limitations in our understanding of consciousnes—'

♦♦♦

THE INTERVIEW WAS INTERRUPTED, MID-SENTENCE, AT THE END OF THE page. There was no follow-on page. No other link to the article. Exasperated, I flicked off the search engine. I could hardly believe this was the full extent of what I could discover about Alice's work. One answer to a blog question, and half an interview in a newsletter that was five years old!

I looked up across the bleak gym room with its white tiles and blistering paint walls. The combination of humidity and air-conditioning had resulted in the high windows fogging up. The scent of whatever cleaning fluids were used to sterilize the place was cloying. Feeling thwarted, I stared into the distance, not knowing what to make of the absence of information.

Which was when I was struck by something else Geshe-la had said: *The only one who comes close to her understanding is Lobsang Mikmar. They worked together, I believe.* Immediately I was back on the phone, keying in both his name as well as hers. The search results produced hundreds of "Lobsangs." I had to flick through page after page. Finally, I came to one which included both Lobsang Mikmar and Alice Weisenstein. Clicking on the result, I came to an article on cognitive development in children and how language was learned.

I was puzzled. It wasn't a subject connected to Alice's field. Nothing to do with the impact of meditation on mind or body.

I scanned the article. It was all very theoretical, written in the language of academia, and many pages long. Going through the whole thing, searching for their names, I reached the end and wondered if I'd missed something. A long list of researchers was quoted, but not Alice or Lobsang Mikmar. Then at the bottom, buried in half a page of references, in small, Italic print, was a footnote. *'Adherence to foreign language protocols: a study of learning. Weisenstein, Mikmar et al. University College, London.'* The date was from five years earlier.

In moments I was on the UCL website, pasting in the name of the research document. Sure enough, a paper attributed to a number of researchers came up, Alice's name being the lead. I clicked it open to find it was password protected. From my own time as a researcher, I knew that studies were often secured this way. Only visitors affiliated with a recognized research institute could get to certain documents without seeking official approval.

My thoughts turned to Harry Saddler. My former boss at the Imperial Science Institute in London had been my mentor for the early part of my career. The model of the mad professor, with his shock of spiky, grey hair, he'd presided over his corner office above Kings Cross railway, usually to a soundtrack of classical music. Although I'd moved to Los Angeles after my Nanobot program had been acquired by a venture capital firm, and then to the Himalayas, Harry and I had kept in touch sporadically. He was still in charge at the Institute. And I knew he'd be willing to do me a favor. I sent him an email, asking him to access the document and forward it to me. I also asked if he'd ever heard of Lobsang Mikmar. Harry was an immensely well-networked person—it was worth asking. The name Lobsang Mikmar wasn't exactly commonplace.

Even after I'd sent the request, however, I remained bewildered. What did 'foreign language protocols' mean? Why had Alice allowed herself to get side-tracked? How exactly was this mysterious Tibetan involved in her world?

♦♦♦

TEN HOURS LATER, I ARRIVED AT DUBLIN AIRPORT. ALTHOUGH I'D MANaged some sleep on the plane, I was weary with fatigue. By the time I cleared Customs and climbed into the back of a taxi, it was the middle of the morning.

'Holiday Inn Hotel,' I told the driver.

I had no reservation, but hotels in the chain were usually central and secure. Fortunately, there was a room available for early check-in. I took the elevator up and made my way along a quiet, carpeted corridor.

I let myself in with the card key and, turning, locked the door behind me. As I did, I felt an unexpected relief. For the first time since leaving Tiger's Nest I was truly safe. Alone in a Western city I felt anonymous, secure.

•••

WHEN I WOKE, THE DIGITAL DISPLAY OF THE BEDSIDE CLOCK SHOWED 5.05 p.m. I was still heavy with sleep but told myself I must get up and start operating on local time. I had plans.

I shaved, showered, and changed into a new shirt I'd bought at Dubai airport. Before leaving the room, I went online, logged into bank accounts that had been largely dormant for most of the past few years, and transferred cash to an account I could access. Then I went downstairs. A short while later I was in the back of a taxi, reading out the address I'd written down on a slip of paper.

Alice's street in the Southside was like innumerable others in Britain and Ireland—three story Victorian terraced houses, most of which were now converted into flats. As the cab driver slowed to check the numbers, I told him to pull over and paid the fare. I could make the rest of my way on foot.

It was cold as I walked along the pavement, yellow lamps casting the streetscape in hazy light. I tried to imagine how it must have looked through Alice's eyes. It was all so very different from where she had lived in Los Angeles. When she arrived, she must have found it Dickensian.

My pace slowed as I got closer to her street number. I knew it was a ground floor flat up a short flight of steps, and I saw light from behind the curtains of a bay window. Her son Josh had been ten years old when I'd last seen him. I remembered him as a super-bright kid. How had he adapted to school in Dublin?

And, as so often over the past few years, I also wondered who else she shared her life with. Michael was obviously more than just a neighbor, having answered the phone the day before. Maybe things had started out that way. Her letters over the years, while warm and supportive, had never been revealing about her personal life. Besides, it hadn't been of immediate relevance, sitting on a mountain in the Himalayas. Now, as I began up the steps, I realized how very little I knew about what happened on the other side of the dark red door with the brass number 42.

To the right side of the frame, the doorbell had a small, lit panel underneath. No name, just the words 'Ground Floor.'

I pressed it. I heard no ringing inside. Nor could I detect any movement. As I waited, I turned, looking across the street. It was quietly residential, just two people in the distance on the other side, walking home after another day at work. A single car driving slowly in the opposite direction.

After what felt like the longest wait, I turned back to the door. Should I try knocking? I was about to do exactly that when it silently opened.

'Alice!'

The door was only slightly ajar, on a security chain.

Her face was mostly concealed. All I could see were the raised eyebrows. The pale, sepia-colored skin.

She was closing the door. I heard her slide the security chain out of its track, before opening it again. She stepped outside, hand on the latch so it wouldn't close shut.

'I thought you were in Kathmandu?' she brushed a fallen lock of hair from her face.

Instantly, I knew coming here had been a mistake. Expression guarded, in the yellow streetlight her face looked grey.

'Long story,' I said. 'There was a change of plan—'

'Mom! Is that Michael?!' came a teenage voice from inside, bright with excitement.

'I'll be a moment Josh!' She called back over her shoulder. Her eyes narrowed. 'This isn't a good time.'

I took a step back. This was all so very different from the warmth of her letters. 'Are you okay, Alice?'

'Would have been better if you'd called,' she glanced down.

Was the darkness under her eyes because of the smoky lighting or was there something else?

'Sorry,' I took a step down. 'Just wanted to give you a surprise.'

'Not a great time for surprises,' she shot me glance of such anguish it drove into my heart.

'Has something happened?'

'I must go.' She turned, closing the door quickly behind her. There was a metallic clink as she slipped the security chain back in place.

I found myself staring at the closed door.

## Chapter Seven

Sinking into the back seat of a cab a short distance from Alice's home, I was too shaken to notice the city streets sliding by or to tune into the low-volume jabber of commercial radio. Numbed and unmoving, I thought of all the letters we'd exchanged in the years I'd been living in the Himalayas. My many fond imaginings sitting under the soaring, solitary pine on the mountain above the monastery where I used to sit and open her letters and savor every word she wrote. While there hadn't been anything romantic between Alice and me, what there had been was harder to put into words. An indescribable connection. A mutual recognition. A sense that we were fellow travelers to the same destination.

From the taxi, I looked into passing restaurant windows where couples were leaning across the table towards each other. Pubs where groups sat in conversation, a wine bar where people were chiming glasses beside a fire. Suddenly, I was ravenous and didn't want to be left alone with my thoughts.

As the hotel came into view, on impulse I asked the driver to stop. There were plenty of bars and restaurants around here. I'd find somewhere convivial.

*Barchetta* seemed to fit the bill. Cozy, Mediterranean, and not too full, it had restaurant tables and also a bar area where I could find a snug booth and have something to eat.

Within moments, a pretty, young waitress with an Irish lilt was bringing over a menu. Food options were on one side of the laminated card. Wines, beers, and spirits on the other.

It took me just seconds to choose a Pizza Margherita.

'Favorite?' inquired the waitress, with a smile as she took the order.

I nodded. I could have added that I hadn't actually eaten one in five years but stopped myself.

'Something to drink?'

I flipped the menu, staring at the options.

"Abandon intoxicants!" The booming voice of Chogyam Bhuti, Chief Disciplinarian of Tiger's Nest Monastery arose, unprompted, in my mind. Alcohol, along with tobacco, weed, and any other recreational drugs were to be abandoned according to one of the five precepts that formed part of the Taking Refuge ceremony.

'Would you like some help?' offered the waitress.

I glanced up at her bright-eyed expression. How to explain that the last time I'd had anything alcoholic to drink was years before? Although I personally hadn't taken the "no intoxicant" vow, wine had never been on the menu at Tiger's Nest.

'I think ...' I scanned the names and varietals until struck by something familiar. 'The Tempranillo.'

'A glass?'

'For the moment.'

I settled back in my seat, scanning the wall in front of me and noticing, for the first time, antique, brass-cornered frames holding in place an entire floor-to-ceiling wine rack, bottles glinting in the reflected, ever-changing glow of the fireplace to my right.

I could remember the last drink I'd had, and it had also been a Tempranillo. I was quite certain, because it had been the last time I'd seen Isabella. I'd driven up from Los Angeles to where she had been staying in Napa Valley to say goodbye. By then we had both come to the bitter-sweet recognition that, as wonderful as things had once been between us, our lives were heading in very different directions.

I wondered what Isabella would have made of my life at Tiger's Nest, so unlike the one I'd had with her. Tempranillo, I remembered her telling me with that expression of Latin intensity, was a smooth red, often used in Rioja blends. I recalled all her evenings of study and tasting, constantly swilling water around her mouth to cleanse the palate. The learning of colors and aromas and the correct lexicon to use—blackberry not to be confused with black cherry or blackcurrant. The nuances of being a sommelier, the subtleties with which different elements of experience were to be expressed seemed every bit as forensic as Tibetan Buddhist instructions on *shunyata*.

It had long occurred to me that sommeliers were among the masters of mindfulness in the West. It was they who had to recognize, describe, and re-create experiences with a degree of refinement that far surpassed the vast majority of people. Their commitment was dedicated to the perfect sensory, or outer, experience rather than the inner one pursued by great yogis. Such being the traditional priorities of West and East.

Across the bar, my waitress was chatting to the barman as he poured my glass of Tempranillo.

*Abandon intoxicants.*

A layperson was required to accept only one of five precepts – to abandon killing – the other four being optional. I'd been willing to accept that precept, along with the vows to abstain from theft, sexual misconduct, and lying. But the idea of never raising another glass of champagne in toast, never enjoying an effervescent gin and tonic on a summer's evening, never accompanying the perfect meal with a glass of wine—all that had seemed a step too far when I'd taken my precepts for the first time with Geshe-la.

I had listened with interest when Chogyam Bhuti had warned about the dangers of alcohol. Monks were required to observe many more rigorous rules than lay people, including abstaining from alcohol. The danger of intoxication, the Chief Disciplinarian always made very clear, was that it impaired judgement.

My waitress was bringing over the glass of Tempranillo on a tray. And once again, I suddenly felt I was looking down at myself from a location in space above me. Time slowed as she reached my table, lifted the glass from her tray, and placed it in front of me.

'Enjoy!'

I smiled up at her. 'Thanks.'

She stepped away, and I observed myself observing the wine. Rolling the stem of the glass between my fingers. Lifting it to better reflect the firelight through the liquid and taking in the swirl of ruby and plum colors. Bringing it to my nose to catch the released fragrances like berries and herbs, at once intensely familiar but, in the same moment, seeming to belong to a different life, an earlier age.

Tilting the glass to my lips, I took my first sip, the burst of tastes across my tongue followed in an instant by a sharp twinge in my jaw. And in that same moment, a thought as imperative as a voice right next to me: *leave it till later. You must keep your wits about you!*

The jolt I recognized from before. Tannin could do that to me. It had been so long since my last drink of wine, my palate was unprepared.

As for the command, I had no idea where that came from. As I glanced around *Barchetta*, where diners were settling in for the evening, there was no immediate threat. Later, when the waitress arrived with my pizza, served on a wooden platter, I decided it was the food I wanted anyway. Peeling a first segment off the platter I took a hungry bite, enjoying the crunch of the perfectly thin crust giving way to the delicious creaminess of mozzarella, basil, and tomato.

Leaving the restaurant a short time later, the waitress glanced at my full glass of Tempranillo.

'Was it off?' her brow was furrowed.

I shrugged. 'Just not in the mood.'

•••

BACK AT THE HOTEL, BECAUSE I'D SLEPT THAT AFTERNOON, I WAS WIDE awake. I knew what I needed. Taking a cushion from the armchair, I placed it on a pillow so that it was just the right height for meditation. I removed the ancient metal cylinder from around my neck, and put it on the bedside table, then sat in the center of my bed, lights dimmed. Even though it had been less than a week since I had returned from solitary retreat, the frenetic events of the past few days made it feel as though the retreat belonged to a different lifetime.

I closed my eyes, all appearances seeming to dissolve into sky-like clarity, a spaciousness that was both at once tranquil as well as imbued by the vibrant promise of all possibilities.

*By this practice, may I quickly, quickly achieve enlightenment to lead all other living beings – wherever in the universe they abide, equally and without exception – to complete and perfect enlightenment.*

Through force of habit, the words arose unbidden in my mind, and along with them, the settling practice of the nine-round breath meditation. For three breaths I focused on inhaling through the left nostril and exhaling through the right. Then inhaling through the right and exhaling through the left for three breaths. And, to complete the cycle, focusing on the sensation in both nostrils as I inhaled and exhaled for three breaths.

The objective of this meditation was not to control or manipulate the breath in any way. Certainly not to try to breathe through only one nostril. Rather, it involved placing the attention on one nostril then the other.

From the most recent novice in a monastery, to the most advanced yogi, the nine-round breath cycle was used to help settle the mind, balance the subtle energies of the body – left and right – and to offer access to an experience of non-duality. This is a state where, instead of the meditator as observer, and breath as object of meditation, there is only a singular experience. A sensation of oneness with the breath. Of being breath itself.

And arising out of the pristine clarity of this experience, came Lama Tsering, not in the form I knew him, but with a radiant, lapis-blue Buddha's body in the nature of light. He was at once both intangible and vivid as a rainbow. Seated in a meditation posture and wearing beautifully embroidered monk's robes, he was holding a small branch of cherry plum tree in his right hand, with delicate white flowers and glistening red fruit. Resting on his left hand, at his navel, was a bowl of vibrantly colored celestial nectars.

This was an image and a practice with which I had become deeply familiar in my training at Tiger's Nest. But not one that had been offered lightly. Only after Lama Tsering had been personally satisfied of my sincerity as a practitioner and diligence in meditation, had he invited me into the candle-lit gompa at Tiger's Nest one evening. There he had offered me initiations in a secret ritual Ih had been passed down from lineage master to student for hundreds of years. And which it was now my daily privilege to recollect, repeat, and embody. I had become so used to it, that even during incidental moments such as these, I only needed to close my eyes, take a deep breath and exhale—and I was there. Back in the benevolent presence of my lapis-blue lama with his expression of supreme compassion.

It was not a static image, but a dynamic one, the radiant lapis-blue of his body, and the vivid intensity of the rainbow-like nectars moving like aurora borealis, the Northern Lights, emanating from his heart and the bowl he held, and streaming through my crown and into my own body.

'The lights and nectars pervade your whole body,' Lama Tsering used to tell me. 'Every organ, every cell, every atom becomes suffused in the rainbow-colored nectars and the qualities they represent.'

It was an immersive experience, a transfusion of all the energetic qualities represented by the colors; a resonance not only with my kind and precious teacher, but with all the capabilities that he embodied. It felt like plugging into enlightenment itself. A state of being in which time held little meaning.

•••

AND WHEN I RETURNED TO THE PRESENT, I WAS VERY CLEAR ABOUT what to do next. Taking out my phone, I went online and keyed in the name 'Grayson Dalberg'. This, more than anything, was what I needed to do. Everything that had happened since I'd returned from Tiger's Nest, it seemed to me, came down to Dalberg. The man in whom the abbot had such faith but whose motivations, I recognized, as I rolled that strange, metal cannister in my hands from one to the other, I'd struggled with right from the start.

Now, for the first time, I had the opportunity to search online. As I did, I opened up hundreds of search results, most of them for specific items sold in the past by Dalberg Antiquities. The breadth and depth of Dalberg's representation of Asian artefacts was instantly evident. Along with evidence of his encyclopedic knowledge. For along with pages and pages of catalogue references of the most august auction houses from

Beverly Hills to Geneva, were interviews with Dalberg in high-end art magazines, and references to him in society pages at the castles, palaces, and on the yachts of his über-rich clients.

There was the face I had first encountered in the courtyard of his Kathmandu home, the one I'd had such difficulty reading. *I gave all that up years ago for more contemplative pursuits* he had told me in that high-born voice of his. I'd wanted so much to believe in his integrity—for the abbot's sake, as much as anything.

But nothing could eradicate the terror of those moments being pursued through Kathmandu by the two Khampas—Dipesh at the wheel of Dalberg's car. How Dispesh had been waiting for me outside my hotel, that intense expression on his face when I disobeyed orders.

Searching for 'Bhutan Temple Theft' I came across media reports of the massive heist ten years earlier. How twelve of the most precious statues, wall-hangings, and reliquaries in Bhutan had gone missing within days of each other. It had been a steal-to-order crime, meticulously executed and never solved.

What it had done was bring an abrupt end to the ability of visitors in Bhutan to take photographs in temples. Bhutan's religious and artistic heritage was quickly reshuffled, transferring certain rare items around the countryside and replacing others with replicas, so that few now knew the provenance of any items in their temple or monastery.

Coming across an interview in an academic Indian journal about religious art, I scanned down paragraphs where Dalberg defended himself against the 'ridiculous accusations,' saying that his mission to catalogue Bhutan's Buddhist heritage had been not simply a labor of love, but part of his Dharma practice. The idea of stealing such peerless items was anathema to him. Besides, he had demanded of his interviewer, given the demand for his services as a dealer, why would he have gone to such elaborate lengths to steal items he would have had the greatest difficulty selling?

I wanted to believe in him and in his well-argued case. But I just couldn't trust him. I remembered his words from that evening in the courtyard of his Kathmandu home: *Comrade Ziu is the usual suspect.*

*He's been restocking Buddhist temples in and around Lhasa with as much original artwork and statuary he can lay his hands on.*

What if Comrade Ziu had been willing to pay top dollar then, as now? If that was so, Dalberg would have had no difficulty selling the purloined goods for spectacular sums.

Keeping the article from the academic journal open, I used it to cut and paste names of the individual items stolen into search fields. Was there an online record of what any of them even looked like?

I recognized the *yiddams* described in the line entries—though the size and quality in each case was evidently what set them apart. A statue of Shakyamuni had been fashioned from twenty-four-carat gold, adorned with rubies, emeralds, and diamonds. Thangkas of Avalokiteshvara, the ultimate expression of compassion with his thousand arms, Green Tara, the female spiritual protector, a Wheel of Life wall-hanging larger than any I had ever seen. There were zero results each time I entered a fresh search. But I kept on going until I reached the tenth item when I was suddenly rewarded with very different findings.

A statue of Manjushri, the Bodhisattva of Great Wisdom, from Kurjey Lhakhang temple, which was neither large nor fashioned from high-value items, had apparently made a brief, inexplicable appearance during the setting-up of an exhibition of Himalayan art in Zurich, only to disappear within minutes. A retired German academic, and frequent traveler to Bhutan, who lived in the same suburb as the gallery, had taken a keen interest in the items being put on display on the day in question. An authority on Buddhist statues, being the author of "Buddhist iconography in the Himalaya Region," Professor Karl Schneider explained how he had hardly believed his own eyes when he saw the Kurjey Lhakhang Manjushri being set on a pedestal five minutes from his apartment. Hurrying home to get his camera, by the time he returned, the statue had vanished.

"I have no doubt at all it was the Kurjey Lhakhang Manjushri," Professor Schneider had reported to a Himalayan Art bulletin board online, seven years earlier. "His presence was enough to make you melt. It was unmistakable. I felt it a dozen times in Bhutan and sensed it again that morning."

The bulletin board went on to note that the exhibition, held under the auspices of APEC nations, had been curated by none other than Grayson Dalberg.

I got up from my chair and walked across the hotel room. Down below at street level, the traffic of buses and cars and cabs was constant, with groups of people still out on the town.

What was it about the abbot, I wondered, that made him so believing of Dalberg, when so many other didn't? Others including government ministers in Bhutan, who had their own intelligence services? Perhaps, when the abbot got my message with the account of what had happened, he would revise his opinions.

I checked the time on the screen and calculated. It had been twenty-six hours since I'd emailed him.

# CHAPTER EIGHT

Next afternoon

SHE WAS STANDING WITH HER BACK TO ME, ARMS FOLDED, AND PURSE strapped over her shoulder as I stepped into the lobby. Dressed in a dark, patterned suit, her blonde hair cut short, it was unmistakably her—but a very different version from the one I knew.

'Alice?'

She turned, wearing a strained smile.

As I hugged her briefly, she kept her arms crossed, as if clinging to herself for dear life. Stepping back, she looked at the floor.

This morning, after attending to important business at the bank, I'd sent her a text message apologizing for my surprise visit. I said I'd like to meet whenever worked for her. I'd been relieved when she'd suggested this afternoon. She had a two o'clock meeting which she expected would last up to two hours. Right now, it was just after 3.00 p.m.

'Quick meeting?'

She shook her head. 'No show. Was supposed to see Jack Bradshaw.'

It disturbed me to see her so wound up. So very different from the poised and easy presence I had first encountered on the teaching throne at the Buddhist center in West Hollywood.

I gestured towards where comfortable-looking sofas faced each other in a soft-lit corner of the room, unoccupied.

'Shall we ...?'

She shook her head. 'Need to walk.'

'Okay.'

She started towards the hotel entrance. I followed. As we headed down the street to where the River Liffey made its way through the city, I decided to leave it to her where to take the conversation. She was obviously distressed. I had no idea about the cause—or even if she'd be willing to tell me what was going on.

We walked in silence, finally reaching the river, before turning right to go upstream. It was a couple of minutes after that when she said, 'Turns out you've landed less than ten minutes away from where I work.' She jerked her head towards a soaring stone building crowned by a cupola with a cross on the top.

'Institute of Information Medicine?' I confirmed.

She raised her eyebrows momentarily. 'Trinity College,' she said. 'They've a whole bunch of research partnerships. Ours is one of very many.'

'I'm guessing one of the more interesting ones,' I observed.

I felt the full force of her scrutiny. 'Why d'you say that?' she asked, guarded in a way I'd never known her to be.

It was a few steps before I replied. 'I don't know what you're researching,' I admitted. 'I know it was a long-term study—'

'Five years.'

'—and that the fieldwork's complete. You said that in your last letter. It must be getting to the final stages for you and your team.'

I could remember the anticipation very well. I had experienced it with my own trials, approaching the moment when I found out if all my hard work and hypotheses would be validated. Or not.

'Just one thing,' she seemed mollified by my ignorance. 'There's no team.'

'You're Research Director, right?'

She nodded. 'Alone in my ivory tower.'

'Fieldwork management?'

'Contractors.'

'Analysis?'

'Contractors.'

'Lots of contractors.'

'None of whom can see the whole picture. Condition of funding.'

'What about oversight?'

She took a deep breath. 'That's where Jack Bradshaw comes in.'

She'd sent me an article about Bradshaw when I was in the Himalayas. He was highly credentialed. Fellow of Trinity College. Global reputation in the field of epigenetics. The photo had revealed a tall, lanky man almost completely bald.

'And the money? When I looked online—'

'You won't find anything.'

I nodded.

'Swiss-based foundation. Very low key.'

'What are they like?'

'I've only met one of them.'

'In all these years?' When I'd been running research programs, my sponsors had been breathing down my neck for updates.

'Jack's their point of contact. Even the guy I met seemed more interested in Jack than in me.'

'And what's up with Jack?'

Tightening her grip around herself as she walked, she replied eventually, 'That's just it. Her face was filled with anxiety. 'I've got no idea.'

•••

THE PROGRAM HAD BEEN HEADING SMOOTHLY TOWARDS ITS CONCLUSION, she told me, as we continued our walk. Bradshaw had been as eager as she was to have the fieldwork analyzed and the results finally revealed. Then, three months before, things got tricky.

Three months before, I noted, was when I'd gone into solitary retreat, a decision which, unknown to me, had triggered my own problems. An interesting coincidence.

Alice's study was a rigorous double-blind, meaning that neither the participants nor the experimenters knew which of the samples were engaged in which activities. Neither Bradshaw nor Alice would know the results of the trial until the double-blind was removed.

Just before this happened, Bradshaw had called her in to say he wanted the results audited by a third party. It would be in their best interests if they demonstrated they had gone to the utmost lengths to ensure methodological rigor. He had never mentioned this step to her before. She'd been caught by surprise. And struck by the embarrassment on his part as he'd made the suggestion.

Impatient though she was to get the findings, she'd had no choice. He was her clinical supervisor.

He'd given her the impression that the audit would be high level, pushing the timeline back a week at most. After a week and a half, when she checked in with a member of the audit team, she discovered that Bradshaw had told them to undertake a detailed review. For the very first time in five years, it seemed that she and Bradshaw were no longer on the same page.

Confronting him with what the analyst had said, Bradshaw had blushed. His words may have been taken out of context by the auditors. What he had intended was that quality shouldn't be sacrificed for time. This was too significant a project for the results to be anything other than impeccable.

How could she challenge that?

Following the audit, results would be sent to Bradshaw. As soon as he received them, all would be revealed.

Only, by that time Bradshaw was preparing for a conference in Prague on another of his projects. Seldom in the office, he was responding to emails at odd hours of the day and night. Prague became all-consuming. He relayed the message that the results would have to wait till post-Prague. At which point, when he was back at his desk, he could give her project his undivided attention.

It was days after his return before she actually met with him. He was making real progress, he told her, looking unfamiliarly flustered. He would soon be in a position to move to the final stage. Then they would go through the results together.

A date one week into the future had been set to do exactly that.

Then he cancelled.

The same thing had happened twice again.

This last time he'd seemed very sure. Something in his tone had changed, Alice said, as if he'd dealt with some unknown obstacle she had sensed but couldn't identify.

The date for the big reveal had been set for today. 2 p.m. at Trinity College. Last night, she'd no sooner got home than a call came through on her landline from a public call box: Bradshaw in a state of unprecedented anxiety.

There was a lot more going on than he'd been able to explain, he told her. He wanted to go ahead with the meeting, but not at work. He proposed a coffee shop with private booths where they could talk in confidence. He was no longer in control, he'd said.

What about the results? The verdict on her past five years of work?

He didn't yet know, he said. But he soon would. He planned on working on the project tonight. He'd give her the results when they met.

Except they hadn't. She'd turned up at the coffee shop and he wasn't there. Nor was he answering his phone. He'd left no forwarding information with college administration. He'd even missed a lecture he was supposed to have given that morning.

'Your program,' I decided to be direct. 'Can you tell me what it's about?'

We had walked some way upstream and there was less traffic around. Instead of replying, Alice shot a glance over her shoulder that made me regret asking the question.

'It's okay,' I said. 'Under wraps. I get it.'

But I didn't. Not really. I was shaken by the distrust. Just as something about her manner sent a chill down my spine. That same, almost tangible, unspoken trepidation I'd sensed at her front door last night.

'All I know about what you're doing,' I tried to continue a normal conversation, 'is from some online blog.'

She grimaced.

'Are there other people working in, like, related areas?'

I was fishing, of course. She rattled off several names I recognized from conversations we'd had before I'd even gone to Bhutan. References much too broad-based to be of relevance.

'What about Lobsang Mikmar?' I queried.

It felt like she was looking through me, across the road. As if our conversation had become secondary to some other activity. 'They told you about that?'

'Not much.'

'It was a while ago.'

I was digesting this information when suddenly she stepped into the road. She waved, frantically, at a taxi which had its "For Hire" light on. It was driving at some speed, evidently not expecting to be flagged down on this quiet stretch. With a short screech of brakes, it came to a halt.

Alice tugged open the back door and leaped inside.

'Quick!' she gestured, face filled with consternation.

I followed her in, slamming the door shut.

'Get out of here as fast as you can!' she ordered the driver.

A burly Middle-Easterner with a luxuriant moustache, he looked startled.

'I'm being followed!'

The driver glanced in his side mirror as he accelerated sharply. I turned to look out the back window. Sure enough, there were two men on the pavement, running towards us. One was tall, bald, and snarling. He had a dark blue tattoo up his neck. Beside him, a shorter, stocky man pounded the pavement, his right leg swinging heavily which each step. Gazing menacingly towards us from beneath his dark hoodie.

I looked back at Alice. She was terrified.

'Who are these people?'

The tall man was enraged we'd got away. He let out a roar from an oblong-shaped mouth that looked like a fire grate.

'I've no idea!'

I was immediately recalling being chased through Kathmandu. 'You said *you're* being followed?'

'They were getting closer and closer.'

We were approaching an intersection. 'Straight ahead!' Alice told the driver. 'Right at the next lights.'

'This happened before?'

She shook her head.

'Why did you even suspect—?'

'Things haven't been right,' her blue eyes had turned grey as she stared at me. Her jaw was taut. 'I've had this ... gut feel.'

'About being followed?'

'About bad things happening,' her eyes bore into mine with unyielding dread.

I glanced behind us, reflexively, although the men had fallen out of sight. 'If you're being followed,' I said, 'going home might not—'

'Already left,' she said. 'This morning. Michael has a place out of town. With everything that's going on, Josh and I are moving in.'

'Uh-huh.'

We were approaching the center of town, not far from where I was staying. 'You're going there now?' I asked.

She nodded.

The driver was slowing down for a red traffic light.

Alice was rubbing her arms around herself in the far corner of the cab. Looking into the rear-view mirror. Desperate for the lights to turn green.

I leaned over and spoke in her ear. 'Let's get out here and switch cabs. We don't know anything about this guy.'

Next moment, we were climbing out of the taxi. I paid the fare. We crossed the road in front of the cab just before the lights changed. Traffic from the opposite direction was flowing smoothly around the corner into the road that ran perpendicular to where we'd stopped. We were able to grab another taxi in a few moments.

Alice directed the driver to a nearby train station.

'We can drive all the way,' I told her, as she sat back in the seat.

'Trains are much quicker,' she said. 'They leave every ten minutes.'

# Chapter Nine

After seeing her train pull out from the station, I returned to the hotel, using a basement entrance in case anyone was out the front. Alice had been convinced that it was her the two pursuers were after. Terrified, she'd been unable to say why. What were two hoodlums doing pursuing a research scientist through the streets? Unless it had nothing to do with her work situation. Or nothing to do with her at all.

Only days before, *I* had been the one having to shake off the Khampas. What if whoever was behind that, was also behind what had happened right now, in Dublin? But who could have any idea that I was even in Ireland?

In my room, I checked if there was a message from the abbot. There wasn't. But an email had arrived from Harry Saddler. He had retrieved the study by Alice and the mysterious Lobsang Mikmar. Clicking on a link, I opened the document and began reading. Behind the academic jargon, the program had been quite simple.

"Foreign language protocols" turned out to be mantras, and how they were to be recited. The study, which had taken place over a six-week period, looked at how quickly people were able to learn and recite mantras by heart. And how much they kept up a practice of reciting them for ten minutes a day as requested, but not enforced, by the research team.

The mantras were in Sanskrit, Tibetan, and Pali—languages with which none of the mostly English-speaking subjects were familiar. The focus of the study was that while one sample was given well-known, traditional mantras to learn which had been chanted by spiritual practitioners for hundreds, even thousands of years, another sample was given made-up mantras. These were of equal complexity to the traditional ones, and used syllables from the relevant languages, but they had been invented for the study by the researchers. Prior to the program, they had never been recited before.

What Alice, Lobsang Mikmar, and the team wanted to find out was whether or not the fact that a foreign language mantra was well-established and practiced made any difference to the speed at which it was learned by people unfamiliar with it. Anecdotal evidence suggested that very well-known nursery rhymes or songs in foreign languages seemed easier to learn than those which were less well known—Frère Jacques, Volare, Bamboleo. Was there any truth to this phenomenon, when studied under clinical conditions?

The study had revealed a very significant difference. On average, people learned the well-established mantras in around half the time they took to learn the made-up ones. They found it significantly easier. What's more, asked to recite the mantras for a short session a day over a period of six weeks, adherence to the program was a third higher among the 'proper' mantra group, versus those who were using the made-up versions. So they were also a lot more willing to maintain their practice.

Given the clarity of both the research objectives and findings, when I reached the end of the report I was baffled. The conclusion that had been reached was unequivocal—but no explanation had been offered to account for it. Exactly why were well-known mantras so much easier to learn than made-up ones? Why were people more willing to keep on chanting them? Even the most cautious researchers would normally have allowed themselves a paragraph or two to hypothesize about an explanation. The researchers' silence on the subject was conspicuous.

At the end of the report was a comprehensive list of the researchers, and their qualifications and the research institutions to which they were attached. I noted that Lobsang Mikmar was also associated with Trinity College—or at least, he had been when the report was published. After some sleuthing, I came up with a phone number for him. It seemed a long shot, but I sent him a text, requesting a meeting.

Pacing the hotel room, my mind was filled with questions. Like why the project had been categorized under the title that it had—almost designed to frustrate, rather than ease discovery? And what was so sensitive about the findings that they were concealed from public view?

I'd hoped that the project might give some clue about Alice's current program. Was the reason for the absence of explanation about the difference between genuine versus 'fake' mantras because that was exactly what she'd gone on to study? Had she spent the past five years trying to find out why people find learning one mantra easier than another? But what did that have to do with Information Medicine? And would it really be the cause for thugs to chase her through the streets of Dublin?

The violent aggression of the men had been shocking. I remembered the expression of horror on Alice's face. The visceral dread as my own heart had pounded in my chest: the same feeling as being pursued through the streets of Kathmandu. But while I knew there were wealthy collectors who'd stop at nothing to acquire unique Himalayan artefacts, I couldn't imagine why Alice's research would attract such animosity. What exactly had the two men been planning to do if they'd got to her anyway?

I was wondering exactly that when my phone rang. The screen showed 'Private Number.'

'It's Alice,' she said when I answered. She sounded desperate. 'I've tracked down Bradshaw. He's in Intensive Care at Saint James Hospital. I can't go to see him in case they're watching. Can you go for me?'

♦♦♦

***Saint James Hospital, Dublin***

IT WAS SHORTLY AFTER EIGHT IN THE EVENING WHEN I PUSHED through the revolving doors of the hospital. Alice had told me ICU patients weren't allowed any visitors except immediate family members. Nursing staff changed shifts at 8 p.m. Amid the bustle of ICU activity, often busiest in the evenings, could I slip in to see him unnoticed?

'Visiting hours ended quarter of an hour ago,' a no-nonsense nurse was standing at hospital reception.

'But what about—' I gestured to a group gathered around a patient on nearby sofas.

'On their way back,' she dismissed me with a glance, turning to a pair of ward assistants who were approaching with a patient in a wheelchair.

Alice told me how she'd continued trying to track down her supervisor from the time I'd left her at the railway station. Bradshaw wasn't answering his phone. No one in the apartment block where he lived could confirm seeing him. Trinity College couldn't say where he was.

According to Alexa Singleton, a colleague who worked on the same floor as him, he'd still been at his desk last night around 8.40 p.m. So busy, he'd told her, when she put her head around the door, that he still hadn't eaten lunch. But he planned on going home soon, picking up something to eat on the way. On his desk, still in its plastic container, had been a chicken sandwich he'd bought for lunch hours earlier.

Alice worked out that he must have called her from a public phone. Probably using one of the phones dotted about campus. Had he been working on her project last night? Had he seen the results? What else, realistically, could be keeping him so late?

Her thoughts returned, several times, to the uneaten chicken sandwich. A lean, rake of a man, for Bradshaw food was little more than fuel. Necessary nutrition to hold together body and mind.

He ate the same thing every day. She'd been there plenty of times when the lunch cart came around, usually pushed by an undergrad student earning extra cash. Bradshaw would always order a chicken sandwich, handing over some coins and placing his purchase on the desk, to be returned to when reading a paper or trawling through something on screen.

Struck by a thought, Alice had phoned several of the city's major hospitals asking to speak to their patient, Jack Bradshaw. In each case she'd been told there was no patient by that name. Until she got to Saint James. There, reception had told her that it wasn't possible to be connected to patients in ICU.

•••

I MADE MY WAY OUT THE REVOLVING DOORS OF THE HOSPITAL, AND once I was outside, I watched. And waited.

The no-nonsense nurse had finished with the wheelchair patient and was being beckoned in the opposite direction by a suited man with a commanding manner. Meantime, a gang of thirty-somethings were accompanying a friend in jeans and hospital slippers who was on crutches. Amid much hilarity they poured through the revolving door, evidently accompanying him back after an extra-mural trip to the pub.

'Visiting hours are over,' a nurse reminded them.

'Just showing him to the lift!' explained a friend.

'In case he tries to escape again!' announced another to much laughter.

The no-nonsense nurse was blanking the gaggle. Suited me. Merging with them, I moved across the foyer. As soon I was through, I followed the arrows in the direction of the Intensive Care Unit.

It was along brightly lit corridors and up a level. Alice had given me the number of the ward and, walking quickly, I headed in the right direction.

I knew that even if I was able to identify Bradshaw I might be stopped before I got to him. *And* that he may not be responsive. But I had to try.

Pulling myself upright and looking as confident as possible I strode into the ward, which consisted of twelve beds ranged about the walls.

A couple of visitors stood next to a very elderly man beside the door. On the opposite side, an emergency procedure was underway, a nurse drawing across curtains as several others headed in her direction, one pushing a cart of equipment.

As I walked, a nurse looked at me inquiringly, 'I forgot this,' I used my phone as a prop. 'I'm going now.'

She didn't stop. Nor did I, continuing to walk till I reached a particular bed.

I wouldn't have recognized Bradshaw from his faculty photograph on the college website. The whole right side of his face was a red welt, the inflammation so bad it had forced his eye shut. Taking in the gruesome evidence, I had no doubt he had been struck on the side of the head.

And, in that same instant, I wondered what would have happened to Alice if she hadn't seen the two pursuers before they got any closer.

'I'm Matt Lester, Alice Weisenstein's friend,' I told him searching for a sign of response in his open, left eye.

I felt bad asking anything of him in his condition, much less a signal of understanding. Alice had said Bradshaw knew about me. They had talked about me in the past and the fact that I was a researcher, like them.

'I'm only here because Alice didn't feel safe visiting. She thinks she's being followed.'

On the pillow, Bradshaw seemed to nod subtly, his left eyelid closing heavily.

'She wanted to know if you've seen the results of her work. Did you remove the double-blind?'

'No!' Bradshaw moaned, surprisingly loudly, as though in pain.

There was attention from a nearby nursing station. Out the corner of my eye, I saw a nurse approaching. Instantly, I regretted asking him two questions instead of only one.

'Is there a message you'd like me to pass onto Alice?' I asked.

Bradshaw's jaws were trembling as struggled to form a word. Before he blurted out, 'Pass. Stolen.'

'Stolen?'

His left arm flailing, he seemed to be pointing towards my lapel. 'Pass,' he repeated.

'This patient is not to be disturbed.' A middle-aged nurse had her hand on my arm and was calmly, but forcefully guiding me away.

'What pass?' I asked, bewildered.

We were halfway towards the door when his voice rang out behind, his voice thick but words unmistakable, 'Lab pass!' he yelled. 'Tell Alice to hide!'

•••

I WAS ALREADY TAKING MY PHONE FROM MY POCKET AS I MADE MY WAY downstairs. Heading towards the hospital lobby, I stepped inside a deserted, darkened waiting room and pressed speed dial.

Alice answered within a few rings.

'Just saw Bradshaw upstairs,' I told her. 'Doesn't seem like he knows your results.'

'You're not sure?' she asked.

'I hardly had any time with him. But he understood the questions. He was ... responsive.'

I wanted to spare her the details of Bradshaw's condition.

'What d'you think happened to him?' she asked.

'Blow to the head. Bruising. I don't know if there's any broken bones—'

'They got to him,' she said.

'Who's "they" Alice?'

'That's what I need to know!'

'And what do they want?'

'The results. I'm guessing.'

After a pause I told her. 'There's something else. I asked if he had a message for you. He told me his lab pass had been stolen.'

When there was only silence from the other end, I asked, 'How ... bad could that be?'

'Jack is old school,' she said after a while. 'He likes printouts. Highlighters. His office is full of reports.'

I registered the gravity of what she was saying. Was a hard copy of her research sitting in his office? 'And building security?'

'None to speak of. You got a pass, you have access.'

'You better call them right away.'

'No point calling now. After hours.'

'Even for an emergency?'

'I don't think Stan Sutton would think this is an emergency.'

'Stan Sutton?'

'In charge of services, including security.'

'How could he not?!' my voice rose. Checking myself, I said, 'Bradshaw had another message for you—but you're already doing it.'

'What was that?'

I took a breath to calm myself before saying, 'He told you to hide.'

# Chapter Ten

The Caledonian, a pub near the end of a narrow, cobbled alley, was soft-lit and secluded. Stepping through its doorway was like being admitted to a private club. I could see why Lobsang Mikmar, Alice's one-time research partner, had suggested we meet here. During a brief exchange of messages, we'd agreed on 9 p.m.

The pub was busy but not crowded. Drinkers lined the sweep of the narrow bar, facing mirrored shelves that reflected back a hundred different bottles of gleaming spirits. Whisky barrels served as tables, nestling against baize-green walls. I scanned the room. I had no idea what he looked like. Would he be in robes? Monk or not, how many Tibetans were you likely to come across in a Dublin pub?

Most of the tables were taken, but I found an empty one near the back. I glanced at my watch. Two minutes before nine.

As I sat, I recalled Jack Bradshaw's face. The inflamed, red welts reaching all the way from his temple across his cheek. Had it been the snarling, bald man with the neck tattoo who'd smashed him in the face? Or the bull-like hoodie-wearer? Had there been a pursuit of some kind, or did they come at him from nowhere?

More than anything, I was hoping that Lobsang Mikmar might help explain what was going on. And why Geshe-la had been so insistent that I needed to know all about whatever it was that Alice was studying.

A bespectacled fifty-something man in a tweed jacket and jeans approached me.

'Matt Lester?' he asked with a Scottish burr.

As I nodded, he offered a handshake, before sitting opposite. 'You can call me by my Dharma name if you like. Most people round here know me as George.'

'George?' I repeated, rapidly revising my mental picture.

'George Forbes. Birth name.'

Behind his glasses, George Forbes had the clearest of blue eyes. He had such a lightness about him, that for a moment I felt like I was back in the presence of the Tiger's Nest lamas. Beings so lacking the solidity of ego, so gentle in aspect, they seemed almost ethereal.

I went to get us both drinks – ginger beers – returning a short time later to the table.

'Thanks for meeting at such short notice,' I said, passing George his drink.

'Something urgent?'

'A few days ago, Geshe Wangpo told me to learn all I could about Alice Weisenstein's research program. It's turning out to be a lot more difficult than I thought.'

He nodded. Evidently Geshe-la's proper name was one he recognized.

'As part of the whole thing, I read your report on learning mantras—original versus fake. Intriguing,' I met his eyes. 'Though it left me with a lot of questions.'

He observed me with equanimity.

'The title was cryptic?'

'When we were ready to publish,' replied George, 'Alice had funding agreed for her current program. One of the funding conditions was to give it an innocuous title. And restrict access.'

'Are sponsors allowed to do that? I mean, they didn't sponsor that first program, did they?'

'No, they didn't.' He regarded me evenly, 'But they can pretty much ask whatever they like. Alice wasn't about to walk away from a commitment to fully fund her program. I was relaxed about it. I was relieved to have had a job for a few months when I first got back from Tiger's Nest. It helped me land on my feet.'

'You were at Tiger's Nest?'

George held my gaze steadily for a long time. 'They didn't tell you about me?'

'Only in relation to Alice,' I responded. 'Why?'

'I don't suppose there's any great secret.' He seemed to be deciding on something, before saying, 'I was there as your surrogate.'

My eyebrows jolted upwards as I absorbed this.

'It was a relief to everyone when you found your way to Lama Tsering. Geshe-la had sent word about you and it all seemed promising. But until you were actually on your way,' he shrugged. 'Samsara, this realm we live in, is uncertain.'

Until this moment, I'd had no idea that there had been a Plan B. That someone else might be trained in case I didn't show up. Much less that that someone was the Scotsman sitting across the table from me.

'Your background before going to Tiger's Nest was—?'

'Quantum science. Like yours.'

Not for the first time I recognized that there were others who knew very much more about my purpose than I could have guessed. Others about whom I knew nothing at all. And why the emphasis on quantum physics?

'I knew I was being prepared for a particular purpose,' he said. 'I never got to find out exactly. Only met Lama Tsering a couple of times.'

'And then I arrived.'

'Leaving me free to return to geekery,' there was a glint in his eye. 'Which was quite a relief.'

There were so many questions I could ask. So many avenues to explore. But I must focus on why we were here. 'Alice's sponsor. The foundation that wanted to hide your research. Is that why I can't find out anything about her work online?'

He nodded.

'Sponsors usually want their names up in lights. All the recognition they can get,' I said. 'Why the secrecy?'

'Because of what's at stake,' he leaned closer, confidentially. 'What she's exploring represents a Copernican-level change.' His gentle demeanor gave way to a look of such unexpected force I felt it physically, like a shove in the gut.

Copernicus was the fifteenth century mathematician who had shown that the sun was the center of the solar system—not the earth. Astronomically speaking, this was revolutionary, going against the sum total of human experience—that the sun rose in the east and set in the west, observably rotating around the earth. Copernicus proved that we'd had it wrong, that it wasn't the sun that revolved around us, but the other way around.

More important were the theological implications. Centuries of religious dogma held that earth was the center of God's creation and that humans, as the most evolved species on it, were His highest and most precious achievement. Copernicus's revelations destroyed this cherished idea in one fell swoop.

Was Alice really on the path to such a massive revelation? Nothing in George Forbes's mild manner gave me cause to think that he was a man prone to exaggeration.

He responded to my look of surprise, 'A lot of the other work that's being done in this field looks at the impact of meditation on stress-related conditions like heart disease. Alice's work—' he lowered his voice, 'is much more far-reaching.'

I raised my eyebrows.

He regarded me significantly before saying, 'What if she can stop people getting sick in the first place?'

'That's what she's studying?' I looked at George, astonished. I had no inkling that her current program was so ambitious.

'Human lifespans ... ' I found myself saying, as my mind raced with the implications.

Sipping his drink opposite, George jabbed a thumb firmly upwards in response.

'The pattern has been strongly up for the past hundred years,' I observed.

'Six hours, last time I heard,' he confirmed. 'That's the rate at which average lifespans are increasing with each day that goes by.'

'Mostly because of disease management.'

'But if the causes of disease were removed before they could manifest physically, her work would be a game-changer.' He held my gaze for the longest time as I sat back against the chair.

'The holistic approach to illness is different from the Western view,' he continued. 'The one and only time I spoke to Alice about her work, she used a metaphor,' he glanced up wanting to recollect it accurately.

I was watching him, riveted.

'You're driving along the road and a warning light shows up on your dashboard,' he said. 'You have no idea what's going on, so you take the car to a service center. Once there, a mechanic turns on the ignition and sees the warning light before spending about thirty seconds fiddling behind the dash and pulling out the light bulb. When he switches the engine on again, the light isn't showing. "That fixes it," he tells you.

I absorbed the story. 'Fixing the symptoms and ignoring the cause,' I said.

George nodded. 'The consciousness model tells you that both ease and dis-ease arise first in the mind. *Then* manifest in the body. Even if you fix what is going on in the body, you are only dealing with the symptoms, not the cause.'

'So, according to this model,' I mused. 'When you get physically ill, you should not only want to fix the illness, but try to eliminate what caused it in the first place.'

'Exactly. Whatever in your inner state is out of kilter. Not such a big leap, really,' he shrugged. 'All doctors accept that stress causes heart disease. That anxiety causes digestive problems. There's no point operating on a cardiac arrest patient and giving them, say, a bypass if they go back to the same lifestyle they had before. There has to be a holistic shift. They have to change their lifestyle, their mental state, or the same thing will happen again.'

'You said earlier that Alice is looking at removing the causes of disease *before* they become manifest?'

'The Holy Grail of mind-body science,' he nodded.

'Why d'you think she's onto something?'

George regarded me closely for a while before he replied, 'Because no one yet has studied resonance?'

I tried to place the concept.

'Quantum science applied to biology,' he prompted. 'The discipline we shared that was one of such importance to the monks at Tiger's Nest.'

'I understand the idea about how most medicine is still based on Newtonian physics,' I said. 'The ball and stick model of matter.'

'People in our line of work,' he agreed, 'people in physics, moved on from that decades ago. The idea of talking about matter, in isolation, without referring to the underlying field—'

'Can't be done,' I was shaking my head. 'Particles can't be separated from the field. They're a manifestation of it.'

'Biology still pretty much ignores the field,' his face was serious. 'But resonance is a way of studying things holistically.'

Something in my deep memory was being triggered—from back in the days when I'd been a researcher. The theory of how, just as magnetic, electrical, or gravitational fields exert invisible but powerful influences on physical activity, so too the quantum field affects humans at a biological level. In the most basic terms, each one of us resonates, at a biological level, with the invisible but ever-present field of our own mind.

The most powerful forces in this field are our habitual patterns of thought, speech, and action. The jobs we work in, families we grow up in and create, the habits we take up, routines we get into—all these impact on our consciousness in ways that are both seen and unseen.

Our brains physically change depending on what we give our attention to. I recalled the words of Canadian scientist Donald Hebb—*neurons that fire together, wire together.* The brains of meditators, I knew, became subtly different from those of non-meditators. And changes in the brain inevitably sparked changes in functioning throughout the body.

But we also resonate at a level that goes beyond what's happening in our conscious thoughts. Subconsciously we are also resonating with fields of energy we're unaware of. In particular, the habits and understanding of those who are close to us, or even not so close. Those who have gone before.

'Resonance theory,' said George, 'may explain otherwise unaccountable riddles: why is it, for example, that people can more easily learn a very well-known mantra in a foreign language, than a mantra of similar complexity, in the same language, which has just been invented?'

'Your study!'

'Exactly.'

'You showed what happened. But you didn't try to explain why.'

'Alice intended to—till the sponsor of her current program stepped in. Wanted it taken off the table.'

Because it was the first clinical evidence of resonance, I wondered?

'Why do people find the QWERTY keyboard easier to learn than an ABC keyboard, even though the latter should be logically faster? George confirmed. 'Studies have been done showing people find QWERTY easier. Why do IQ test scores increase over time – a phenomenon known as the Flynn Effect – until the test is reset? It's not because people are becoming more intelligent. The resonance hypothesis is that when we do something, *anything*, that resonates with what many other people have done, or are doing, we find it easier.

'Resonating with the field around us, patterns of thought become more and more deeply ingrained. And translate into physical form. Chronic stress may manifest as high blood pressure, heart disease, or inflammatory conditions. Social connection or, put another way, positive resonance with others, is a better predictor of long life than any lifestyle factors, like diet or exercise. The combined impact of what happens in our consciousness manifests physically. So: you are what you eat, but you are also what and who you resonate with.'

I was following George's explanations intently. 'If negative resonance is the cause of disease, then being free from disease requires us to resonate with something in the field that's incredibly powerful and positive.'

George was nodding.

'That's what Alice is studying?'

'I'm guessing. But I don't know the specifics.'

I was contemplating exactly what such a positive energy might be when a teenage boy came through the pub door and stopped at our table. Wearing a tracksuit and trainers, his face flushed, he had evidently just finished a sports game.

'We're outside,' he spoke to George directly.

'Matt, this is my stepson Jordan.'

Jordan pushed a mop of dark hair away from his face and smiled, as George reached into his pocket and drew out his wallet.

'Will ten do?' he handed over a note.

Jordan accepted the money with an impish smile. 'Can always go to the casino.'

'Don't you dare!' responded George, as the boy turned away.

'Jordan has the unlikely distinction of being the only 16-year-old to be banned from the Park Lane Casino in London,' he said, replacing his wallet. 'Can hack his way into anything. He worked out how to get all the slot machines in Park Lane to simultaneously spew out all their coins for two minutes straight.'

'Long time to be giving away free cash,' I mused, watching the retreating figure.

'The casino wasn't happy,' said George.

•••

TIME WAS SHORT AND THERE WAS STILL SO MUCH I WANTED TO KNOW. 'Alice's sponsor—how much do you know about the Swiss sponsor?'

'Almost nothing. He came on board as I was moving onto the next project. All I know is that he's immensely rich.'

'He? I thought it was a foundation?'

George shrugged. 'A legal entity based in Geneva.'

I revealed that Alice had only ever met one man.

'Any idea who he might be?'

'I'm guessing the same guy who wanted to suppress the findings of our previous research. Pascal Lascelles.'

The name meant nothing to me.

'One of the wealthiest men in Europe.'

I raised my eyebrows.

'And one of the most reclusive. A man with something to prove.'

'He is?'

'The Lascelles family keep themselves out of the public eye as much as they keep their company front and center. It's JB Pharmaceuticals.'

I was startled. JB was one of the biggest pharma giants in the world, with household name brands from painkillers to beta-blockers.

'This ... Pascal Lascelles, owns JB?'

'Used to,' said George. 'Had a major falling out with his brother and sister. Ten years ago, maybe more. Because it's a private company, there's fewer disclosure requirements. Pascal wanted to take the company in the direction of holistic wellbeing. His siblings were sticking to the tried and tested drugs portfolio. There was a titanic struggle—I've heard he's a seriously brilliant individual. But in the end, it was two against one.'

'They bought him out?'

George nodded. 'Which left him on the outside. Free to pursue his own interests.'

'Like funding research which could one day bring down the entire basis of his siblings' wealth?'

'Like I said—' George was nodding, '—he has something to prove. And he's been keeping the whole thing tightly under wraps.'

Now that I had some understanding of what was at stake, and who was funding Alice, for the first time I realized who might be out to cause her harm.

'Big pharma—' I began.

'Her work threatens their whole business model,' confirmed George.

Heading out the door of The Caledonian a short while later, making our way up the cobbled lane, I asked him, 'By the way, do you know Grayson Dalberg?'

'Art dealer?' he queried. 'We've never met.'

'Abbot Lhamo seems to rate him highly.'

'Despite his reputation?' George asked rhetorically.

'I just wondered if you knew anything about him?'

'I heard something once from a friend of my brother. He and Dalberg were in the military together. Way before he got into antiquities.'

'The military?'

'SAS, to be precise.'

Dalberg's physical poise assumed an even more menacing significance in light of this revelation.

'Apparently he was one of the most focused warriors in the squad.'

'Really?'

'He had a reputation. Focused and connected to military types around the world. Once he sets his mind on something there's no stopping him.'

# Chapter Eleven

At 8.45 the next morning I was scanning the rush hour crowds pouring out of Heuston Station. Alice had never commuted into the station before. There was no reason anyone would know she was about to show up. All the same, I'd insisted on escorting her the short distance to her office, to report what had happened to the head of security at Trinity College.

She saw me first in the crowds flooding from the platforms.

'You okay?' I felt a tug at my elbow and was soon being swept along beside her.

I noticed the darkness under her eyes. The tightness of the muscles in her face. Didn't look like she'd had a moment's sleep.

She led the way to the part of Trinity College campus where she worked—not a grand, neo-classical building, but an anonymous, 80s style, glass-fronted block. All the while, we were constantly scanning around us.

'Can you tell Stan Sutton I'd like to see him?' she asked the woman at Reception when we arrived. 'It's urgent.'

The receptionist dialed a number. I was surveying the wall behind her. On the shiny, glass panels was a long list of all the registered research entities and partnerships housed at the center, in alphabetical order. No mention of an "Institute of Information Medicine."

Heading up several flights of stairs a few minutes later, Alice turned to me, 'His big thing is roses.'

I must have looked confused.

'Flowers,' she confirmed.

She led the way along a corridor of nondescript offices, floor to ceiling transparent panels revealing desks, chairs, and IT equipment, before stopping at an open door which gave onto a desk dominated by a bowl of rose blossoms.

'This is my friend, Matt Lester,' she introduced me, stepping inside.

It was hard to look past the vase of large, dust-pink flowers and the fragrance that filled the room. A fragrance that transported me in an instant to Tiger's Nest. In the background, leaning back in his chair, arms folded, a plump and bespectacled middle-aged man was taking me in.

'We've a stolen lab pass to report,' Alice told him.

'Yours?' he raised his eyebrows.

'Jack Bradshaw's.'

'He hasn't reported it missing.'

'He's in hospital.'

'He was attacked,' I spoke for the first time. 'Badly injured. His lab pass was stolen.'

Sutton didn't move from his reclined position, expression unchanged.

'He told you it was stolen, did he?' he asked Alice.

'He told Matt. Last night.'

'An attack on campus?' he glanced at me.

I shrugged. I could see where he was going with this. It confirmed exactly what Alice had warned me about.

'It's a security matter if it happened on campus,' he confirmed. 'Even then, it's down to the police.'

'And the lab pass?' asked Alice.

'If I had a pound for every "stolen pass" story I heard, I'd be a rich man,' he grimaced. '"Lost," is the better word.'

'I'm worried he had hard copies of my research in his office.' Alice's voice sounded panicky in the face of Sutton's cynicism.

'And the thieves used his pass to steal your data?' he pulled a humorless smile.

As Lama Tsering had taught, I fixed my gaze on a nearby object – the rose bowl – and took a mindful breath to manage my rising anger. Having seen Bradshaw's face for myself, there was no doubt the attack had been intentional. We needed Sutton to do his job.

Sutton evidently took in my expression, mistaking my stare for interest in his roses.

'The rosette form. And delicate fragrance. A masterpiece of design.'

Along with the scent in the room, Sutton's use of the word "rosette" triggered a memory of Lama Tsering bent over a rose bush on a dazzling Himalayan morning. It had been in the hermitage gardens, Tigers Nest's greatest secret and the closest place to heaven on earth. The pristine air had been filled with the delicate fragrance of fresh blossoms as my lama had told me about this very rose while holding one between his fingers.

'David Austin,' the name emerged, without effort, from my subconscious.

'Ah!' Sutton's face lit up. 'He knows his roses!' He returned to vertical from his leaned-back posture and unfolded his arms. He glanced approvingly towards Alice.

'Alice would be ... extremely grateful,' I made the most of the moment, 'if you could check if Bradshaw's pass has been used in the last 24 hours.'

Sutton turned in his chair, fingers performing a tattoo on the keyboard. Within moments, something appeared on his screen, which he flicked round for us to see. Next to a security photo of Bradshaw appeared a list of times and dates. The one at the bottom read 23:13 from two nights before.

'Working late?' Sutton's demeanor had shifted.

Alice leaned closer to the screen. 'That late?' Her pale face was reflected eerily blue. 'Alexa Singleton was the last person who saw him at his desk. She told us 8.40 p.m. He told her that he would soon be going home. Needed to eat.'

Sutton turned the screen back, rapidly scrolling upwards through months of entries. 'Not usually a midnight owl. At least, not here.'

Picking up his desk phone, he keyed in four digits.

'Can you run some CCTV footage, Danny? Two nights ago. 23:13. And an ID check.'

Sutton replaced the receiver, looking at Alice.

'A Luddite, you say?' he asked her.

'Wouldn't go that far.'

'Data print-outs in his office? You know, I can do something about the integrity of our systems. But if staff choose to leave sensitive documents lying around on their desks ...'

'I'm not saying he did. But I'd like to check his office.

'Can't do that if you're saying his office may be a crime scene,' he returned with a bleak expression.

Alice's face was filled with anxiety. So much that she seemed unable to speak.

'Alice's concern is an IT breach,' I wanted to get the ball firmly back in his court. 'We don't know where Bradshaw kept his passwords.'

'In his head,' replied Sutton.

'Really?' It was my turn to play the skeptic. 'All 53 of them? Every code for every platform—work, bank, business, government, social?' I kept my tone as neutral as possible. 'Like most people I think he probably wrote them down somewhere. And that somewhere may well have been here.'

If Sutton was concerned by this suggestion, he wasn't showing it. But nor did he have a smart-ass come-back.

A notification appeared on his screen and he opened a message—evidently the CCTV file from two nights before. Tilting the screen halfway in our direction, he pressed Play, and we watched a full screen black and white image of the ground floor lobby with a digital clock at the top left-hand corner flicking through tenths of a second.

The foyer was deserted until 23:13 at which point a figure appeared outside the main door and swiped the card reader. As he stepped inside, directly into the facing camera, Sutton pressed pause. We all leaned in to get a better view.

He was thickset with a dark hoodie tugged over his head. Alice and I exchanged a glance. He was one of the two who had pursued us when we were walking yesterday. Keeping his face down, we couldn't make out any identifying features. But the hoodie, his shape, the way he moved were unmistakable.

Releasing the pause button, Sutton let the file play, with coverage from the inside corridor cameras. The man had arrived with a duffel bag under his arm. Shown emerging from a stairwell at 23:14 and a few seconds, there was no hesitation about the direction he was taking. He pushed open a fire safety door and proceeded without hesitation towards Bradshaw's office with that particular heavy, swinging gait.

Even Sutton's eyebrows twitched at the directness of his route.

There was no CCTV once the man stepped into Bradshaw's office. We had no way of knowing what was going on in there. But the cameras caught him again, twenty minutes later, emerging, duffel bag still under his arm and making for the front door.

Sutton replayed the footage several times, before nodding towards the screen, 'Security breach. I'll advise the police. We'll check our IT systems.'

'When—' Alice began. 'I mean, how long ...?'

'You'll hear from the police pretty quickly. Next few days.'

'Days?!'

Sutton flashed a glance towards her, 'They'll want to interview Dr. Bradshaw. He's the starting point.' Then seeing her expression of anguish unchanged, 'The pass was stolen to access his office by the looks of things. Okay. But why? As long as I've had this job, unauthorized entries like this,' he gestured towards the screen, 'have been rare. Three or four in ten years. And it's always been animosity. Professional rivalry. Never about intellectual property. If it was your results they were after, they'd be trying to hack into the system. Not sniffing around in the hope of finding print-outs.'

He swiveled in his desk chair to face her directly. 'You worried about your intellectual property?'

Biting her lip, Alice nodded.

'Bradshaw has a dozen projects going on any one time. Why do you think this is connected to yours?'

'That guy,' she pointed at the screen. 'He was chasing me yesterday.'

'Chasing?' he was folding his arms.

'Outside. On the street.'

'I was with her. We had to jump in a taxi to escape. There were two of them.'

Sutton regarded me without conviction. Evidently, I had used up all my David Austen credits.

'That's something you can talk to the police about,' he said. Forehead wrinkling, he scrutinized Alice carefully for a while. 'I remember you telling me once about your program. You said if it was successful, no one would ever make money out of your intellectual property. Is that so?'

Alice confirmed this with a tilt of the head.

Eyeballing her closely he asked, 'So, who would want to steal it?'

•••

In silence, Alice led the way back along the corridor, down two flights of stairs to the floor below, where there was a similarly bland stretch of offices. She paused outside the door of one, reaching into her handbag for keys.

'This is your office?' I asked.

She nodded.

'Don't you think it's risky inside, I mean, to talk?'

She looked dumbstruck for a moment. Then she was putting away her keys. 'I know somewhere,' she said.

She showed me back down the stairs and into the basement. Along a winding corridor that led past a generator so deafening we walked as quickly as we could to get away from it. Minutes later, having made our way through a labyrinth, we emerged up a short flight of stairs into the semi-darkness of a marine biology laboratory.

A vast aquarium fronted one entire side of the room. It was like having a window into a cavern at the bottom of the sea. A huge coral reef stretched from one side of the tank to another. Anemones were swaying in the underwater currents. Looking into the ultramarine depths, there were signs of movement in the distance. From time to time there was a flash as a deep-sea fish materialized briefly in the foreground before disappearing back into the darkness. The constant dull throb of a pump.

'Marie-Lise is a friend. This is her lab,' said Alice heading towards the glass.

I nodded.

She turned, hugging herself with her arms, and jerking her head in the direction of upstairs. 'You saw the reaction.'

'He's cynical and lazy,' I agreed. 'But not stupid. The question he asked—it is *the* question: who *is* trying to get at your results?'

'Whoever's been following me,' her voice rose. 'Whoever put Jack in ICU.' She shook her head. 'You know, my thought when I was phoning round the hospitals was that he might have food poisoning. Salmonella. Never this!'

'The sooner you speak to Jack—'

'Already called from the train. Immediate family only today. In the meanwhile, I can't just sit around—'

'I agree. What you told Action Man upstairs about no one getting rich on your research. It's true, but it's not really the point is it?'

'How d'you mean?

'The point is—who's going to *lose*? If you prove your case, the commercial impact on Big Pharma will be catastrophic. It's the ultimate existential threat.'

At that moment, a giant eel, several yards long, appeared from the depths of the tank behind her, mouth snapping threateningly and teeth glinting as it swept a plume of sand in its wake.

'That's if what George Forbes told me is true,' I continued.

'You've spoken?'

'Seemed like an idea.'

'Big Pharma is why you'll find nothing about the program online. Of course, they're the primary suspects. But who in Big Pharma exactly? What do they want? If those thugs had run me down yesterday, what were they planning to do? Even if they'd killed me, the work's still there.'

'Only, no one can get it.'

'Exactly what I spent all last night worrying about,' she stepped forward, fiddling restlessly with the handle of her purse. 'What if the plan is to put Bradshaw and me out of the picture. Access the data. And deal with it.'

'Sabotage?'

'By the time we're back on board, *if* we're ever back on board ... '

I'd been wondering the same thing. Going over all that George had told me the night before.

'Maybe it's time you took matters into your own hands,' I said.

'How?'

'Get a look at your own results.'

Her eyebrows jolted upwards.

'I've met George. I've also met his stepson, Jordan.'

'Banned-from-gambling Jordan?'

'If he can get past Park Lane Casino, I reckon he'd find Stan Sutton a walk in the park.' My eyes narrowed. 'What do you say?'

For the first time that morning her jaw seemed to relax. She was taken aback by the suggestion, but she was thinking. Eventually she said, 'Worth a try.'

'Good.' I nodded. 'I'll make the call if you like—'

'There's no need,' she jumped in. 'I'll ask George.' For the first time that morning, there was a glimmer of hope in her voice.

'Another thing,' I said. 'Perhaps it's time you reached out to the foundation.'

'I only met the guy once. Years ago.'

'Lascelles?'

She nodded.

'You have his contact details?'

'We've never been in direct contact,' she said. 'It's always been through Bradshaw. Why do you think I should be reaching out to him now?'

'Bradshaw has been hospitalized. You've got people on your tail. Sutton is up there smelling his roses. If you were bankrolling this project, wouldn't you want someone to tell you what the hell was going on?'

Alice turned away, walking along the side of the aquarium, where flashes of dark scales swirled behind her, rolling and roiling through the ocean waters. Clutching the strap of her purse in her right hand and running the thumb of her left round and around her fingertips, she seemed absorbed in some thought that she was unable to articulate. Deep in a place of uncertainty.

Eventually, after walking all the way to the end of the tank and back, she returned to face me. 'I can't put it into words, but I just have this feeling.'

'Feeling?'

'There's something here,' she tapped her heart with her left index finger.

It was unlike Alice to refer to intuitive feelings—at least, in a professional context. Not because she didn't have them, but because the research scientist in her knew that evidence-based rigor was the only thing that cut it in the materialist world.

But the fact she was referring to a feeling that she was willing to tell me was more right brain than left, didn't mean I took it any less seriously.

'Like I don't want to make things even worse than they are now,' she said.

'From what George told me, it's not Pascal Lascelles who might be the problem. It's his brother and sister.'

'I get that. The whole thing bewilders me.'

'Do you know anyone, besides Bradshaw, who can tell you what Lascelles is like to deal with? Anyone who can help work out—'

'Yeah,' she glanced over in agreement. 'I know what you're saying.' She was scanning with her eyes, from left to right, trying to remember.

'There is somebody,' she was working it through. 'Yes.' She pointed her forefinger upwards. 'Dr. Qi.'

'Chee?'

'Her real name is Lindsey. No Lin. Dr. Lin Jiang. Expert on Qi. You know, life force. She needed money for a program. I said she should try the foundation. This was three, four years ago.'

'And did she?'

Alice was nodding. 'Jack put her in touch with Lascelles. She went to Paris to meet him. He invested some money. Don't know what happened after that. Haven't seen her for ages.'

'Where's she based?'

'Here. Dublin. But always on the go.' Alice was slipping her handbag off her shoulder and reaching inside for her phone. Opening it and scrolling through her contact list, when she reached Dr. Lin Jiang, she looked at me, eyebrows raised.

I nodded.

## Chapter Twelve

An hour later we were on a train heading out of Dublin. Sitting opposite us, Dr. Lin Jiang. Travelling to a two-day conference in Galway, she'd offered us some time—if we didn't mind traveling.

For the first half hour of the journey, Dr. Jiang was on a conference call at the other end of the near-empty carriage, using an in-ear headset, and speaking rapidly from time to time into a microphone at her chin. At the end of the call she beckoned toward us, tugging ear buds away from her face.

Alice sat down directly opposite her. I was next to Alice, taking in the tousled, brown hair, brisk gestures, and mercurial expressions of the woman we were facing. My most immediate impression was of a rapier-sharp mind. The ability to sum a situation up in a single glance.

'We're hoping you can tell us something about the foundation,' began Alice.

'Pascal Lascelles?' Dr. Jiang's eyes narrowed. 'Isn't he still funding you?'

'Yes. But Jack Bradshaw's always been the one—'

'Arm's length.' Dr. Jiang was nodding. 'I remember. How is Jack?' Her expression was warm.

'In hospital. He was attacked yesterday.'

Dr. Jiang looked shocked. She also seemed to be turning something over in her mind. 'Aren't you about to finish up around now?'

'Yes.'

'Are you alright, honey,' she zeroed in, reaching over to take Alice's hands in her own.

Alice's gaze fell to the table.

Dr. Jiang shot me a glance.

'It's a difficult time right now. This thing happened to Jack, and there's other stuff going on and we think perhaps we should let Monsieur Lascelles know. Only, I've never had much contact with him.'

It was a while before Dr. Jiang asked, 'You want to know what he's like?'

Alice nodded.

Letting go of Alice's hands, Dr. Jiang sat back in her chair, and stared out the window at the passing countryside. 'I didn't spend a lot of time with him,' she said. 'Part of a weekend three years ago.'

'And?' Prompted Alice.

'He's brilliant. Borderline genius. Courtly and quite chivalrous in the way some European men can be. Encyclopedic knowledge about our world,' she spun her hand around. 'Mind-body science,' she confirmed. 'You know about the family?'

'JB Pharmaceuticals,' Alice nodded. 'The falling out between Pascal and the other two.'

'I heard that the siblings wanted to keep the family firm heading down the same tracks,' I confirmed. 'But Pascal Lascelles wanted to invest in the next big leap. So there was a falling out.'

'That was some of it,' agreed Dr. Jiang. 'He wanted to take their research and development in a completely different direction. But he also wanted to deepen involvement with the World Health Organization. He's spent a lot of time in Geneva developing high level relationships. He sees the future of global health as collaborative.'

'Sounds philanthropic,' said Alice.

'In part,' agreed Dr. Jiang. 'He also sees the World Health Organization as a treasure house.'

'Meta-data?' I queried.

'Exactly. They collect statistics like no other organization on earth. They have their own reasons for doing so. But that same data can be mined by organizations for different purposes. Pascal saw the benefits of close collaboration. His siblings didn't.'

'What kind of meta-data?' asked Alice.

'I know he has an interest in Asia. He was involved in some studies there. Something to do with the impact of vitamin deficiencies. It wasn't related to my own work. I didn't look at it.'

'How did that study of yours go with him?' asked Alice.

'Useful,' she said. 'Only, like a lot of work in this area, it left us with more questions than answers.'

I already knew that there was one question, in particular, that consumed Dr. Jiang. Waiting while she'd been on her conference call, I had checked her out online. An expert in Qi, the body's electromagnetic energy, or life force, it turned out that she had originally trained as an acupuncturist in San Francisco.

The underlying principle of acupuncture is that Qi is the animating force in all life. In the human body, Qi circulates freely and abundantly unless interrupted or blocked by causes such as emotional or physical stress, injury, or infection. Acupuncturists remove such blockages by accessing specific points on energetic meridians that exist throughout our bodies using needles so fine they don't actually feel like needles.

Practiced for over five thousand years and validated in the West to the extent that even health insurers paid for it, as I knew from personal experience, acupuncture can be dramatically effective, especially for pain management and digestive problems.

From what I'd gathered, Dr. Jiang's career had been spent trying to answer a very specific question: trying to define exactly what Qi is—hence her nickname of 'Dr. Qi.'

Across the table from her I asked, 'Did the research help you define Qi?'

She flashed a glance towards me. 'I think it defined the limits of present-day technology.' Leaning forward in her seat she said, 'One way or another, all the smartest scientists around the world working in this area, are trying to find the answer to a single question. The question is simple. The answer almost certainly isn't.'

Alice and I bent closer.

'The question is: at what point, exactly, does energy become matter? When can you say "this is the place where something that didn't previously exist materially, now does exist." Or, if wave and particle really are impossible to isolate, at what point does the wave, or the field, impact on the particle? How does Qi interact, biologically, to support what functions and to counter what doesn't?'

'At a cellular level?' questioned Alice.

'Even more fundamentally. At an atomic level,' responded Dr. Jiang. 'What interests me is how energy manifests as form, how it affects form. At what precise instant does subtle energy impact on matter, or even become matter?'

I remembered my conversation with George Forbes. How he'd described most medicine as being stuck in the Newtonian, ball and stick view of biophysics, even though we now knew that things were a lot more complex, and less predictable, than that much earlier theory.

'I suppose the way that energy affects matter, or manifests as matter, depends on the energy,' I suggested. 'Aren't the two the same thing? All arises from mind.'

Dr. Jiang met my gaze with the same, keen-eyed scrutiny as a Tiger's Nest lama.

'Are you trying to measure, to quantify what's going on?' I asked.

'That's what you wanted Monsieur Lascelles to invest in, wasn't it?' questioned Alice.

Dr. Jiang nodded. 'Quantum science would tell you that when you have a lack of electron density in the body, you have ill health. Electrons take part in all manner of physiological processes. Oxygen is a powerful electron acceptor. When we breathe, we are literally boosting the proliferation of electrons in our bodies.'

'So—electrons are what Western scientists call Qi?' I asked.

'That's what I have been exploring,' she nodded. 'All living tissues give signals in electron-spin resonance experiments. It's only in the past few years researchers have been focusing on the role of electrons on health. It seems to be the case that when you have an inadequate supply of electrons, you have all kinds of disorders from sleeping problems to chronic inflammation, which can be a precursor to cancer.'

Alice and I were following her closely. I knew that electrons are stable, sub-atomic particles found in all atoms and the primary carriers of electricity in solids. I had never before heard it proposed that electrons could be the Western terminology for Qi or prana. But the suggestion, once made, was irresistible.

'How far did you get with your measurement?' I asked.

Her eyebrows furrowed. 'It's tricky,' she said. 'We know that all biochemical processes are ultimately driven by electron transport. Right now, we know how that works at a cellular level. We know what happens to organs when the cells in them are electron-depleted. The challenge is in observing that precise moment when an electron moves or doesn't move. When it becomes present or is no longer present.'

Alice was nodding.

'How is it that something arises from the field of all possibilities?' Dr. Jiang continued. 'It's going on within and around us at every level constantly—the quantum level, the cellular level, the organic and bodily level. But it all starts,' she was pointing to the table with her two forefingers, 'right here. At the sub-atomic level when things first come into being. And the problem,' she looked from Alice to me, 'is how to monitor the movement of an electron at a sub-atomic level. Following electron movement is something we're not able to do yet. Even if we were able to attach something to them, say, a radioactive tag, that would probably change the way they are transported.'

'The act of observation itself changes what is observed,' I quoted a familiar quantum concept.

'Exactly,' she nodded.

Alice glanced out the window, to where deep-green fields were flashing past. Then turning back to Dr. Jiang, she met her eyes with a direct expression. 'Could you say that intention is a form of energy?'

'I would say that it's *part* of the most subtle form of consciousness, which also includes energy.' Dr. Jiang regarded her significantly. 'Intention doesn't exist in isolation. You can't have intention without a mind; a consciousness giving rise to it. Intention, an aspect of knowingness, is one element of our most subtle mind. The other element is energy. Qi.'

'Knowingness and movement. Two parts of the subtle mind.' I agreed. 'And where the mind goes, energy flows.'

'When we understand the mechanics of that—' began Dr. Jiang.

'—we understand the mechanics of creation.' Alice finished for her.

As I followed what was being said, Alice was saying, 'I can see why you were such an inspiration to Monsieur Lascelles.'

Dr. Jiang leaned back in her chair and fixed Alice with a sharp-eyed scrutiny. 'And you need to know if you can trust him.'

'Can we?' she returned.

'The starting point is that his intention,' she nodded towards Alice, 'to use your word, is for enlightened healthcare. He thinks we're on the cusp of a technological revolution that will see quantum science transform medicine. He believes that we'll come to see chemical methods of treatment, with all their toxic side-effects, with the same collective shudder we now regard medieval surgery. That's where he's headed.'

Behind her words, there was an ambivalence.

'But?' prompted Alice.

Dr. Jiang's eyes narrowed for a while. 'Watch out for his ego.'

'He's ... self-absorbed?' I asked, wondering where she was going with this.

'He didn't talk very much about himself at all, that weekend,' said Dr Jiang. 'He doesn't operate at that level. But I never doubted that he was driven. Messianic. And he needs the validation.'

I recalled what George Forbes had said. *He has something to prove.*

Looking at Alice, Dr. Jiang observed, 'I've no doubt his lack of contact with you is deliberate. Not because he doesn't value what you're doing, but because he doesn't want to taint it.'

Alice raised her eyebrows. It was evidently the first time she'd considered the reserved stance of her benefactor this way.

'I don't really know what you're researching?'

'It's pretty much under wraps,' confirmed Alice.

'Sounds like a Lascelles directive.'

'You say he's Messianic,' Alice wanted to be clear. 'How d'you think that would come into play if I told him I was having some problems with the project?'

'If he thought that his baby was somehow under threat—' Dr. Jiang's regarded her closely, '—he'd move heaven and earth to help you!'

•••

DR. JIANG'S PHONE VIBRATED ON THE TABLE. A SCHEDULED CALL FROM London. Our time was up.

We returned down the carriage, Alice stepped into a space between seating compartments to make a few calls, one of them to George Forbes, with a specific request for his son, Jordan. Jordan's response was, apparently, both immediate and casually confident: when did she want the results, and where should he send them?

By the time Alice returned, the train was starting to slow. Glancing out the window I realized we were arriving at Galway.

'Shall we find somewhere quiet to talk and—,' she held up her phone. I took the gesture to mean that we should call Pascal Lascelles, whose number Dr. Jiang had given her.

I nodded. 'Encouraging, what she said,' I tilted my head behind me in the direction of Dr. Jiang.

Alice met my eyes, nodding.

•••

AT GALWAY WE GOT OFF THE TRAIN AND WALKED THROUGH THE STAtion building outside. Eyre Square comprised a stretch of paving ahead of us, giving onto a grassy park with avenues of trees. We made our way across a paved area, next to the lawn, towards buildings on the opposite side of the square where there were signs for hotels and restaurants.

About halfway across, Alice turned to me, eyes suddenly filled with dread.

'Don't look. They're behind us,' she murmured.

'You're sure?!'

'Nuh. But I think.'

'The two same guys?'

'One's like the guy in the security video. Black hood.'

'How close?'

'Twenty, thirty yards,' she was picking up the pace.

'Here's what we do,' mind racing, I was working out a plan. 'Straight across the road. See the Terrace Hotel? They'll have CCTV. Security. You'll be safe in there.'

'And you?'

'I'm going to keep walking. We'll wave, like I'm going somewhere. I'll head up the road, past the bank. I want to come back and check them out.'

Her face was ashen.

'Okay?' I asked. We were reaching the street on the far side of the square.

'Okay,' she confirmed.

The pedestrian crossing was turning red. On the other side of the street, three steps led up to the lobby of the Terrace Hotel. There wasn't much traffic. I grabbed her hand and we ran across the road, moments before a bus headed towards us from the right, and a motorcyclist appeared on the left.

'Inside!' I told her, as we raised our hands to wave.

She headed up the steps.

I continued walking, facing the street ahead of me for about five seconds before turning back, glancing towards the hotel entrance.

Which was when I saw them. The same two. The tall, pale one with the neck tattoo. The swinging-leg black hoodie. There was no sign of them entering the hotel, or even hesitating at its steps. They were following me.

Had they seen me, noticing them?

Digging my hands in my pockets, I walked faster. *This* wasn't an option I'd considered. I, we, had assumed they were after Alice. There were no shops, pubs, or other entrances immediately ahead. Just a long stretch of polished stone, until steps led up to the bank.

Maybe they were checking out where I was headed.

There were only a few pedestrians around. Light traffic on the road. I could hear their tread on the pavement behind me. Getting closer.

At this rate they would catch up with me before I even reached the entrance to the bank. I glanced across the road, wondering if there was an escape route on the other side.

But opposite there was just another bank. One with dark reflective glass. And as I looked in it, I couldn't help myself looking at them.

They noticed. And were immediately racing towards me.

# CHAPTER THIRTEEN

I BROKE INTO A SPRINT.

Tugging my hands from my pockets, I scrambled as fast as I could towards the bank entrance.

There was no pretending now. They were after me. But why? What possible use could I be to them. I had no idea about Alice's program. Didn't they know?

Instants before I was about to run up the bank steps, the brass-handled doors swung open. Two deliverymen guiding a pallet loaded with files, occupied the entire entrance. They completely blocked it.

I had to keep running.

After the bank came a series of shops selling clothes, jewelry, home-wares. Pursued through the streets of a foreign city, what to do next? I could burst into a quiet retailer. The men would follow. The presence of a shop assistant would offer no defense.

I needed protection. Pounding the pavement at full tilt, people were turning to look. My pursuers were undeterred. I could hear them directly behind me, their footfall hefty. I sped down the pavement, willing on the appearance of a policeman, a soldier—a member of any security apparatus. Driven by adrenaline surging through my system. Taking in unexpected fragments of sounds and odors. I'd never felt more wired as I checked through every option for safety.

I'd seen what they'd done to Bradshaw. His bloodied, inflamed face lying against the Intensive Care Unit pillow was vivid in my mind.

When I reached the row of food outlets, I knew what I must do. There was a line of them selling everything from burgers to baked potatoes to fish and chips. I darted from the pavement into a juice bar. Brightly lit, with fruit color walls, I raced to the stainless steel counter, slid across it, and rushed into the kitchen. Operating a juicing machine, a staff member looked up in shock as I raced past him to a door leading outside. Unlocked.

I pushed the door, finding myself in an alley. The doors of several of the other food outlets opened onto it. Some of them were ajar. As I heard the commotion from where my pursuers were bursting through the kitchen of the juice bar, I stepped into the darkness of a storeroom, closing the door behind me.

I'd bought time—but how much? There weren't many shops in the row. I could hide in a corner and hope they didn't find me. That didn't seem viable.

Instead, I stepped from the storeroom into what turned out to be Tangaroa Tattoos. A large, Māori man was sitting in the tattooist's chair, bent over the morning newspaper as I appeared from the back of his shop.

Looking up, as our eyes met, I saw his broad features were inked heavily in a wrathful depiction of what could be waves of the sea, or flames of fire.

Halfway to the open door I murmured an apology as he launched out of his chair with surprising speed.

Moments later, this was followed by a roar. Instinctively I knew what it meant. Glancing behind, I saw the Māori man standing, legs astride in his tattoo parlor, my two pursuers on the other side of him.

I raced from his shop. Turning right into the street, I was searching for safety. Anywhere that CCTV cameras and a security presence might offer protection. Where was the police station in Galway? The town hall? Putting as much ground between me and my pursuers, it would be only instants before they were back on the chase.

A large, corner building coming up on the right housed a covered market. There was a produce stall on the ground floor, a butcher further on. Behind them, the usual mix of market stalls. Somewhere to disappear? To throw them off completely?

I made my way inside and headed to the back of the building as quickly as possible without creating a scene. I wondered how long it would take them to work out where I'd gone. How far they were behind me. Nearing the back of the market, I knew. A woman shrieked with indignation as she was shoved out the way.

Being a corner, market building, I was expecting entrances on both sides of the premises. But reaching the other side, I found myself up against a wall. Stalls backing onto it. Instead of being a smart move, coming into a warren of stalls, open on several sides, I'd hit a dead end. Nowhere to escape. The only point of exit was the way I'd come in.

There was a bakery on the mezzanine level with a café attached. It was a risk. But with a loud crashing, only a few stalls away from me, and the chaos of scattering wooden beads as a craft stall caved in. I had to keep moving. Up the stairs. Into the back of the café with its view of the whole covered market. An open, upstairs storage area running the full length of the market to a window above the produce stall at the end.

Heart pounding, I sidled towards the edge of the café, taking extreme care of how much I was exposed to the market below. Scanning the people milling around the stalls. Searching for my pursuers.

Having reached the back of the market, they were checking every place I could be hiding. Under counters and behind hangers of clothes. Overturning packing cases and throwing shelving racks aside. It was like watching a rapidly moving vortex of chaos from above. One that lasted only moments before the men decided to try upstairs.

The café was cottagey: lace napkins, dainty bone china tea teacups, and a glass-fronted display laden with cakes. A counter offered the only hiding place, but as I hurried towards it, the stout matriarch of the establishment barred my way. Behind me was a commotion on the stairs. They would appear in seconds.

With nowhere to hide, I had only one option. I raced to the balustrade, vaulting over a 'No Entry' sign. I quickly worked my way behind stacked cases and crates of the storage area. Behind me was a chaos of smashed crockery. A loud wailing from the café. They were on my tail, leaping over the balustrade.

I was flinging packing chests and furniture in my wake. Even though I knew I could be cornering myself, I scrambled to keep them at bay.

Trying to dodge missing floorboards. Throwing back as many obstacles as I could find.

I reached the end of the mezzanine floor. An old, frosted window was at waist height. I smashed it with my right shoe, a sudden gust of cold air coming in.

Directly below were the produce stall's awnings. Just beyond them, having off-loaded produce, an open farmer's truck was idling.

From the other side of a collapsed wall of tea chests came a massive shudder. The head of an axe appeared between boxes. I glimpsed the side of the taller man's face. The tattoo of a tarantula spider, its dark blue legs clutched around his neck. His frenzied expression as he raised the axe to strike again.

There was only one option: I had to get through the window. I kicked at the jagged shards of glass sticking out of the frame. Crouched on all fours to clamber onto the sill. Drawing up, I threw myself from the sill. Flew over the awnings in that curious double-speed of heightened intensity. Part of me was hurtling through the air. That other part, observing it all, moment by moment. Unfolding my legs. Preparing to land. Noticing, at that precise instant, the crunch of gears. The lurch as the truck took off.

It quickly picked up speed in the light traffic. Behind me, my pursuers were momentarily framed in the empty window. Peering through it, the hoodie gesticulated furiously. The pale-head with the tattoo slowly drew a line from one side of his neck to the other.

•••

The truck made swift progress for several hundred yards. If the driver had noticed the lurch as I'd landed in the back, he wasn't stopping to investigate. At the next intersection he turned left. We were now well out of sight of the covered market. As the vehicle slowed behind a double-parked car, I jumped off it, heading into the nearest shop, which sold paint. There, I pulled out my phone, opening a ride-share app.

Two minutes later, a Toyota appeared with an Asian man at the wheel. I confirmed a destination I had just found online—a car-hire firm on the outskirts of town. Via the Terrace Hotel. I slouched out of sight, onto the back seat and sent Alice a text to confirm I was on my way.

There wouldn't have been enough time for my pursuers to get to the Terrace, even if they'd returned immediately. I wondered if there was anyone else outside the hotel, or if it had been only those two.

As we pulled up at the side steps, Alice was running down. Joining me on the back seat, she looked shocked by my disheveled appearance. The perspiration running off the sides of my face.

'What?!' she mouthed as the driver pulled away into the traffic.

'Later,' I murmured. 'We're hiring a car. They were the same two from yesterday. We've shaken them—for now.'

Horrified, she threw a glance over her shoulder as we headed out of Eyre Square, and away from the town center. Meeting my eyes, her face was filled with remorse. She reached over, taking my left hand, and held it between her two, before looking straight ahead out the windshield, fighting to hold it together.

•••

The rental firm had two cars available. We arranged a one-way hire to Dublin. Between Alice and me, we had the required ID and contact information. But it still took time. Half an hour before we were finally in the Volkswagen, heading for the main road.

We were soon surrounded by patchwork fields and lush vegetation, country lanes and distant farmhouses with blue-grey smoke curling from their chimneys. Turning down a narrow road, I headed towards a copse of trees behind which we could stop for a moment, shielded from the road. After the most terrifying pursuit of my life, I just had to get out of the car, stand outside, and breathe.

Alice understood. She seemed in need of the same thing. For the longest time she stood, arms folded against the wind, staring across the rolling fields which fell into the distance, her abdomen rising and falling.

After a while I walked towards her. Turning, she held my eyes, face clouded.

'There's something I need to know,' I held her gaze. 'When was the first time you knew you were being followed?'

She raised her eyebrows before glancing away. 'Things have been going wrong for weeks.'

'Was it before two nights ago, when I visited, you know, as a surprise?'

'I had this feeling I was being watched before then,' she said.

'Watched as in followed?' I had to be specific.

'Hard to explain.' She was shaking her head. 'I knew something was going on.'

•••

'BEFORE YESTERDAY, WHEN WE WERE WALKING TOGETHER. DID YOU ever *see* anyone outside your home? At the lab? Tailing you?'

'Not like that,' she admitted.

I exhaled heavily.

'Why?'

'The two guys today were the same as yesterday. They came at me hard,' I shook my head. 'It was quite the performance.'

'Oh Mattie,' she reached out to squeeze my hands.

'That's when I realized. It's not you they've been following. It's me!'

She looked startled. 'But they were outside the lab when I left work yesterday! They were around again after the two of us left the hotel. After we'd been walking for a while I knew for sure.'

'They were following you,' I nodded. 'Hoping you'd lead them to me. They didn't know where I was staying. I only just got here.'

'If that's true—' she asked, '—what were they doing in Jack's office?'

'That's where I'm stuck,' I was shaking my head. 'I've no idea.'

'How did they know I was on my way to see you?'

'Maybe they didn't. But if they followed you long enough—'

'How do they even know you and I are connected?'

Not for the first time today I recollected Grayson Dalberg's face the evening I'd visited him at his home in Kathmandu. What he'd said about "the circle of our fellow Buddhists involved in the arcana of quantum science."

'They know a lot more about us than you'd imagine,' I said.

'Who are these people, Matt?' She was desperate.

'I don't have the answers,' I nodded. 'But there's something you must know.'

•••

I TOLD HER ABOUT KATHMANDU. THE *TERMA* THAT HAD GONE MISSING from the statue. Being pursued through the streets of Patan by the car with the two Khampas driven by Dalberg's driver. How I'd fled across the border to India, before flying to Dublin.

'What sort of man—' Alice couldn't contain herself, '—has people all over the world, chasing after targets—'

'One of the most notorious art thieves in the Himalayas,' I said. 'Grayson Dalberg.'

She frowned. 'Isn't he the guy the abbot sent you to?'

I was nodding. 'George Forbes told me something else. Dalberg is ex-SAS.'

'What?'

'Long before he got involved in trading antiquities. Obviously, he still has plenty of military connections.'

'It doesn't make sense! The abbot said you could trust him.'

'Yes,' I agreed. 'And I'm sure he believed it. But when you look at everything that's happened since I went to see him. Who else has the network? The motive?'

Alice turned, looking out across the emerald countryside, as a chill breeze blew across the fields.

'You're saying the abbot got it wrong?'

There was a long pause before I replied, 'When people have been closeted away in monasteries for years, even decades, maybe they're not the worldliest.'

'But he said you could trust Dalberg?' She returned to the same question.

'Uh-huh. He's probably one of very few people in Bhutan who would say that.' I felt disloyal, speaking against the abbot, but there was no point pretending. 'Dalberg was banned by the Government of Bhutan after the biggest art heist in the country's history. He denied having anything to do with it, of course. But it doesn't add up.'

'How do you think Dalberg managed to hoodwink the abbot?' Alice was still battling to understand.

'I think the abbot wants to see the best in him.'

Alice turned to meet my eyes directly. 'He's also clairvoyant. Like Geshe-la. Like Lama Tsering—I'm assuming?'

I felt the fierce blaze of her scrutiny.

'However unworldly, however closeted, he can *see*.'

'Is clairvoyance enough,' I challenged her. 'There's plenty of clairvoyant monks in the monasteries of Bhutan, but it didn't stop the art heist.'

Alice considered this for a while before asking, 'Did you bring the *terma* with you to Ireland?

About to reply, I suddenly remembered a phrase the abbot sometimes used, which summed things up. 'It's probably best that I don't burden you with that knowledge.'

For a moment she raised her eyebrows. Before saying, 'Okay.' She wore a small smile. 'For my own good.'

'Pretty much,' I agreed.

•••

FOR THE NEXT HOUR WE DROVE TOWARDS DUBLIN. WE TALKED ABOUT Bradshaw, and when he might be released from ICU. We didn't know how much damage had been inflicted. Even if he'd already been transferred to a general ward, and was up to receiving visitors, there was no guessing how much he would remember. What he would he be willing to say. Plus, the police would also be lining up with questions.

We talked about George Forbes's son, Jordan, and his casual confidence that he could get access into Bradshaw's account.

'What about Dr. Jiang?' Alice asked after a pause. 'What did you make of her?'

'Impressive,' I said. 'I'd never heard it suggested that Qi and electrons might be the same thing. I loved the way she got straight to the heart of it. How thought, how intention can manifest at an atomic level. How things are created. It's like she's on the brink of this whole new approach to healing.'

I glanced over, catching a spark in Alice's eyes.

'Or have I just described your research?'

She fixed me with an ironic expression. 'Its's probably best that I don't ... burden you with that knowledge.'

'Oh really?' I snorted. 'Touché!'

We travelled further before I said, 'What she told us about Lascelles's background was also kind of intriguing.'

'JB Pharmaceuticals,' she said, wryly.

'For someone with an inquiring mind, he must have found it suffocating.'

Alice nodded.

'Were you reassured by what Dr. Jiang said about him?'

'Moving heaven and earth?' she mused. 'We could sure use his help right now.'

'I agree,'

'I'd have tried calling already, only the signal's too weak.'

'Where's your phone?' I was surprised. I hadn't seen her touch it since we were on the train.

She adjusted the grey, cotton scarf at her neck to reveal her mobile, tucked into a pocket. 'Useful for hands-free,' she said. 'I'll keep an eye on the signal.'

'Uh-huh.'

After continuing in silence for a while I said, 'There's something I've wanted to understand about healing practices using meditation, visualization, that kind of thing.'

Looking across, I checked I had her attention.

'We know that something's going on. Whatever it is that you and Dr. Jiang and others are studying. We know it can be incredibly powerful.'

She was nodding.

'But we also know that it doesn't always work.'

'You mean—'

'People with a disease—say a cancer tumor of some kind. They're being treated by specialists. They're doing all the right things by Western medicine. They're also being very diligent applying healing meditations, doing whatever practices their teacher has told them. But instead of getting better, their condition deteriorates. The tumor metastasizes. Perhaps they even end up dying.'

'Yes.'

'So,' I shrugged. 'Doesn't that make this whole area unreliable?'

'Oh, I see,' she said. 'You mean, the results are too hit and miss?'

'Exactly!' I was relieved she was taking the question in her stride.

'Depends on what you monitor and the timeline you apply. Are you monitoring the impact of practice on the symptoms of the disease? Or on the cause of the disease?'

'By the symptoms you mean?' I prompted.

'The growth of a tumor. The impact on inflammation.'

'Most people would say those *are* the disease. Different aspects of it.'

'If you go with that argument you have to ask: where did the disease come from? What caused it to arise?'

'Chronic stress?' I shrugged. 'Genes. Exposure to toxins?'

'That sounds to me like hit and miss,' she said with conviction. 'If you have a family with the same genetic inheritance, why are the genes triggered in some family members and not others? If chronic stress, say, causes heart disease, how come some seriously stressed people are in great physical shape, while others, who have little or no stress, keel over with heart attacks?

'Genes, stress, et cetera, may be contributing factors,' she continued. 'The hypothesis I'm working on, is consistent in that the underlying reason for disease comes from mind itself.'

'Okay,' I said. 'When you say that measuring healing practices depends on what you monitor, what do you mean?'

Next to me, Alice sighed.

'A practice either works or it doesn't, right?'

'Exactly.'

'If you have a well-established, effective meditation practice, either it has an effect or not.'

'Depending on the ability of the practitioner,' I said.

'Of course. But for a regular person with ordinary levels of concentration who takes up the practice, it either has an effect or it doesn't.'

'Sure.'

'What happens if you have a large enough sample of people using the practice over a long enough period of time and hardly any of them show physical symptoms of disease. What could that tell us?'

'That the practice prevents disease?'

'One,' she nodded. Holding up a finger. Before flicking up a second. 'And two?'

I couldn't think of anything else, so I shook my head.

'As important as the first one,' she was wiggling her fingers. Eventually, she answered her own question.

'It proves the hypothesis that disease arises from mind. From consciousness. That's the origin. The source of ease or dis-ease.'

'Okay. But for some people, it comes too late. The practice might be helping their minds—'

'That's why I said it depends on what timeline you apply,' she nodded. 'If you step back from the materialist view of death as the end, if you are open to the idea that the mind continues in some subtle form, then what's better: having consciousness continue with the presence of disease, or without? Even if it's too late to stop the symptoms overwhelming you in this lifetime, what about the future? At some point you will have to deal with the source, the root cause, or it will just manifest again and again.'

'So the healing you're talking about isn't only about this lifetime.'

'We have to move away from that short-term view. When we see consciousness in a more panoramic way, healing practices become even more important. We are healing not only for now, but for very much longer.'

I met her eyes, and the conviction in them, and I thought how closely the perspective she'd just shared chimed with what I'd learned at Tiger's Nest Monastery. How she was articulating the same insights and practices with which I had become familiar, under the care of Lama Tsering.

•••

AS WE CONTINUED, THE SKY DARKENED. AND OUR STOMACHS BEGAN to growl. We needed to eat. We also had to work out where exactly we were headed next. Setting out from Galway, my single-minded goal had been to escape the pursuers—but not by train. I'd assumed we'd head towards Dublin, where I would leave Alice at the safe house outside the city owned by her mystery man Michael.

As we drove and talked, we realized it may be better to keep clear of Dublin. As long as we were in the countryside, somewhere between Galway and Dublin, how could our pursuers possibly find us? Tomorrow, I would take Alice home and we'd speak to Lascelles. For my own part, I'd need to decide what I was going to do next. One thing I knew for certain: there was no way I could return to the hotel.

It was already twilight by the time we reached Tullamore. It wasn't a large town, but driving along the main street we saw a few pubs and places to stay. We made a couple of circuits before coming to O'Meary's, a traditional Irish pub with ornate script on the outside of the building, glowing windows, and the promise of hearty meals. A blackboard at the front announced "Accommodation Available."

The landlady was a matronly woman with apple cheeks and a pair of Jack Russell terriers at her feet. Asked about a room for the night, instead of leading us upstairs, as I had imagined, she showed us to the back of the property, across a parking lot towards what once had been stables, and had subsequently been converted into guest rooms. As she stood at the front door to one of the rooms, searching for the right key, we looked around.

A few yards away, on the other side of the parking lot, was an orchard. The branches of trees were etched as dark silhouettes in the dusk. A subtle, sweet fragrance drifted to where we were standing.

'Pity it's so late,' said Alice. 'I'd like to have explored.'

'Maybe tomorrow?'

Finding the key, the landlady threw open the door and ushered us in. 'You'll find the bedroom with bath to the right, so you will,' she told us. 'Keep on walking for the sitting room.'

The furnishings were basic but clean. I walked right through to the sitting room. When Alice joined me, after pausing to check out the bedroom, I nodded towards the couch. 'That'll do me.' I murmured.

•••

BACK IN BHUTAN, I'D USED TO IMAGINE MEETING UP WITH ALICE AGAIN, for the first time, and how it would be. During the months, then years of our old-fashioned correspondence, I'd wondered where our mutual connection might take us.

How would it be, when we first saw each other again? Whether the closeness that ran as an undercurrent beneath Alice's words would be as tangible as I sensed it, turning the pages of her letters beneath that lone pine tree on a Himalayan mountainside. How would it be, sitting in her presence, across the table at a café or restaurant? How would it feel, just the two of us?

Since Lama Tsering's death, and my hasty departure from Tiger's Nest Monastery, nothing had been as I'd imagined. Including the way things were with Alice. That evening, as I returned to our pub table from having placed our food orders, was the closest things had come to normal. And even that wasn't very.

'Two lemonades,' I set our glasses in front of us. 'And two vegetarian lasagnes ordered. The landlady probably thinks we're a pair of freaks.'

'At least we're hungry freaks in need of a bed,' she said. 'Can't be all bad.' She raised her lemonade.

'May all beings be free from disease,' I held up my own drink.

We clinked our glasses.

♦♦♦

AFTER EATING, WE RETURNED TO THE ROOM. ALICE TRIED PHONING Pascal Lascelles. The reception signal was strong for a rural town, but there was no reply, and no voicemail on which to leave a message. She tried several times again, with the same result. Was he on a plane somewhere? Having dinner? She'd call again in the morning.

I used the shower in the bathroom and came out to the sitting area to find that Alice had turned the sofa into a bed for me.

'Not the ideal arrangement,' she acknowledged, eyes meeting mine.

'But under the circumstances?' I replied.

'Exactly.'

She gave me a hug before going to her room.

•••

IT WAS MORE THAN ONLY A PHYSICAL SHOWER THAT I NEEDED. I ALSO wanted to wash away the horror and the trauma, to leave behind all the bewildering uncertainty, and to reconnect with what was enduring and beyond all this.

I set up a cushion for meditation, wrapped a blanket around my body, and closed my eyes. I took a few, very deep breaths, filling my lungs to capacity and when I let go, I let go of everything—all thoughts and sensations, memories, and emotions. I visualized that I was breathing in prana or Qi, in the form of cleansing light, like the pristine air of a Himalaya morning, and that my exhalations were like smoke, dark with the experiences and trauma from which I wished to be free. Every cycle of breath was both purification and release. An absorption of the positive and liberation from the negative.

*By this practice, may I quickly, quickly achieve enlightenment to lead all other living beings, wherever in the universe they abide, equally and without exception, to complete and perfect Buddhahood.*

For a while I practiced nine-round breathing to settle, re-balance, to let go of Matt the meditator and simply become one with breath. A state of boundless clarity, free from concept or identification, a feeling of primordial peace, without beginning or end.

And, emerging naturally from this state, like a wave out of the ocean, came Lama Tsering in vibrant lapis-blue. Seated in meditation posture with the branch of cherry plum in right hand and bowl of celestial nectars resting on his left, he was looking at me with a love and compassion beyond expression. The embodiment of Sangye Menla, Supreme Healer, Medicine Buddha himself.

Colored lights were radiating from every pore of his body, especially powerful at his heart, as well as at the bowl of nectars on his left hand, emanating dazzling rays with a profusion that were soon enveloping my whole body, pervading my physical form.

"Each one of these colors represents transformational qualities," Lama Tsering had taught me. Through practice, I had become familiar with vividly different sensations arising from the experience of each.

White is the color of purification. All negativities, be they physical disease or unhappy emotional states, all hindrances and suffering, are eliminated through the cleansing radiance of white light. Permeating my whole being, there was nowhere the light didn't reach, not the subtlest element of body or mind that wasn't purified. And, along with the purification, I felt the experience of peace, boundless and all-pervasive, not restricted to my physical form, dissolving all myopic beliefs about being a bag of bones, and revealing instead a far more expansive, subtle reality of awareness as having no limits, no definition within time or space. The tightly-held sense of self was gone, and in its place, simple consciousness with no beginning or end.

Next I sensed blue, the color of healing. A universal archetype, the radiant, lapis-blue color was both dynamic and curative. It had the power to instantly remove pain, inflammation, blockages, pressures, hindrances, and all aberration, turning the tide on disease and washing the body-mind continuum with wave after wave of vitality and vigorous good health. Profoundly impactful and without limit, its purpose was to bring wholeness to consciousness as much as to the body, to eliminate all origins of disease in the mind. Here and now, without any conscious effort on my part, drinking in the deep-blue light strengthened my resilience. Simply abiding in its presence empowered a sense of profound wellbeing.

Red is the color of energy. The flame of passion to create and make vibrant, red is a color that overturns apathy. "Spiritual attainment is not possible without great energy," Lama Tsering used to say. The energy to persevere with enthusiasm along the path of meditation, even when it is rocky. The zest to hold true to one's search for meaning even when at risk of being overwhelmed by circumstance. Red is the force that enlivens a sense of purpose, that gives fire to hopes and dreams. When empowered by red lights and nectars I felt recharged on a level beyond the physical.

Green brings harmony. The profoundly soothing tones of green, the colors of nature, are a visual reminder of our physical origins. Balance is restored. The disconnect that comes from living too much in our thoughts, and too little in the direct present, green is the antidote that reconnects us to nature. Suffused by green lights and nectars I was, once again, restored to myself. Reminded of what was simple. Re-aligned with my authentic roots. I came home.

Gold is the color of joy. The dawn of hope that makes all things possible, the celestial symbol of abundance and optimism. When pervaded with the dynamic energy of gold, there is a buoyant radiance, a welling up of cheerfulness. Gold reminded me of my incomprehensible good fortune—for unlike most beings on earth, I had an inclination to the Dharma and its treasury of practices, a precious opportunity to cultivate bodhichitta, the mind of enlightenment, for the ultimate benefit of both myself and others. If happiness is an inside job, how more incomprehensibly fortunate could anyone be than to have access to the most powerful practices ever devised to cultivate profound wellbeing? With gold came the uplifting recognition: how lucky am I?

That night, I remained in meditation, receiving light and nectar therapy. Exactly what I needed to rebalance and restore. Afterwards, I fell asleep easily.

•••

I awoke to an eerie light. For a few moments I had no idea where I was, being aware only of a greyness, without any shape or form. A coldness that made me huddle under the blanket. For a while I lay, eyes half open, aware only of pearly luminosity. The chill that seemed to come with it.

Where I was, and events of the day before streaming back into my consciousness, I turned my head one way to see the back of the sofa. On the other side were drawn curtains, running the length of the room. It took some moments to get my bearings and to tilt myself up so that I was looking along the short corridor to the bedroom and, beyond it, to the front door. Open.

I remembered Alice turning towards the orchard, already in darkness when we'd got here yesterday evening, the ambrosial fragrances blowing over from the trees. How she'd wanted to look around. I imagined her waking and deciding to walk among the trees at dawn, before anyone else stirred. She must have left the front door off the latch, and it had blown wide. Cold air was pouring in. I was waking fast.

I sat and, as had become my habit in recent days, touched my chest to confirm the presence of the mental cylinder about my neck. As I stood, I pulled the blanket around me as a shawl for warmth. I began walking towards the front door, intending to close it.

On my way, I paused at the bedroom and looked inside. Empty.

Reaching the front door, I had my fingers on the handle when something stopped me in my tracks: a sound from outside. Part-whimper and part-gurgle, it sounded like a trapped beast. And made my hair stand on end.

As soon as I stepped outside, I saw Alice. On the other side of the empty parking lot, in the cold, dawn light. Kneeling under a tree, hog tied with black cable and her mouth gagged. The hooded man with a fistful of her hair in his left hand, wielding a knife with his right, was staring directly at me.

As she saw me, her eyes flooded with tears.

And in that same instant, I lurched to my knees, my legs kicked out from under me. I felt a sharp, rigid thrust in my back.

'You've got something from the statue,' came a voice above me in an Eastern European accent. 'You give!'

# Chapter Fourteen

I raised my hands towards my neck. Instantly, pain seared like lightning up my arms as I slumped to the ground.

'No move.' He commanded. 'Where is it?'

'Neck,' I croaked, so shaken that I could hardly speak.

I felt the blanket grabbed from me and thrown to the ground. My shirt collar tugged back to reveal the twine cord. I was looking at Alice all the while my captor pulled the cord from under my shirt. Both of us were caught in the intensity of this moment of revelation. The grave transgression it signified. Reaching the end of the cord, the man behind me reached the cylinder that he grabbed from around me. Out of the corner of my eye, I saw him thrust it into the air, victorious.

◆◆◆

Next thing I knew, I was coming around on the doorstep.

Beside me, Alice was working frantically at the cable binding her wrists behind her. As she did, she was watching me, crying.

She tried to say my name, but she was so tightly gagged, all that came out was a rasping sound. Bewildered, I looked around, trying to make sense of where I was and what I was doing here.

It took me a while to realize that I could move. My arms and legs were responsive. Even though I was groggy, I managed to roll onto my side slowly and hitch myself up. I still couldn't recall what had happened. How

I got to be here. But Alice was in trouble and needed help. She turned so that I was able to start tugging at the cable around her wrists.

It was minutes before I was able to free her from the tight knot. More time passed as I kneeled behind her, working to remove the gag from her mouth, while she pulled at the noose around her ankles.

As I finally released the cloth at her mouth, she spluttered, bending to draw a deep breath, and gasping for air before coughing soundlessly as she exhaled. She repeated this several times, before wiping her mouth carefully with the back of her arm. The sides of her lips were swollen from the cable.

As our eyes met, I took her into my arms and we held together, on the doorstep.

'Do you remember what happened?' she asked as we broke apart.

I looked into her bloodless face. I hadn't until a moment ago. But it was coming back. The horror of seeing her held hostage on her knees. The recognition that our two pursuers had cornered us. The jab in my back.

I raised my right hand to my head and touched where it felt damp. I looked at my fingertips. They were covered in blood.

'Painkillers,' she was getting up.

She led the way back inside and took a pack of Paracetamol capsules from her bag. I swallowed two. The pain in my head wasn't so much like a headache, more a rawness of a wound from where I'd been struck.

'So.' Staring at me, in distress her blue eyes seemed to have turned grey. 'It *was* you they were after.'

I nodded. 'We've got to get out of here!' I moved to grab my jacket from a chair.

'Why would they come back?' her eyes widened.

'Maybe they think I have more to offer.'

'Do you?'

'Best we leave ASAP.'

Moments later, we were walking to the car. 'How did they even find us?'

'The car hire place?' she suggested, as I clicked the doors open.

'They didn't know what road we'd take. How far we'd go. Not even *we* knew.' Behind the steering wheel, I looked over and we held each other's eyes, sharing the dread of what we'd been through. Apprehension about what lay ahead. I turned the key.

'It just feels like we're ... adrift,' she said.

I nodded, tracking back through all the time I'd been at Tiger's Nest, fixed in a daily routine, but always certain about why I was there and what I was doing. How innocent those days seemed, and how comfortable. Now, like Alice said, there was no certainty of any kind. Our purpose being threatened at every turn.

I had just turned onto the main road that would take us back to Dublin, when my phone rang. Private Number.

Alice held the phone for me, putting it on speaker.

'This is the abbot,' his distinctive voice sounded, as clear as if I was standing right next to him on the worn, embroidered carpet of his office. And instantly conveying with it, that imperturbable, all-knowing authority.

It was in those four words that I was summoned not only to the physicality of his office at Tiger's Nest, but more importantly, to the reality of his presence. 'Remember when you left here, I asked you to see Dalberg?' he said.

I recognized his tone of voice. It was the one he assumed when a monk who'd failed to follow instructions found himself in difficulty and, once again, the abbot had to guide them, like a wayward child, back to the path.

'Yes,' I replied. 'But things went very wrong.'

I told him how I'd gone directly to Dalberg from the airport. How, the very next morning, I'd learned that the *terma* had been separated from the Buddha statue. My subsequent retrieval of the *terma* in Patan before being pursued through Kathmandu and even Ireland.

'You think Dalberg is behind this?' he asked.

'Who else has the means and the motive? I've been chased through the countryside—'

'I know,' he cut me short. 'I can see you, like watching TV.'

Alice and I looked at each other.

'Then you'll know what's been going on for the two of us.'

'Yes, yes.' He took this as a given. 'Death not happening.'

It took me a moment to process this. It was a phrase I'd heard him use before when counselling those around him who were hitting the panic button. Death not happening. The ultimate perspective-setter.

But beneath what he was saying, the abbot seemed to imply that the reason why things had gone wrong was because I hadn't kept in touch with Dalberg. After everything that Alice and I had been through, the accusation was insufferable.

'I *do* have a plan,' I told him.

'What plan?'

'There's a man, a wealthy philanthropist called Pascal Lascelles—'

'Don't trust Lascelles,' he cut me off instantly.

Beside me, Alice was aghast.

'You *know* Lascelles?' I was shocked.

'He was here, in Bhutan, with the World Health Organization. Pretending to be a benefactor, the great savior of monks and nuns. He said he was going to give us all multivitamin pills because we had inadequate diets. He didn't really want to help us. He wanted us to help him. We had something he wanted, only he didn't understand what it was. He even came here, to Tiger's Nest. He showed extraordinary interest poking behind every statue and *thangka*, convinced we were hiding something in plain sight.'

There was that phrase again. The guiding message I'd learned at the feet of Lama Tsering.

'What did Lama Tsering say?' I asked.

'Refused to meet him. Even though Lascelles promised a large donation. We sent him on his way.'

Worried for Alice, I told the abbot, 'Lascelles put up all the money for Alice's research. It's got to the critical phase where the results are about to come out. But there's been shocking interference.'

The abbot didn't skip a beat. 'Dalberg will direct you on what to do next.'

For a moment I was too startled to react. Not only because of the malevolent force behind my pursuers. But also because the abbot was conflating Alice's work with mine.

'Dalberg?' I repeated, in disbelief.

The abbot left the name, suspended in silence.

'Are you saying—' I needed to be clear '—there's some connection between the *terma* and Alice's research?'

'Of course.'

'I don't even know what she's studying!'

'Maybe it's not only Himalayan people who like secrets.' Irony had crept into the abbot's tone.

Alice and I were startled.

'When she tells you,' the abbot seemed to be concluding our conversation, 'I think you'll already know.'

'Okay.'

'You understand what to do now. Thank you and goodbye.'

'Abbot, one last thing?' I cut in.

'Yes?

'Did you travel down the mountain to phone me?'

There was a sigh from the other end before he said, 'A concession to the modern age. After the attack on Lama Tsering, I bought a satellite phone for the monastery. Airtime is expensive. Emergencies only!' he declared. Then hung up.

•••

'DALBERG?' I WAS STRUGGLING WITH THE INSTRUCTION AS I PUT DOWN the phone. The abbot was saying everything I'd come to believe about our pursuers was wrong. We weren't up against an antiquities thief with military training and deep connections in the criminal underworld. Other forces were at work. Worse was the clear inference that I'd somehow made things difficult for myself by disobeying orders. If only I'd kept in touch with Dalberg, he seemed to suggest, things might look a lot different.

'What he said about Lascelles wasn't great,' I glanced over at where Alice was looking out the windscreen, eyes filled with apprehension.

She nodded. 'I'd heard about the WHO work.'

'WHO?"

'World Health Organization. In the early days Jack told me about Lascelles being involved. I thought it was a good thing. Humanitarian venture.'

'What kind of work were they doing in Bhutan?'

'Population health measurement. The kind of study they do in most countries. Lascelles paid for a more detailed measurement of the monastic population. Apparently, there were concerns about monastic diets. Like the abbot said, there was talk of Lascelles providing iron and vitamin supplements. I don't think anything came of it.'

'Not at Tiger's Nest,' I confirmed. In the five years I'd been there, no vitamin supplements had been handed out to the monks. Not that they were needed. The ready supply of fresh vegetables and fruit in the monastery had surprised me—until the secret dimension of the hermitage had been revealed.

My thoughts turned back to Dalberg and the abbot's explicit order that I must call him. How he would 'direct' me on what to do next. The abbot's view of Dalberg I could hardly credit. I hadn't had the chance to tell him about the exhibition in Zurich. How Professor Karl Schneider, an expert on Himalayan antiquities, had identified the stolen Manjushri statue. How it had mysteriously vanished by the time that the exhibition had officially opened.

Reaching up, in what had become an automatic gesture, I touched my chest. Instead of the metal tube—nothing. I wondered where it had got to, right now? Where was it being taken? When might it be opened?

The idea that I should, once again, voluntarily hand myself over to Dalberg troubled me. As I was trying to get my head around what that entailed, beside me Alice said, 'I was amazed when he said there was a connection.'

I glanced over, meeting her eyes.

'Between the *terma* and my program.'

'Yes.'

'Almost like he assumed we knew.'

'That we should have worked it out.'

We travelled in silence for a while, before she said, 'Maybe it shouldn't come as such a great surprise. After all it was Geshe-la who put me onto it.'

'Your program?'

'Now I think about it, he led me there, step by step. Not that it was quite so obvious to me at the time.'

'Skillful means?' I asked.

"Skillful means" was a term used in Tibetan Buddhism whereby more realized people could propel others towards their enlightenment—sometimes without them even recognizing what was going on.

'Exactly,' she said. 'In retrospect, he set it up.'

'What you're saying,' I tried to clarify after a while, 'is that this whole thing has been masterminded by Lama Tsering with the support of Geshe-la?' I pictured my lama, with his timeless features, sitting by the window at Tiger's Nest, with the spectacular Paro Valley sprawled out below. All that had happened in order to bring me from my life in London then Los Angeles, to sit at his feet. Everything Alice had done, and her own move from Los Angeles to Dublin and her research study.

'He has always been at the heart of things,' she agreed. 'I've never had any doubt that Geshe-la did exactly as Lama Tsering requested.'

'Good guru yoga,' I agreed, acutely aware that in my own relationship with both Lama Tsering and, more recently, the abbot, I'd allowed my personal convictions to override their instructions.

'Do you think Lama Tsering told Geshe-la to guide you? Or did Geshe-la just ... know?'

Both of us knew Geshe-la to be a master yogi in possession of perfect clairvoyance. Just like his teacher, Lama Tsering.

'Does it matter?' Alice shrugged. 'At that level, things probably become ... '

'Self-organizing?'

She nodded. Then after we'd been driving for a while, 'Maybe it's time, at our level, we got more organized.'

I thought I knew what she meant but was unsure. The moment the abbot had made his wisecrack about keeping secrets, I wondered if he'd persuaded her to tell me about her program.

I nodded.

•••

WE STOPPED AT TYRRELLSPASS. THE SIDES OF ALICE'S MOUTH WERE still swollen from where she'd been bound, and I needed to wash the black cable smudges from my hands. We found a place that did breakfast and sat down with two coffees while our food was prepared.

Across the table, I met her eyes with an expectant expression.

'Where to begin?' she asked hypothetically, looking from me to the scene outside, where a short lawn rolled towards a thick, verdant hedge.

'I guess with what Dr. Jiang was saying,' she continued. 'About the question a lot of researchers are working on right now: how energy intersects with matter at the most subtle level. Or, as I prefer to think of it, how consciousness intersects with matter.'

I nodded.

'We've always taken it for granted that they do. If someone gets embarrassed, they blush. If they get a shock, the opposite—white as a sheet. If mind and body were separate, that wouldn't happen. Why would the blood vessels in your face dilate or constrict because of a mere thought? A mere emotion? So the intersection has always existed. The most obvious example being sexual arousal. All it takes is for certain thoughts, ideas to arise in the mind of a person and ... ping! A complex chain of physiological events happens effortlessly.'

I met her expression with a grin. 'Yeah.'

'So, how to harness this intersection for the purposes of healing?'

'In a way that's verifiable?'

She regarded me closely. 'In a way that's observable, repeatable, and measurable. A mental software which reliably promotes ease and removes disease. Which has verifiable impacts across the full range of metrics that support longevity.'

'Meditation of some kind?' I asked.

'A form accessible to everyday people who may not have great concentration. It's no good validating a technique that only yogis can use.'

I took a sip of coffee. 'Sounds like something Geshe-la would say.'

She looked at me curiously. 'It *was* Geshe-la who said that. In almost so many words.'

I was nodding.

'Like so much wisdom, it seemed like common sense once he'd pointed it out,' she told me, spelling out the logic in clear, simple terms. 'In ordinary human beings, people with no special abilities, the most subtle way in which consciousness becomes matter is through sound.'

'The thought becomes the word?'

'Exactly. The vibration of vocal cords. The movement of our mouths. That's the first physical manifestation of thought. Sound might not be solid, but it is quantifiable. It has metrics. Unlike thought, sound can be measured.'

'You're saying that sound is energy made form?'

'The wave or the field becomes the particle,' she was nodding. 'As it happens, the idea that words, in particular, are the physical representation of consciousness isn't only a Buddhist idea. It was present in much earlier, Hindu traditions. And much later, in the Bible, the very first line of the Gospel of John: 'In the beginning was the Word, and the Word was with God, and the Word was God.'

I was leaning closer in my chair.

'Where it gets really interesting is the impact of sound on the body. Which isn't something studied in any depth in the West—not yet anyway.'

'Although when you think of music, it's everywhere,' I gestured to speakers on the wall above me.

'Exactly. Music, the language of the emotions,' she nodded. 'We all have our special favorites. They make us feel a particular way. They change us, physiologically. We know this. We just haven't given it the scientific attention that it deserves. Tried to work out what particular sounds correspond to what particular changes. How much these are defined by culture, age, upbringing.'

'Until—' I gestured towards her.

'Kind of,' she admitted. 'While standing on the shoulders of giants. Three thousand years ago, in India, highly realized yogis, or rishis, who had purified their consciousness through meditation, *they* were the ones who understood, in precise detail, the impact of sound on our bodies. They knew, through clairvoyance and personal experience, that our physical body is actually a manifestation of a more subtle body – the astral body – comprising channels and chakras.'

'Dr. Jiang's energetic meridians?'

'Yes. The rishis knew how sound vibration affects the subtle body and the energy, or prana, within it. They knew, for example, that when you make the sound 'Ah,' you are not just making a noise with your vocal cords. That's only what's happening at a gross level. At a subtle level, the vibration of sound rises upwards to the chin, the cheeks, the forehead, the crown, and loops down to the heart. There are five distinctly different positions of the palate, corresponding to different locations of the body, and vibration produced by these different palate positions resonates to promote ease and remove disease. The rishis even developed a language to embody healing: Sanskrit.'

I had met a yogi at the Tiger's Nest hermitage who had told me as much. A man who had spent over twelve years in solitary retreat, and was believed to possess *siddhis*, or special powers, he had explained to me how Sanskrit was the most spiritually powerful language ever conceived. How it had been created in the very distant past by spiritually evolved beings who understood the power of words and sounds to embody different energies.

I remembered reflecting at the time how very different the Eastern world view of evolution was from the Western. In our hemisphere, we were perceived to be on a journey of advancement from the primeval swamp. In the East, the most evolved times were thought to belong to the past. We were the descendants of beings of light, our journey was one less of evolution than devolution.

What if both were right, depending on the yardstick used? What if the technological progress of the West could be harnessed to create a renaissance of Eastern wisdom?

Aloud, I said to Alice, 'I know a lot of the chants we use are in Sanskrit, even though the people teaching them speak Tibetan.'

'And Bhutanese. And Hindi. And many other languages. But the impact of Sanskrit words at an energetic level is understood and implicit in the fact we rely on it so much. When you manifest intention through the sound of that intention, you achieve healing. Wholeness.'

Alice seemed to have summarized an approach to physical wellbeing that seemed at once extraordinarily simple, and at the same time, revolutionary.

'The most precious gift of the rishis,' she lowered her voice, 'was to leave us energetic formulas, condensed into single phrases. Sequences of sounds designed to shift prana, or Qi in specific ways to attain specific goals.'

'You're talking about mantras?' I confirmed.

'Exactly. Mantras to achieve all kinds of purposes. To cultivate inner peace. Abundance. Harmony. To bring about change at the deepest level.'

As she spoke, confirming what I'd thought she might be researching, but had been unable to ask, I felt the hairs on the back of my neck begin to prickle.

'You've been researching the impact of mantra on healing?'

'Yes,' her eyes held mine. 'If there was any language designed for the purposes of healing, it's Sanskrit. Through sound, through vibration, we can embody the healing energies that we already possess. We channel patterns of wholeness at a subtle level, which manifests at a physical level. By chanting mantras, we draw on these energies and magnify them, creating a ripple throughout our entire system, subtle and physical.'

The way she had answered my question made me sure of it now—agreeing with what I asked while avoiding saying exactly what the mantra was. I was remembering what the abbot had said: When she tells you, I think you will already know. Just as I was also remembering one particular afternoon when Lama Tsering had summoned me to his room.

•••

IT HAD BEEN ABOUT EIGHTEEN MONTHS AFTER MY ARRIVAL AT TIGER'S Nest and I had thought it would be a regular meeting about my meditation practice and study, but it had turned out to be far more significant than that.

To begin with, he'd asked me to bring some *po cha*, or butter tea with me. I had learned how to make this drink just the way he liked it in the kitchen of Tiger's Nest. Comprising tea leaves and hot water, along with butter and salt, it was quite unlike the English breakfast tea I'd grown up with, and the oily, savory taste was one I had yet to acquire. But when Lama Tsering asked me for it, the arrangement was that I would prepare his drink while also making a more conventional mug of tea for myself and, if they were available, bring some biscuits to his room.

On such occasions, our conversations were less formal than when he was teaching me, but just as instructive. Often more so, because in the tales he told me of his long and extraordinary life, and in the many stories of spiritual accomplishments he shared, there were always insights, or truths, which set fire to my imagination.

That particular afternoon, there was a quality about Lama Tsering which I had come to recognize from whenever he had just returned from a few days in retreat. I didn't know that his retreats were always at the hermitage, a dimension of the monastery I wasn't even aware existed at the time. The most closely guarded of secrets, it would be still be months before the energetic heart of the monastery was revealed to me. That afternoon, however, began my initiation.

Across the Indian rug, seated on the mattress that served as his meditation cushion, bed, and day chair, my guru met my eyes with a glowing radiance that belied his 96 years of age. His hands unshaking, and gaze lucid, there was a lightness about him; an ethereality as though he'd just come back from another world. Which, in a way, he had.

As always before drinking, Lama Tsering dipped the tip of his left ring finger in the liquid, before flicking droplets in the four directions, offerings to all the unseen Buddhas. Only then did he raise the mug of butter tea to his lips and close his eyes while taking his first sip, swallowing it and nodding towards me with a smile of appreciation. No doubt I had become used to his small stature, narrow face, and ascetic features during my first two years at Tiger's Nest. For when I was with my teacher, I no longer saw an ordinary person, but rather felt a presence harder to define, his physicality representing only a small part of a much greater totality. It was like being enveloped by a benevolent awareness, a knowingness from which there was no escape and yet, at the same time, which communicated the profound feeling that all was well.

We sat for a while without speaking, just drinking tea and listening to the sound of the wind outside, rattling at the shutters. From a nearby window ledge came the cooing of doves. The sound of them continued, more and more insistently.

After a while, Lama Tsering asked, 'You know the story of Vasabandhu and the pigeon?'

I shook my head.

A smile lit his face. 'Vasabandhu was an Indian pandit, a great scholar, well-versed in many teachings, and especially the Abidharmakosha, an ancient Buddhist text. He loved the Abidharmakosha, and even wrote a commentary about it. He knew the verses of the text so well that he would recite them out loud while bathing.

'As it happened, there was a pigeon,' he pointed towards the sill where the doves were gathered, 'who used to sit at the window of the bathroom and listen to him reciting the verses. Over and over. Many times.

'After some years, the pigeon died. Vasabandhu, being clairvoyant, tuned in to see what had become of his little friend. He saw that the pigeon had been reborn as a boy to a family in a nearby village. Very high rebirth for a pigeon!'

I nodded.

'In time, Vasabandhu went to visit the family. As he grew, the boy showed an inclination to the Dharma. Vasabandhu offered to be his teacher. The boy became a novice, and then a monk, and in time he turned out to be a great scholar, just like Vasabandhu. In fact,' Lama Tsering's shoulders began to shake with mirth, 'it was said that his knowledge of the Abidharmakosha was greater than that of Vasabandhu himself!'

I chuckled.

'This is why I like to say mantras and texts out loud,' he was pointing again towards the pigeons. 'They are like us, yes? *Sem-chens,* in Tibetan. Mind-havers.'

'Even though they don't understand what the mantras mean?'

Lama Tsering had raised his right index finger as was his habit when he wanted to emphasize a point. 'Imprints,' he said. 'Our mind is a continuum, yes? Formless, but it keeps flowing because it has an energy to it, a subtle energy. When we repeat a mantra, it leaves an imprint on the continuum at this subtle level because our recitation has an energy too. Intellectual learning, great scholarship, these are part of the personality we acquire in this lifetime. But they dissolve away when we die. They are never seen again. What remains are the energetic imprints. Karmic propensities and habits. This is why,' his eyes were bright, 'enlightenment is possible.'

I was following him closely.

'If we were fixed as the beings we are, if the acquired personality was permanent and solid, we would be stuck with our limitations, our negativities. It is because there is nothing fixed or concrete whatsoever that we can change. We can shape ourselves, transform ourselves. Rise above the mud to flower as a transcendent lotus. All depends,' he nodded significantly, 'on creating positive imprints. Abandoning harmfulness. Cultivating virtue. This is what Buddha meant when he said in the Dhammapada:

*Arrow-smiths fashion arrows.*

*Carpenters shape wood.*

*The virtuous mold themselves.*'

I took a while to absorb what he had said, the two of us sipping our tea in silence accompanied by the wind and the sound of the doves. Before I asked, 'Lama, is there a particular mantra I should learn to create positive imprints?'

For a few moments I felt that I was being held in his awareness, before finally he nodded. 'It is time,' he said, and I knew that I had reached some inflection point in my journey when I was about to be entrusted with a spiritual teaching more precious than I had ever received before.

That afternoon, Lama Tsering taught me a mantra. Known only to him, as well as those relative few he had expressly authorized. A mantra to be held in the strictest secrecy. It was a mantra of unique and extraordinary healing power. Sanskrit syllables packed in a potent formula to bring about transformation first at the subtle, then physical level.

Lama Tsering had also shared with me a visualization to accompany the vibratory energy of the mantra. And a preparatory meditation to optimize the practice, so that the most profound and beneficial imprints were created.

It all began with a nine-round breathing meditation to settle the mind and create an energetic balance. Before the visualization of a lapis-blue Buddha holding a small frond of cherry plumb in his right hand, and a bowl of healing nectars in his left.

Only towards the end of that teaching from my guru had I become aware of a movement beside him, on the mattress he used as bed, chair, and teaching throne. Up till then, I'd given no attention to what was beside him, in the shadows, but there could be no doubting—something moved!

Following my gaze, Lama Tsering reached down and gently touched whatever was at his side. A moment later, the front paws of a cat stretched out from the mattress into space and quivered tremulously. A mouth opened wide in a yawn.

'I didn't know,' I smiled.

'Usually she stays in the hermitage. Sometimes she likes to come this side. I think she wanted to meet you,' he said.

'What's her name?'

'Sorrow,' he said.

I must have misheard. That was far too unhappy a name for any being. 'Sorrow?' I confirmed.

'You will see,' recognizing my confusion, he pointed to his eyes.

I did see. Moments later, the cat drew herself up beside him, looking directly at me. She was a black and white cat, with beautiful markings. And while the fur at her chest and shoulders was white, around her eyes and ears she appeared to be wearing a perfectly symmetrical black mask.

'Zorro!' I said.

She meowed.

'Like this!' Lama Tsering laughed.

I met Zorro's large, golden eyes, delighted by the discovery of her presence, as well as such an unlikely element of Western culture in this remote part of the Himalayas. Meantime, lightness was spilling out from Lama Tsering, filling his room, and Zorro and me, with a playful energy.

'Human. Pigeon. Cat. All *sem-chens*,' he chuckled. 'All possess consciousness and therefore Buddha potential.'

♦♦♦

'THERE WAS A PARTICULAR MANTRA YOU WERE RESEARCHING?' I ASKED Alice now, across the table.

There was no avoiding the directness of my question.

Leaning even closer, I whispered the mantra I had learned at Lama Tsering's feet.

She looked startled.

I explained how Lama Tsering had taught it to me. 'The most powerful of all healing mantras,' I said.

She held my gaze directly. 'I believe so.'

For a while the two of us sat facing each other, registering fully, for the first time, how even though we had spent the past five years pursuing what we believed were our own endeavors, in reality we had been part of a much greater and more important plan. One which had taken me to the Himalayas and Alice to the end of a research project of unprecedented scope: a contemporary, scientific validation of what had arisen in a pristine era of spiritual knowledge and conveyed to us through an unbroken lineage of Tibetan Buddhist masters. The scope of it was simply beyond words.

•••

Over coffee I asked her about her research: how had she set out to establish the power of the secret mantra?

She told me how she'd set up three samples, each comprising a significant one thousand people, with the study conducted over a period of five years. All participants were aged between sixty and seventy years old. A control sample provided the benchmark. Test sample participants were trained in the practice of the mantra and had committed to repeat it for twenty minutes at least five times a week. A second test sample made the same commitment—and were given a made-up mantra of similar length and complexity.

The study she and George undertook had shown that people found it harder to learn made-up mantras and were less likely to keep up the practice of recitation. But it was important to have a test group with a made-up mantra to reveal how much the impact of whatever happened arose from the placebo effect, versus the mantra itself. The placebo effect, as we both knew, was responsible for a large proportion of all healing.

In any trial of a new drug, some people would benefit even when taking chalk pills, simply because of it.

She talked me through the research challenges they'd faced. As a former researcher myself I had always admired her rigor, and the creativity she'd used to design programs that went where no previous studies had gone before. This program was designed to be precise and definitive, while at the same time testing the mantra across an array of metrics to assess impacts on biological functioning and aging markers.

'Anecdotally, I've heard some pretty amazing stories over the past five years,' she told me, eyes shining. 'Of course, I don't know who has been given which mantra.'

'It's so exciting,' I agreed. 'Like you said earlier, what you're doing is validating something already understood when the rishis first conceived of mantras millennia ago. I mean, *we* know from our own experience that mantras have an effect. But they've never been validated in a research setting.'

She nodded. 'The "corpus callosum" is what Jack calls this project.'

I looked at her, questioningly.

'You know, that part of the brain that connects the two hemispheres, east and west?'

'I get it.' And as I nodded, I thought of all the different mantras with their great variety of purposes. 'What you're doing is more than testing a single mantra. You're validating, from a Western perspective, the whole concept of how subtle energy can be harnessed.'

'Exactly,' she was smiling.

'Your findings can be applied to every aspect of consciousness.'

She was nodding, and I was remembering George Forbes's phrase: Copernican-level shift. 'Maybe it's not surprising,' I said, 'there are forces out there that want to get their hands on it.'

She raised her eyebrows before reaching over to touch me with her fingertips, pressing at the place where the *terma* had been suspended around my neck.

'Yours too,' she said.

'What if it's the same mission?' I asked. 'Only we didn't know it.'

'A mission conceived by Padmasambhava himself?' Our eyes were locked together as we contemplated the possibility that it was the intention of one of Tibetan Buddhists most famous yogis, one and a half millennia ago, which had brought us to where we were, here and now. A purpose we had only begun to recognize over breakfast somewhere half a world away?

There was a buzzing sound at Alice's neck. She removed her phone from the pocket in her scarf and looked down to find a message.

'It's from Jordan, George's son,' she looked up with intense anticipation. 'He's sent me a link.'

# Chapter Fifteen

Alice clicked on the message from Jordan. He had successfully hacked into Stan Sutton's 'impenetrable' IT system and retrieved her research files. They were in a zipped document which took time to download. As the separate files came up on her phone, she became totally focused. Then frustrated with the time it took to open each one, every file containing huge volumes of data. She was trying to navigate through complex tables on a tiny screen.

'I'll give you a few minutes,' I said, as she flicked her finger across the screen. So engrossed in what she was doing, I don't know that she even heard me.

I got up and took a walk through the restaurant, which was located within an old castle, and went outside. It was a large, grey stone building fortified with ramparts and a parapet. To the one side was the busy road on which we'd arrived. To the other, a short wall gave onto lush green fields. Walking to the wall, I shoved my hands in my pockets, taking in the scenery as I thought about that morning's call from the abbot, and what he had asked me to do.

His insistence I contact Dalberg again and take orders from him went against all my instincts. I'd had doubts about Dalberg from even before we'd met. I remembered standing in the gallery of his home in Thamel, taking in the spectacular *thangkas*, the transcendent music, and suddenly becoming aware that I was being watched. How Dalberg had professed to not having the connections he self-evidently did. What had happened the very next morning in Patan, when I'd gone to visit Rakesh Sharma and things had gone badly wrong. Dalberg had seemed implicated in it all.

George Forbes' revelations that Dalberg had been in the SAS just went to prove he was a man with unknown networks he could call into play at any time.

But the other thing, first suggested by George and confirmed by what I'd heard subsequently, was something I couldn't ignore. If the contents of the *terma*, and Alice's work, posed a threat to Big Pharma, then what if *they* were the forces we were up against? A global cartel of big businesses, present in every country and overwhelmingly powerful?

My phone buzzed. Reaching into my pocket I found a message from George Forbes. 'Following up, just thought you'd like to see this—one of the few photos of Pascal Lascelles.'

I clicked on the image, waiting for it to appear. I knew that Lascelles was an intensely private man, which was probably why I had no idea what he looked like. After a few moments, up came an image on the screen. Lascelles had a formal demeanor—a broad forehead, steel-rimmed spectacles, and grey hair receding at the front that was brushed back from his face. Clean-shaven, he was dressed in a suit. Just a regular-looking European man, albeit one with an air of privilege.

It was the person he was with that made the image more interesting. He was presenting a *khata*, or white scarf, to a monk I recognized as a highly revered abbot from a monastery in the Bumthang Valley, Bhutan. As he made the traditional offering of respect, the expression on his face seemed to be one of anticipation.

It made me recollect my conversation with my own abbot. I wondered what it was Lascelles had said or done to incite such distrust. The abbot's suspicions about Lascelles were as hard for me to understand as his insistence that I should speak to Dalberg.

•••

RETURNING TO ALICE SOME MINUTES LATER, I FOUND HER IN A STATE of exasperation. 'How am I supposed to make sense of this?'

'Trouble downloading?'

She was shaking her head.

'Screen size?'

'Worse.' She murmured, preoccupied.

I sat down again, deciding to keep quiet till she was ready to speak.

'What I'm seeing,' she flashed a glance in my direction after a while. 'Looks like Test Sample 2 did way better.'

'The group with the made-up mantras?'

She nodded. 'The group with the real practices, the real mantra, was like this tiny blip better than the control group.'

She was swiping through pages of numbers, trying to work through the different parameters.

'You're sure?' I asked.

'Not 100%. On this thing ... ' She shook her phone in frustration.

'We need to get you onto a bigger screen—'

'I'm sure enough.' She met my eyes, her jaw beginning to bruise from where she'd been tied, and her expression deeply troubled. 'I've checked the key markers.'

'It doesn't make any sense,' I replied. 'How could a fake mantra—?'

'Dunno,' she was skimming through pages of tables. 'Placebo drugs work. Placebo surgery works. Why not a placebo mantra?'

'You're saying the Sanskrit mantras had an effect, even though they were jumbled? That, itself, would be—'

'Yeah, but not the purpose of the study,' she shook her head.

'You're sure the double-blind was removed?'

'First thing I checked. It's all across the top of the document.'

I paused before suggesting, 'What if the two test groups were switched?'

'Thought of that,' her tone was somber. 'But they're consistent with the sample sizes.'

'How d'you mean?'

'As we know from my previous study with George, there's a lower adherence to fake mantras. More people drop out. The sample is smaller—still statistically robust, but smaller than the real mantra sample. But here we have the larger sample,' she was shaking her phone, 'the people with the real deal, showing practically zero benefits.'

'Maybe we need to call Jordan?'

'At school?' her tone was caustic.

'Just to ask about the integrity of the material.' I was clutching at straws.

For a long while we sat in silence, trying to deal with a disappointment so great it felt somehow unbelievable.

Eventually, face still buried, she said, 'I'm sorry. I shouldn't be so reactive.'

I reached over with both hands, holding her by the shoulders, my forehead touching hers. 'It's okay,' I whispered.

•••

WE WALKED OUT TO THE CAR AND WERE SOON BACK ON THE MAIN ROAD to Dublin. She sent a text to Jordan. She needed to be sure there were no other research files. But even as she keyed in the message, the futility of what she was doing seemed self-evident.

After pressing 'Send' she asked, 'Are you making that call?'

'Call?'

'Like the abbot said. To Dalberg.'

'I've been thinking about it,' I said.

'What's there to think about?

I shrugged. How to put it into words?

'The abbot told you to call him.'

'So I should?' I knew it sounded petulant. But after everything that had happened, I was finding it hard to change direction so suddenly. I wasn't a robot that could smoothly execute a 180 degree turn at the press of a button. 'Maybe I'm not so good at guru yoga as you are,' I glanced over.

In Tibetan Buddhism, teachers are not simply regarded as people who impart information. Because the practices they share are the cause of enlightenment, teachers manifest the work of Buddhas. As students, we are to see them not so much as ordinary people but, at the very least, as Buddha-like, a process of alignment called guru-yoga.

'Being independent-minded is all very well,' she replied directly. 'But where has it got you?'

I raised my eyebrows.

'One of the meanings of "Dharma,"' she reminded me, 'is "the truth".'

'So?'

'So if a teacher is telling the truth, what's the problem doing as he suggests?'

'Because Buddha also said you shouldn't just blindly accept things,' I was irked by her persistence.

'Sure he did.'

'What if you're told to do something that goes against your experience—'

'When has the abbot done that?'

'This whole Dalberg thing,' I replied. 'It's not only that most of Bhutan believes Dalberg is a con artist. I know what happened to me in Kathmandu. What's happening to us right now.'

'And you still think it's because of Dalberg?' She didn't mask her vexation.

'I don't know what to think,' I retorted.

We fell into silence for some time, before she spoke again in a tone more conciliatory, 'What would you have to lose by calling him?' she asked.

I thought for a moment, before shrugging. 'Revealing where we are?'

'If he's behind all this, he already knows we're in Ireland.'

'Somewhere,' I conceded.

After another pause, she asked, 'What would it take for him to prove he wasn't working against us?'

'That's easy,' I flashed her a glance. 'He could provide a convincing explanation.'

'Isn't it worth giving him a chance to do that?'

I shrugged.

'After what the abbot said about Lascelles,' she told me. 'I'm not trying him again. Anyway, with my results ... ' she turned away, looking out at the passing countryside, her expression downcast.

•••

I KNEW I MUST DO SOMETHING—FOR ALICE AS WELL AS FOR ME. WE'D hit rock bottom. Our pursuers making off with their trophy from around my neck. The revelation that Alice's own treasure, her program, having apparently come to nothing. We were heading swiftly towards Dublin. What then?

Would we still be relentlessly pursued, or had this morning's attackers got all they'd come for? Was Jack Bradshaw still lying in ICU, or would he be able to speak? Even if he was available, would it make any difference? What was I to do next? And Alice?

'*The mind is like tissue paper blowing this way and that,*' the words of Lama Tsering came to me suddenly. And the memory of him, sitting in his room overlooking the Paro valley, using his right hand to indicate something flimsy and unsubstantial blowing and curling in the breeze. '*Clear direction is what we need if we are to attain progress, yes?*'

I remembered nodding at the truth in what he said.

He was leaning forward in his seat, as he always did when wanting to emphasize a point. '*Where do we find clear direction? From the lamas.*'

Even the word "lama" he had explained to me, implied this point. It was the combination of two Tibetan words. *La* or *bla,* meaning higher in spiritual experience or virtue. And *ma,* meaning mother. A lama gladly accepted responsibility for the spiritual nurturing of others.

I looked at where Alice was sitting in the passenger seat. 'I'll call Dalberg,' I told her. I nodded towards where my phone was in a compartment between us. 'Can you look up his number please?'

•••

'YOU'VE BEEN LYING LOW,' DALBERG'S CUT-CRYSTAL ACCENT SOUNDED through the car speakers, within a few rings of Alice dialing. We were using her phone because it had a stronger signal.

'It's been a busy time.'

There was a pause before Dalberg replied, 'We lost track of you after the Khampas hijacked Dipesh. They did him serious damage. His right arm is broken in two places.'

Usually I would have been dismayed by this news. But how did I know he could be believed?

'I sent him away from outside my hotel.'

'I know.'

'I called you, wanting to pass on some news.'

I remembered ignoring his call in the taxi to Patan. 'What about?' I asked. 'The statue?'

'That too. Mainly to tell you that you were being watched.'

'What?'

'Men outside your hotel. Dipesh tried to warn you.'

I recalled his intense, indecipherable expression.

'I told him to follow,' said Dalberg. 'Then Khampas arrived. Got rid of your taxi. Hijacked Dipesh.'

This was a very different version of events from the one I had imagined.

'We delayed the Sangye Menla statue going out,' he continued. 'It still went to Hong Kong, the next day. I thought it would disappear behind the red curtain. Become one of Comrade Ziu's Lamaland exhibits. But after two days on the ground, it was loaded onto a different carrier. Right now it's on an aircraft headed in the opposite direction. It's bound for Milan.'

'Right,' I observed.

'We couldn't get access to the statue before it left Kathmandu,' he said. 'But … intermediaries installed a GPS locator in the container.'

I hardly needed reminding of Dalberg's network of influence.

'Once it gets to Milan, and comes out the container, we can only guess where it goes next.'

'But you have an idea?' I responded to his tone.

'I've been thinking about little else,' he responded. 'And making inquiries. Being in Kathmandu, I'm on the wrong side of the world to prove the theory.'

'Which is?'

'That the individual who ordered the theft of the Sangye Menla statue did so expecting it to contain a *terma* of inestimable value—not financially, but because of the instructions it contains. He didn't know that statue-stripping comes as standard in Kathmandu. When he heard the *terma* had been removed in Patan, he sent the Khampas after it. And, by extension, you. In the meantime, he arranged to have the statue sent to one of his homes.'

'Why does he want the *terma*?'

'For years he's been in pursuit of *elixir vitae*. The secret to prolonging life indefinitely.'

•••

ALICE AND I EXCHANGED AN ELECTRIFIED GLANCE.

'It's *my* belief,' said Dalberg, 'he's convinced the recipe for this is contained in the *terma*.'

'Why?' I asked.

'I don't know precisely. It seems that he's comes across something unusual about the monks at Tiger's Nest. You would know more about that than me. Do they live to a particularly advanced age?'

I was immediately thinking of the hermitage and its resident monks. The radiant glow with which Lama Tsering used to return from retreating there.

'Monastic communities are often long-lived,' I replied cautiously.

'Tiger's Nest perhaps more so than usual?' he returned.

I remembered what the abbot had said about Lascelles coming to Tiger's Nest wanting to see everything "poking behind every statue and *thangka*, convinced we were hiding something in plain sight." Dalberg's theory was making sense.

'He's made a connection of some kind. He's an immensely wealthy man. Well-connected globally. I think you'll find, Matt, that he'll stop at nothing to get the *terma*.'

'I think I—' I was meeting Alice's eyes again, '—we, have already found that.'

'Ah,' he paused. 'And his operatives—?'

I knew exactly where he was heading. 'Got what they came for.'

There was a long silence at the other end before he asked, with a solicitous tone, 'Are you okay?'

'Just,' I responded. 'And what you're saying. The guy you're talking about. Is it Pascal Lascelles?'

'The abbot told you?'

'Not a lot.'

'Just about the steal-to-order thefts ten years ago?'

'No,' I was shaking my head.

'He has exquisite taste, Pascal. And the means to acquire artefacts even when they're not for sale.'

'So why—' I decided to ask him directly, '—does the Bhutanese Government believe you were behind the thefts?'

'Pascal Lascelles is a generous benefactor in the Himalayas. They *wanted* to believe him. When he showed them fake invoices from Dalberg Antiquities they saw no reason to investigate further. As it happens, it was the Buddha of Wisdom himself who revealed the truth.'

'Manjushri?'

'At a small exhibition I curated in Zurich. I invited some well-known collectors to contribute pieces. They included Pascal Lascelles. One of Lascelles's underlings delivered the wrong statue. I wasn't in the gallery at the time, and the error was quickly corrected. But the statue was recognized by a well-known academic who happened to be passing by.'

'Professor Schneider?'

'You've been doing your homework.'

I'd agreed with Alice that I should give Dalberg a chance to make a convincing explanation. Everything he had just told us had a perverse but irrefutable logic.

'One thing about Lascelles's ... operatives,' I said. It seems that wherever I go, they know where to find me.'

'Lascelles invests in cellular networks,' Dalberg didn't hesitate. 'If they have your phone number, they have your GPS.'

I felt a sudden chill recognizing how naïve I'd been the night before, believing we were safe just because we were deep in the countryside. In reality we had been obvious targets. Just like we were right now.

'In that case, I'd better ditch this SIM card as soon as possible.'

'A wise precaution,' he agreed. 'Perhaps an unnecessary one if Lascelles already has what he wanted. I have a feeling that the timing of all this has been dictated by him.'

'The timing of the *terma* theft? Or what's happening with Alice?' I realized I hadn't, so far, referred to Alice. Or even revealed where we were. I was asking not so much to seek an answer to my question, as I was to find out how much he knew about where I was and who I was with.

'I was talking about the *terma*,' he returned, immediately. 'Alice is your scientist friend?'

'Yes.'

'If her work is in some way related, no doubt it would be of keen interest.'

'You mentioned timing,' I returned to what he'd said. 'Why the urgency?'

There was a pause at the other end before Dalberg asked, 'Have you ever heard of an organization called the *Accademia del Cimento*?'

'Can't say I have.'

'A very ancient and elite scientific society going back to the days of Galileo. Nobel prize winners and other eminent scientists. Each year they hold a dinner, amid great ceremony, followed by a short presentation by one of their members. Lascelles has been bankrolling them for years in the hope that the day would finally come when he could offer a presentation of his own.'

Alice and I looked at each other in immediate recognition. So this was behind everything she'd been experiencing in recent weeks. It was true that he must have drawn an inspired connection between her work and my *terma*—a connection that neither Alice nor I had made during the past five years. But that had been for reasons of professional confidentiality on Alice's part, which Lascelles himself had done his utmost to enforce.

'So there's a gathering of the *Accademia del Cimento* coming up?'

'Indeed.'

'And Lascelles is the speaker?'

'No doubt one of the more intriguing presentations in the Society's history. If he was able to prove the case for his *elixir vitae*, in whatever form it takes, there could be no more triumphant endorsement than theirs.'

'Earlier you said this whole thing is just a theory,' I said to Dalberg. 'But you're not on the right side of the world to prove it. What side of the world would that be?'

'Somewhere in striking distance of Milan. That's where the statue is landing. And that's where the *Accademia del Cimento* holds its annual meeting.'

'The abbot has told me I must return the statue and *terma* to Tiger's Nest,' I explained.

'And where are you now?'

'Ireland.'

There was a long pause before he said, 'You're closer than I thought. But you'd still have to act swiftly. The Sangye Menla statue is due to touch down in Milan at lunchtime.'

I glanced at the dashboard clock. Just after ten a.m.

'And when is the *Accademia del Cimento* dinner?' I asked.

'Tonight.'

## Chapter Sixteen

As soon as we reached Dublin, we bought new SIM cards for our phones, having buried our previous ones at the side of the road as soon as I'd ended with Dalberg. Then we sped to the airport. There was a flight that would get us into Milan early in the afternoon. Between buying two of the remaining seats and boarding, we picked up fresh clothes.

I was firm with Alice that she didn't have to come with me. The abbot had set a particular mission that was mine to undertake. I had no idea what I was getting into. It might put me in further danger. At the very least I wanted to confirm if Dalberg's theory was true: if the Sangye Menla statue showed up at Pascal Lascelles's Italian home, it would confirm that he had masterminded its theft and all the violence that had followed both Alice and me, culminating in the horror of dawn this morning.

Given what we had learned about Lascelles's long-held ambition to be the messiah who stopped aging, the man who halted entropy in its tracks, it would also put him at the center of whatever had been going on with Jack Bradshaw. Had he gained access to the results several weeks back, Alice wondered? Had the delays and obfuscation been about Lascelles putting pressure on Bradshaw to manipulate the results? To fix the findings to support his grand vision?

Alice was still reeling, hardly able to believe the results. She had spoken to Jordan during the morning. Soon after I'd called Dalberg, she'd heard from Jordan during his morning break. He'd confirmed that the files were exactly as he'd found them on the system. As they spoke, he had even gone back into her network to scrutinize their edit history. Since the double-blind had been removed, he confirmed, the results had not been tampered with. They had been locked, saved, their integrity protected. The results were the results.

He had also confirmed that all the files had been manually downloaded by the hooded intruder the night Bradshaw's pass had been stolen. One way or another, Lascelles was involved. Why exactly he'd sought to steal findings that were to be revealed anyway, was unfathomable right now. Unless, of course, he'd wanted to appropriate them for himself, to show off to his friends at the *Accademia del Cimento.*

•••

In the airport departure lounge, I waited for Alice to return from the bathrooms where she was freshening up. I was still reflecting on the conversation with Dalberg. How right, I thought ruefully, that Alice had been to insist that I make the phone call. The skill with which she had persuaded me. Dalberg *had* been able to provide a very coherent explanation. Lascelles's motivation for wanting to lay his hands on the *terma* also made an undeniable sense, given his conviction about the value of what it contained.

I had also been startled by Dalberg's account of how it had been Lascelles who was behind the greatest art heist in Bhutan's history. How, with the aid of deep pockets and falsified receipts, he'd been able to distract the authorities into believing otherwise.

But there was one thing, above all else, that kept coming back as I mulled things over: Dalberg's phrase "he's made a connection of some kind." And his questions about the longevity of monks at Tiger's Nest. I had never really considered the subject properly. Of course, I knew of Lama Tsering's ripe old age a long time before meeting him. I had no preconceptions about the age of other monks that I would meet at the monastery—and they varied greatly from novices through to old men. But there was no doubt that residents of the hermitage were all of advanced years. They didn't show it—and I guessed that was the point. In terms of years lived, they may be old men, but the way they behaved and interacted, the lightness of their beings, the vibrancy of their presence, was timeless.

Youth or old age had never come into my mind, because they didn't seem old.

Alice came back to the lounge, refreshed and purposeful in a new, blue top and jeans. Her blonde hair brushed sleek about her shoulders and freshly made-up, there was no sign of what she'd been through this morning apart from a slight swelling at the sides of her mouth.

'I keep going back to what Dalberg said about Lascelles making a connection,' I said as she sat on the lounge chair beside me.

She nodded. 'Tied in with what the abbot said.'

'So what's the World Health thing you mentioned?'

'The WHO regularly publish reports on health metrics in most countries.'

'Dalberg suggested the monastic population in Bhutan is long living.'

She nodded.

'And you told me before that Lascelles paid for a more detailed measurement of them.'

Alice was already pulling her phone out of the grey, cotton scarf at her neck. 'Life expectancy. He probably found they were significantly older.'

'You mentioned something about iron and vitamin supplements?'

'Now we know his agenda,' she said, opening a search field. 'That was probably just a cover.'

'Exactly how detailed do the reports go?' I asked.

She nodded towards the phone. 'That's what I want to find out.'

'They're publicly available?'

'Some are,' she had already navigated to a website and was keying in some words. Then, waiting for a page to download she said, 'Hey, it was good what Dalberg said about the scooter?'

I smiled, nodding. At the end of our conversation, Dalberg had dropped in that Dipesh had told him about the purple Mahindri scooter I had "borrowed" in Kathmandu. One of his staff had located it, at the bottom of a stupa in Durbar Square. With the help of the police, and using the registration plate, the owner had been traced, vehicle returned and, what Dalberg had described in his upper-crust voice as a "vexation fee" had been paid.

'That was a clincher for me,' I admitted.

'Thought it might have been,' she was looking back at the phone as a table appeared.

After a few moments she pointed to a row of figures, 'Life expectancy of Bhutan is higher than neighboring countries,' she said. 'Not unusually so.'

'Any breakdowns of the figures?'

'Not here. Small population anyway—only 800,000.' She scrolled down the page till she found what she was after. 'Country representative,' she read the name.

'You know her?'

'We've had dealings,' she pressed the hyperlink. 'Let's see what she has to say.'

She got up from where our part of the lounge was filling up and moved to a quieter part near a deserted newspaper rack. I watched her engaged in conversation, walking up and down holding the phone to her face with one hand, the other folded about her waist.

A group of fellow travelers got up and hurried to the departure gate. This was followed by an official announcement that boarding had commenced. It wasn't a large aircraft and processing didn't take long. Alice remained in animated conversation as people streamed through the gate. She only ended as the departure lounge had completely emptied. We were the final passengers to step into the airbridge.

'Useful?' I asked, as we headed towards the aircraft door.

'Ever heard of the "Bhutan Blip?"'

I shook my head.

'The country as a whole has a strong longevity figure—we saw that. It seems longevity is pretty average in the ordinary population. But the monastic segment pulls the score upwards. Some years ago, a benefactor paid for a more detailed census. Which is how they established the trend they call the Bhutan Blip. They weren't able to give me the name of the benefactor,' she delivered a droll look.

'Or provide the data he paid for, I suppose?'

'They can accept external funding, apparently, but only on the basis that the data are made available for anyone who knows to ask.'

'So we can see it?' I raised my eyebrows.

Alice tapped her scarf. 'I'm hoping it's on its way to me right now.'

'How do they explain the Bhutan Blip?'

'Social integration is what they're saying. It's a more effective predictor of longevity than diet, exercise, and other lifestyle factors. Monasteries are highly cohesive communities. People get taken care of. But that's just a guess. It's not something they've worked on.'

'The WHO are not in the business of discovering *elixir vitae*?' I confirmed.

'I guess not,' she said.

Once we were in our seats, Alice took out her phone again and clicked on the email icon. We didn't have long to wait before an email arrived from her WHO contact, providing a page link. Clicking on it took us to a listing of seven different monasteries—the more detailed census paid for by Lascelles. I recognized the names of the monasteries, located from Paro Valley in the West, through to Trongsa Dzong in the center of Bhutan, right across to the beautiful Bumthang Valley in the East.

Below the list was a graph showing life expectancies across the seven. What was instantly striking was the result for Tiger's Nest, or Paro Taktsang. It was way off the chart. Compared to a life expectancy in the late 70s for the other monasteries – average life expectancy in Bhutan, as a whole, being just 70 years of age – at Tiger's Nest the figure was 93. The single bar stretching out beside the words 'Paro Taktsang' left all other data in the dust.

'Not so much a blip as a spike,' I said, as we peered at the graph on the small screen.

'The woman did say there was one monastery that had much stronger results than the others. She couldn't remember the name. Hasn't looked at the data for years.'

Alice was scrolling down the page. The sample numbers for each monastery was shown. Tiger's Nest reported a sample of 150.

'I'm surprised they can fit that many onto the side of a cliff,' she said.

'Bit of a warren.'

'All the same, not a big enough sample to be statistically significant. You'd need multiple times that number.' I knew that was reflecting on her own research.

'Like a thousand?' I murmured sympathetically.

She met my eyes with a pained expression.

'I guess that's why Lascelles was funding you.'

She was nodding. 'Smart guy. He knew about this,' she waved her phone. 'Neither of us did. Which makes you wonder: what else does he know?'

•••

AS SOON AS WE REACHED MILAN MALPENSA AIRPORT, WE WENT TO A car hire place. I took care of the paperwork while Alice called Dalberg for an update.

The Sangye Menla statue had arrived in Milan on schedule, he told her, and the container offloaded from the aircraft. It was Dalberg's opinion that because the statue was hot property, Lascelles would have arranged for it to be processed as fast as possible. Lascelles was a man of means. He quite probably had friends in high places. We should act immediately.

We were soon on the road headed for Lascelles's Italian home—a villa on the banks of Lake Como in Cernobbio. Our maps app told us it would take just over an hour to get there.

Heading swiftly along the Autostrade, we had no definite plans for what would happen when we got to the other end. At the very least, we thought, we'd find a place to keep watch on Lascelles's home. We'd try to observe if a delivery was made.

Even this modest goal was less easy than we imagined. We arrived at Lake Como in mid-afternoon on a perfect, cloudless day. Row after row of ornate lakeside mansions, and their immaculately manicured gardens, ascended from the lake like seats in a theatre. Lascelles's villa, a spectacular three-story mansion directly fronting onto the lake, was accessed by a narrow public road, which curved around the perimeter of the property, barely accommodating one lane of traffic each way. A forbidding, high wall protected the mansion on the street side, with the only access through locked, steel gates. There was a cobbled yard immediately inside the gates, leading to a stately entrance door under a columned portico, with garages on the left-hand side, and a large conservatory to the right.

There was no place to park the car at the roadside and keep discreet surveillance. Unless you were directly outside the gates, and immediately obvious, there was no way you could observe the comings and goings.

'Looks deserted,' Alice observed as we approached the place. The gabled windows along the sweeping front of the house, overlooking the lake, were firmly closed. The terrace lawns neatly trimmed. The cobbled yard beside the garages immaculately leaf-free. The house seemed unoccupied.

On the other side of the road from the entry gate was the bottom of a garden. It belonged to a similarly impressive but deserted residence up the hill. Driving past Lascelles's house, we continued for a short distance, coming to a leafy park overlooking the aquamarine waters. We left the car there, returning to the garden opposite Lascelles's on foot.

There was no barrier to entry besides a low, wrought-iron fence. We headed into the garden from a point far beyond the sweep of whatever security cameras Lascelles might have mounted around his house. We made our way behind a hibiscus hedge, directly facing Lascelles's gate, which offered a vantage point. We didn't know how long we'd be staking out Lascelles's house. For all we knew, we could be waiting for the rest of the afternoon.

•••

As things turned out, we didn't have long to wait. Just under forty minutes after we arrived, an unmarked, white Mercedes Benz Sprinter van slowed down as it approached the mansion. On went the turn signal. It turned into the driveway.

A deliveryman in dark pants and a white polo shirt stepped from the driver's seat. He approached a brass console to the left of the gates and pressed the buzzer. When there was no immediate response, he folded his arms and glanced about distractedly. He walked to the front tire of his vehicle. Tapped it with the toe of his shoe. Looked at his watch before returning to the buzzer, pressing it again.

This time, when there was no response, he pulled his phone out of his pocket and fiddled with the screen before holding it to his ear. Soon, he was issuing a stream of Italian language, gesticulating frustration in the direction of the house before him.

Call coming to an end, he replaced the phone in his pocket and once again approached the buzzer. This time he held his hand on it for a very long time, before jabbing it in exasperated bursts.

It seemed to take an eternity, but finally the front door was opened. A woman in a blue housekeeping dress peered from the darkness into the bright afternoon. She was tall, hawk-faced, her grey hair pinned in a bun. After a brief exchange, she stepped back and closed the door again. The driver returned to his vehicle, slamming the door shut.

Moments later, the gate was rolling open.

From behind the hibiscus, Alice and I watched the driver guide the vehicle towards the house, pulling up parallel to it.

The housekeeper appeared in the conservatory and was unlocking some French doors. Getting out of his seat, we could hear the driver opening the sliding door on his side of the van. He was evidently fetching a delivery box out of it.

'Shall we?' I gestured towards the house, impulsively. Spur of the moment. What risk was there from an elderly housekeeper? I guessed that whatever alarms might have been in place were currently deactivated.

Alice nodded.

Immediately, we were scrambling around the hibiscus hedge. Over the wrought iron fence and across the road.

The gates were already starting to close automatically. Reaching the other side of the van, we saw the driver carrying a box, exactly the right size for the Sangye Menla statue. He was walking behind the housekeeper across a short lawn into the conservatory.

We followed.

Inside, we were hit by a wall of stuffy heat. We continued through the mugginess, passing through a room bedecked with sumptuous sofas and Persian carpets. Heading into the gloomy interior, after the conservatory we were in the hallway, from where the housekeeper had opened the front door. Even with the curtains drawn, it was evident that this was a spectacular salon, with a marbled floor, a sweeping staircase, a central table on which stood a massive vase – currently empty – and huge, giltwood mirrors on each wall, reflecting us as we stepped into the semi-shadows.

After the hallway came a large dining room. Multiple arched doorways fronted onto the picturesque vista of the lake. A huge table ran the length of the room—thirty people, at least, could be accommodated in the polished ornate chairs that ran down both sides. Three enormous crystal chandeliers were suspended from the ceiling.

Crouching behind the table, we continued moving. The voices of the housekeeper and deliveryman were close by. In the very next room? Alice and I crawled between chairs and under the table. We couldn't be seen, so long as we stayed here, could we?

There were brief exchanges in Italian. The deliveryman seemed to be asking for direction.

There sounded like a misunderstanding, as if the housekeeper expected something unanticipated.

Muffled, cracking sounds emerged from the room. The housekeeper kept repeating something snappily. After a pause came a loud thud. Then, after the briefest exchange, approaching footsteps as the two returned through the dining room.

We watched their legs file past, the deliveryman followed by the housekeeper. We heard their footsteps retreating through the hallway. Followed, a short while later, by the housekeeper making her solitary return, muttering grievously under her breath. There was further activity in the next-door room, cracking and brushing. Then the housekeeper's footsteps fading into the distance. A while later, the resounding thud of a far-away door being shut.

We waited in silence for the longest time. Then we crept out from between the chairs, got to our feet and, quietly as possible, walked in the direction that the box had been carried.

Next door wasn't like any kind of room you might imagine in an Italian villa. Even larger than the dining chamber, rising to a second story and with a dramatic vaulted ceiling, massive *thangkas* bedecked the walls on both sides of the room, which faced onto Lake Como. At the opposite end from the lake was an altar on which was set out a magnificent array of Buddha statues. From the handwoven carpet of the expansive chamber, to the brocade curtains on the windows, every surface was decorated with elaborate motifs—the eight auspicious objects of Tibetan Buddhism, mantric symbols, and other ancient emblems from India and the Himalayas. To encounter such a place, set amid the cultivated beauty of one of Italy's most celebrated vistas, wasn't simply unexpected. I remembered what Dalberg had said about Lascelles—*He has exquisite taste, Pascal. And the means to acquire artefacts even when they're not for sale.*

I looked from item to item. There was the wall-hanging of the thousand-armed Avalokiteshvara, along with Green Tara, the female protector. The gigantic Wheel of Life *thangka*. In central place on the altar was the statue of Shakyamuni Buddha fashioned in twenty-four-carat gold, adorned with rubies, emeralds, and diamonds. Next to it, Manjushri, the Bodhisattva of Great Wisdom, that had been stolen from Kurjey Lhakhang. The one I had read about in the online article, glimpsed briefly by Professor Karl Schneider.

As I ran through the checklist of Bhutan's looted statues and *thangkas*, I realized why this place felt so utterly incongruous. It may have been intended as an homage to a Tibetan Buddhist temple. A celebration of the wisdom and compassion, advanced to its ultimate expression by our precious lineage masters since the time of Shakyamuni Buddha himself. But in reality, it was a corruption of all that Buddhism stood for. The *thangkas* and statues may rank among the most beautiful of their kind ever created. But they were stolen. This place had none of what I'd once heard an esoteric teacher describe as "the milk and honey of devotional energy" of the kind you would feel, as a palpable force, at even the most humble mountain shrine in the Himalayas. It was more like stepping into a museum. Every piece immaculately curated and presented. But torn from its intended context, instead of being part of a living, breathing experience of transcendence, here it remained in suspended animation.

'They're all here,' I whispered to Alice.

'Stolen?'

I nodded.

Scarcely able to believe what we were taking in, as we looked around the room, we caught sight of the Sangye Menla statue in the same moment.

Positioned on a lapis-colored plinth to the left side of the altar, we were instantly connected.

We walked across the carpet as though drawn by his presence. Standing directly beside him, I remembered how long he had been an established part of Tiger's Nest Monastery. All those decades since Lama Tsering had brought him out of Tibet. The impact of his presence throughout the monastery. The special *terma*, more than a millennia old, that had remained inside him.

'We should tell Dalberg,' I said.

'I've still got his number,' Alice pulled her phone from her scarf and took a photograph of the statue. Then photographs of several of the other *thangkas* and statues. She added them as attachments to a text message. And pressed 'Send.'

'What next?' she whispered, returning the phone to her scarf.

'Break him out of here.'

In the mid-afternoon, the deserted villa had settled into stillness. Looking out the far side of the room, through the windows Lake Como appeared as serene as a series of framed landscape paintings.

'How?' her eyes held mine.

'Front door,' I tilted my head in the direction from which we'd come. 'I assume there's a gate control through there.'

We turned back to the Sangye Menla statue. I reached out and, for a moment, lifted it off the plinth. There was a loud 'clink' as the nectar bowl fell off the Buddha's hands and rolled into his elbow.

'If you hold the bowl–' I whispered, '–I'll take the statue.'

'You sure?' she swallowed.

Suddenly, there was furious shouting behind us. We turned. Two large security guards were racing towards us. One of the men drawing out his pistol.

We froze.

# Chapter Seventeen

Suddenly we were face down on the floor being body searched. One of the men was grabbing the phone, wallet, and keys from my pocket. The other was frisking Alice. He seized her purse, dumping its contents on the carpet. Pressed down next to her leg, I couldn't see her face.

How had the guards got in? Had they been in the house the whole time? A heel was jabbed roughly between my shoulders. The other man, having gone through Alice's belongings, stepped away. I heard a short burst of Italian. After a pause, another burst.

Next I was being kicked in the legs. Looking up, a large, swarthy man with menacing eyes and a lustrous moustache was gesturing for me to get up. I rose to my feet. As soon as I was standing, he had my arms behind me and was locking my wrists with handcuffs.

Beside me, the other guard, an older man with a shaven head and scar etched all the way down his right cheek, was hauling Alice upwards. He shut cuffs around her wrists too. She moaned in pain.

They were pushing us away from the altar. Ordering us into the dining room. They pulled two chairs from the table. Shoved us into them. In moments, they were cuffing our ankles.

'You can't do this!' Alice suddenly burst out. 'You can't lock us in handcuffs—'

'*Silenzio*!' Roared the older man in her face.

I was surprised by her unexpected outburst. The expression on her face was one of shaken anguish.

Having been placed together a short distance away from the table, the younger man tied our cuffed legs to the legs of the chair, making it impossible for us to move.

The older guard was making a call. After a brief exchange, he set his phone on the table, using Alice's purse to prop it at an angle so that we were facing the screen.

Alice and I looked at each other. There could be only one possible person known to the guards with an interest in talking to us at this moment. The same person who, paradoxically, we had willingly called the evening before, hoping he would come to our rescue.

Was it really possible he'd reveal himself to us, while we were handcuffed to his own dining room chairs? And if he was, what else might he be willing to do? Images of Alice, hog-tied in the orchard at dawn raced through my mind. Lama Tsering, dead on the temple floor. Bradshaw's face as he lay in his hospital bed. The two thugs in Ireland—the tall, bald one with the tarantula tattoo, deliberately drawing his finger across his neck.

There was something bizarrely, despicably out of kilter if a man of such evident intelligence and refined tastes, a man who was willing to prostrate himself before the most realized masters of the Himalayas, also seemed to have no qualms about ordering armed thugs to maim and kill. Could it really be true?

Sure enough, after some moments, he appeared. A distinguished-looking patrician, his silvering hair immaculately coiffed. Sensual lips pursed in disapproval. Blue eyes regarding us through gold-rimmed spectacles with a mix of curiosity and distaste. Wearing a white shirt and black jacket, he stared at us like a pair of specimens for time before saying,

'So this is how you repay my kindness?' His voice was deep and etched with French cadences. 'You break into my house?'

For a while we sat in silence before Alice responded. 'Kindness?'

He puckered his lips, disdainfully. 'All those years I paid for the program. Millions and millions of Euros. Never a quibble. And what is my reward?' He leaned forward towards the screen, face flecked with animosity. 'Colossal failure!' he spat. 'I expected better of you, Dr. Weisenstein. Your supervisor, Dr. Bradshaw, is a plodding administrator. A diligent dullard. You, on the other hand, had the promise of brilliance. It's only a pity that your methodology was so badly flawed. What a debacle!'

'Why did you keep funding the program, if it was so badly flawed?' Alice returned, forcefully.

Lascelles ignored her. 'Your incompetence has been my deepest disappointment,' he continued. 'You have no idea how important my research was in contributing to the grand ideal.'

'*Your* research?'

Lascelles's lips curled in disdain. 'I, alone, have the vision. I have made it my life's work to understand both scientific rigor and esoteric spirituality, analysis and intuition, the contemporary and the ancient. I, alone, have been able to divine what stares others in the face—and yet what they fail to see. They glimpse only parts. They catch mere fragments of their own, tiny reality, when what's needed is the panoramic view. The big picture. Who else sees this, eh?'

Without hesitation I replied, 'I know of several.'

'You,' he was derisive. 'And your dear old lamas. They may be the possessors of certain wisdom. But what do they do with it? Hide it away! Keep it to themselves! Creeping about like moles through their dark caverns and passageways, they conceal it, for initiates only. What do they understand about commercializing an idea? About taking it to the market? About global reach? It is beyond them and their narrow ways.'

'Which is why they guided Alice in her research,' I responded. 'And have been training me. You don't have an original vision at all. Your grand plan is stolen, just like,' I gestured with chin, 'all the objects next door.'

'Enough!' Lascelles thumped the desk. 'I should have had you shot like dogs this morning,' he snapped. 'That is not a mistake we shall be repeating.' Pushing back, he regarded us both with scorn.

'What I have assembled on Lake Como is a treasury of the most exquisite Himalayan art. The purpose of those *thangkas* and statues is to edify, to inspire, to raise our sights to a wider vision. Despite all the inspiration, what good have the Buddhists of the Himalayas ever been to the world? What have they ever done for humanity? What gift have they bestowed to mankind? They don't deserve such art.

'I, on the other hand, have been inspired to offer to humanity the alchemy for which it has always yearned. *Elixir vitae*, the nectar of immortality. The promise of eternal youth. Not some cosmetic cocktail, but much more subtle than that. A secret code. A specific vibration that transforms at the atomic level.'

From his pocket he was producing the metal *terma*, which had been removed from around my neck in Ireland. 'I will be sharing its contents later with a rather interesting group of people. It will undoubtedly be an evening that everyone will remember for all the right reasons.'

He paused, aglow with the anticipated triumph of the evening ahead. Before his expression charged to a scowl. 'I had hoped to share my research results too, but thanks to your blundering –' he glared at Alice, '– that will no longer be possible. Still,' he flipped the metal tube through his fingers, 'I have some compelling data to support my thesis, and the revelation of this will be accompanied by ... a certain theatre.'

'Aren't you troubled that a *terma* should only be revealed under the most auspicious circumstances?' I asked.

Lascelles regarded me contemptuously for a while, before laughing without humor. 'You really have been infected with lama-ism, haven't you? All their endless prayers and rituals. I can think of no more auspicious circumstances than a gathering of the *Accademia del Cimento*, one of the most elite scientific assemblies in the world.'

He paused, staring at the camera for a long while. 'In the meantime, you two present me with yet another problem. I can't make you disappear when there is so much evidence you have been near my home.'

He tilted his head regarding us in silence for a while. 'Every season there is at least one tragic accident on the lake,' he shrugged. 'An inexperienced couple may take a boat out for a romantic evening and find themselves in trouble. It's such a big lake. Unless they are strong swimmers, well,' he shrugged. 'The worst is possible. Exhaustion sets in. Lungs fill with water. Death by drowning. Not that you will know anything about it. You will be asleep, you see. Mrs. Pacchiana will send you on your way, just as she had to end the days of her beloved greyhounds. She's very good at it. Quite the euthanasia expert. A strong dose of Pentobarbital will put you both to sleep, its effect irreversible. Then a final journey to the lake.'

I was aware of movement from behind and glanced around to see the housekeeper approaching. In her hand, a bottle and syringe. As she crossed the carpet, her eyes were narrowed on the two of us, like prey.

'You know, of course, that the word "soul" comes from Old Saxon. It means "coming from and returning to the sacred lake." Appropriate, don't you think, under the circumstances?'

A security guard was speaking in Italian.

'We won't let you get away with all you have stolen from Bhutan,' Alice's voice was icy.

Lascelles regarded us with contempt. 'Buona notte,' he said coldly.

Then he was delivering instructions in Italian. The older guard took his phone back and was responding to Lascelles's instructions, the housekeeper nodding as she followed the conversation.

As the call ended, the guard pocketed the phone. Both he and his colleague stepped towards Alice. Beside them, the housekeeper held the bottle upside down and drew down a measure into the syringe. One man seized Alice by both shoulders. The other held her right arm firm. Because one of the men was standing right next to her, I caught only a brief glimpse of the housekeeper pressing the needle into Alice. Steadily unloading the contents of the syringe into her arm.

The two men stepped away from Alice. She turned and our eyes met. Instantly I felt lifted from my body, and she from hers, and we were together, looking down on the unfolding events. What to say to one another in such circumstances? What had happened in the past days had been so intense that there hadn't been the time and opportunity to share what really mattered. So much emotion that had remained unexpressed.

More than anything right now, I felt the anguish of a mother who would never again see her son. The yearning to protect and nurture her child. A love so powerful, no other emotion came close. None of her professional work mattered at all right now. That was left behind, a white coat cast off on the floor.

My own feelings unvoiced, I was also aware as never before how much hope I had invested in being with Alice. How much I yearned to hold her in my heart. Our journey through this lifetime had been extraordinary. And as I glanced back through time, as was possible in this state, I recognized that this wasn't the first time. Stretching back since beginning-less time, our lives, and those of our teachers and guides, had been entwined, like colored strands weaving in and out of a vast tapestry.

Aware of the past as well as the present of the vivid materiality of our lives, as well as their tenuous fragility, just as I knew and understood Alice's emotions, in this curious state I suddenly realized that she knew mine too. There was no need for words, whose limitations made them superfluous. As we held one another's eyes, side by side, in a different way we were attuned to one another as never before. We understood each other, in our entirety. Despite the passage of time in the mundane world, for a glimpse we shared a different reality where there were no seconds and minutes, where we were in complete understanding.

Alice's head lolled forward. Her eyelids appeared heavy. She said just three words, 'Time to practice.'

Even as the housekeeper turned away from her victim, there was part of me that felt curious contentment. Alice was recollecting the death process, the eight stages from normal consciousness through to clear light, which Tibetan Buddhists rehearsed and rehearsed in meditation. Preparing for the opportunity that awaited all who recognized it, to attain release from the endless cycle of death and rebirth. An opportunity that came but once a lifetime—and was now at hand.

Just as the housekeeper was reaching in her pocked for the bottle of Pentobarbital, there came the sounds of sirens. A large number of them. Approaching the house at speed.

The security guards instantly dropped my arm and raced from the room in the direction of the temple. Glancing at Alice's crumpling form, the housekeeper's eyes widened in horrified recognition as the wail of vehicles came dramatically closer. Taking the bottle from her pocket, she held it vertical and tried to shove her syringe needle into it. But her nerves got the better of her. Hands shaking as the sirens grew ever closer, she fumbled. The bottle fell from her grasp, striking a brass claw on one of the protruding feet of the table, instantly shattering. About turning, she hurried out of the room.

I tried to count the sirens. It seemed like there were at least three that were so loud that they had to be right outside the front gate. I sat, expecting rescuers to smash their way in at any moment, willing Alice's system to slow down and the drug injected into her to have the most delayed reaction. The sirens continued at full wail directly outside. But no rescuers.

'Alice are you with me?' I had to bellow about the clamor to be heard.

She showed no response at all. No sign even of being conscious.

Every second was taking Alice further and further into a state beyond recovery. While I had no knowledge of barbiturates, I had seen the dosage measured into the syringe by the housekeeper. It had been significant.

Trying to get up, legs cuffed and tied to the chair, I found it impossible to walk. The dining chair was well-upholstered and heavy. It was like lugging a huge shell on my back.

I thought of the security around the villa. The steel security gate. The high wall. No doubt Lascelles would have the best available protection. How would the police break through? Were they accompanied by an ambulance? It was critical to get Alice to a hospital if she had any chance.

I wasn't doing her any good sitting here, I reckoned. Amid the deafening sound of sirens, and using the pressure of my limbs, I brought all the strength that I could to bear on the right leg of the chair, shoving and wrenching, trying to get it to snap off the base.

If I could make it across the dining room and through the hall, I reckoned, I might find a gate control. The front door was where the housekeeper had appeared earlier. I didn't know if she carried a remote for the gate with her. Or if there was a control in the hallway.

I was desperate to get there.

Outside, the cacophony was growing even louder. How many vehicles were piling up outside? The road must be completely blocked, I thought, glancing up. Apart from the noise, the view from inside was of a tranquil, late afternoon. Through the windows of the conservatory, the green lawn, blue lake, and deepening sky were all perfectly still.

I was making progress with the chair leg. It was starting to move. On my side, I tried to ignore the chaffing of ropes and cuffs about my ankles. The chair leg was wobbling now. With a few more shoves I felt I could snap it off completely and break free.

I managed to do exactly that. There was a final crack of wood, and the chair leg spun across the carpet. My right leg free, I was soon able to slip my left from the other side.

I got to my knees. Then I was standing. My hands were still cuffed behind me, but I was free to go directly into to the hallway. Except that I didn't. For no apparent reason, I was struggling to maintain my balance. Stumbling onto my side. Falling hard and striking my head on the same side that Lascelles's thug had hit me with a pistol butt.

The whole room was spinning.

•••

NEXT THING I KNEW, POLICEMEN WERE KNEELING OVER ME, WORKING on the cuffs at my wrists. A racket of sirens sounded outside.

'Alice!' I called out. In my bewilderment I thought I must alert them to who really needed help.

'Si, si.'

'Help Alice!'

One of the policemen was holding my wrists still, while the other maneuvered beside him. There was a snap of metal and my hands were free. Automatically, I was drawing them in front of me, feeling a warm surge of blood into the muscles of my upper arms.

During the flurry of activity, a mustachioed face appeared above the crowd. 'You are Matt Lester?'

'Yes.'

'I am Marchetti. Head of Police.'

'How is Alice?'

'We are releasing her now. She is unconscious.'

'They injected her with a high dose sedative. Pentobarbital.'

The policemen were moving back from where I lay on the carpet.

'There is a medical team here,' Marchetti glanced behind me.

I sat up to look round.

The policemen were motioning me to stay where I was.

'We have a doctor to check you,' said Marchetti.

I wasn't going to sit around till I knew what was happening to Alice.

'I'm okay, really,' I said, clambering to my feet and turning. Police officers had already freed Alice from the chair. They were helping a medical crew lift her onto a rolling stretcher. Her body was as limp as a ragdoll. A paramedic was tucking warming blankets around her as the crew began wheeling her in the direction of the hallway.

Policemen were cutting the cuffs from my wrists and ankles. One of them, standing beside me, had his arm around my shoulders for support.

Marchetti, a tall, broad man, every inch of him the police chief, was studying me carefully. The front door was being opened, in anticipation of the stretcher. Outside was a chaos of emergency vehicles—several police cars and an ambulance.

'Will she be okay?' I asked a paramedic, as I began following the stretcher.

He was a middle-aged man with sallow skin and perceptive eyes. 'We don't know how far the drug has advanced. We need to run tests.'

He was promising nothing.

Crossing the hallway and looking into the late afternoon, I saw that the massive steel gates had been cut open. That was what had taken the police so long.

Turning to Marchetti, who was beside me, I said, 'I was trying to get to the front door to open the gate.'

He nodded.

'We're going with Alice to a hospital?' I watched the medical team pushing her stretcher rapidly towards the ambulance.

'We follow,' he agreed. 'She is in good hands. Before we go, perhaps, can you help with a question?'

My confusion must have shown.

'I have been investigating allegations of a major art theft,' he fixed me with an expression that was both determined and also curiously solicitous. 'I was first alerted to it over ten years ago.'

'By Grayson Dalberg?' I asked.

'I can neither confirm nor deny,' he nodded, his leaked, non-verbal communication speaking volumes. 'There are a number of high-value items on an Interpol stolen property list,' he continued. 'My ... difficulty has been gaining access to this property without a warrant. Dealing with a very rich individual, one who has friends in high places, it has been impossible.'

I noted his frustration. And putting it together with the plea for help, suddenly I got it. Having been thwarted from getting inside Lascelles's villa for the past decade, with the emergency call today, an unexpected opportunity had presented itself.

From the hallway I watched as Alice's stretcher was being loaded into the ambulance. Two of the medical team climbing in beside her. The doors being closed.

I remembered the last thing she'd said to Lascelles: *we won't let you get away with all you have stolen from Bhutan.*

I could follow her to hospital. There was nothing Marchetti could do to stop me. But what would I do once there? I'd be left in some waiting room, pacing up and down, filling in the time. Meanwhile, if I was to make good on the last words Alice had said, and if I was to fulfill my own obligations to the abbot, I could help the police chief do his job.

I turned to face Marchetti. 'What can I do for you?'

Marchetti breathed in deeply. 'Lascelles is a big flight risk,' he sighed. 'If he thinks there is trouble, if he goes across the border into Switzerland, I have no jurisdiction. He is gone, forever.'

'You can get him in Milan. Tonight.'

'I want to,' he checked his watch. 'But this is only possible with your help.'

So, it seemed that this all hinged on me.

'Can you identify which artworks were stolen from Bhutan?'

'Of course,' I nodded. 'The ones from some years ago. Also the Sangye Menla statue, recently stolen, that brought us here this afternoon.'

I led the way to Lascelles's Himalayan showroom. Switching on the lights, as twilight shadows lengthened across the room, I led the police chief directly to the stolen statues of Shakyamuni and Manjushri on the altar. As one of the detectives accompanying him photographed the statues, another checked them against the Interpol list. Then I was pointing out the wall hangings of the thousand-armed Avalokiteshvara. Green Tara. The Wheel of Life. We made our way past several other *thangkas* before reaching the Sangye Menla statue stolen from Tiger's Nest.

After a brief exchange with colleagues, Marchetti was satisfied he had the evidence he required. He returned briskly through the house, telling me that while his team continued scouring the lakeside for the fleeing security guards, his own mission was to drive to Milan. He, personally, would be arresting the billionaire.

'I'll have you taken to the hospital,' he said.

Again, my thoughts were with Alice and what awaited her at the hospital. When she arrived, she'd be rushed through to the intensive care unit. She'd be tested, probably hooked up to drips, closely monitored. I almost certainly wouldn't be allowed in. Even if I was, what could I do? Without my phone I wasn't able to contact anyone.

Lascelles, in the meantime, was about to face an elite audience of the most eminent scientists in Europe. I could imagine the smug self-importance as he addressed the room, every idea of any significance that he had stolen from someone else. Building up to his main dramatic prop, he would no doubt weave a tale of towering egotism before producing the *terma* that had, until so recently, been hanging around my neck. Would Marchetti get there before he opened the *terma*? At what point would the police chief make his move?

*We won't let you get away with all you have stolen from Bhutan.*

Suddenly, I wanted to be there to see Lascelles's arrest. To witness the turning point. I thought again about Alice, alone in a hospital bed in a foreign town. But in the same instant I recollected the wordless connection we had shared earlier. There was no doubt in my mind. I knew what to do.

As Marchetti reached what used to be the gateway into Lascelles's mansion, in the gathering dusk I asked, 'Would it be possible to come with you to Milan? To see you put Lascelles away.'

The police chief glanced at me quizzically. 'As a witness?'

I nodded.

He was evidently making a calculation. Weighing up the arguments for and against. Seeing that I had helped provide the evidence he needed, for what would undoubtedly be one of the catches of his career, he found in my favor.

'We return later this evening,' he confirmed.

'Perfect.'

•••

The road trip from Cernobbio to Milan usually takes about an hour. We made it in forty minutes. Traffic melted away at the approach of a fast moving police car. The policeman behind the steering wheel took full advantage, switching on the emergency lights and sirens whenever we approached what looked like congestion.

We were in the lead of several police vehicles. Marchetti sat in the passenger seat, placing and receiving a volley of calls with colleagues in Milan and Como. In the back, I closed my eyes, resting after the tumultuous events of the day. Occasionally, looking out the window, watching twilight deepen into darkness.

On the way, the police chief turned to tell me that the housekeeper had been arrested almost immediately after the police had broken in. Her phone had been removed and checked. She had made no outgoing calls that day. As for the security guards, their boots and other items of clothing had been found at the side of the lake. Unable to exit through the gate, their only option had been to swim. Police officers were in pursuit. A major search was underway.

Then as we neared our destination, Marchetti confirmed. 'We have arrested the security guards.'

'Good.'

'Their phones were checked,' there was the faintest glint in his eye. 'They have not called Lascelles. We are all set.'

'Even better.'

•••

For most of its four-and-a-half centuries of existence, the *Accademia del Cimento* had held its meetings in the home of its founding patron, Grand Duke Ferdinando II de Medici. Ancient, elegant, and discreet, the fortified villa had remained in the hands of Italian aristocrats for most of its existence. Its current owners had redeveloped it as a venue that paying guests who have the right connections could hire for special gatherings.

Unfamiliar with Milan, I had no idea where the villa was located when the small convoy of police cars pulled over at the side of a city block. But looking down the street leading off where we were parked, I observed a stately building, with a portico entrance and a gleaming car parked beneath. Ivy clung to the walls of the villa, and an ancient standard above the entrance drifted grandly in the evening breeze, as it no doubt had since time immemorial.

'You stay here. I talk to colleagues,' Marchetti instructed me, opening his door.

From the backseat, I watched the police chief and members of the Como team walking down the pavement, presumably to ensure that everything was in place. I'd heard the police chief liaising during the constant phone calls he'd made since leaving Como. Even though I couldn't speak Italian, I'd picked up that all the private security guards hired by guests this evening were to be drawn aside during police operations. Exits from the venue were to be secured. Lascelles's car and driver would be detained.

As the minutes went by and twenty minutes became forty, then the waiting time eventually stretched towards a full hour, I hoped that, amid all the logistics, Marchetti hadn't forgotten me. I'd told him about the critical importance of the *terma*. Why it had been the main object of Lascelles's theft of the Sangye Menla statue. How he was planning a theatrical opening of the cylinder before a group of elite scientists he had been cultivating for years.

*Accedemia* members were no doubt already meeting at the Medici villa. It was after 8.30p.m. I didn't know about the format of the evening besides what Dalberg had told us—a ceremonial dinner followed by a short presentation. How many people would be in attendance? In particular how, exactly, was Lascelles planning to open the *terma* in the presence of his A-list audience?

Pondering exactly this, there was a tap on the window. A policeman gestured me to get out. A short distance behind the police car, Marchetti was issuing orders to officers. On the opposite side of the road, a group of chauffeurs in suits and caps were resentful at being corralled by the police. The police chief was conferring with two very large, uniformed colleagues. The three of them were switching their phones and radios to silent. With a nod he signaled me to follow.

We proceeded in swift silence. Down the side street towards the prestigious-looking building. Even though Marchetti, the two large police officers, and I were followed by half a dozen other personnel, our progress down the street was almost soundless.

Reaching the portico, Marchetti led the way behind a highly polished cobalt-blue Bentley Continental and up a short flight of marble steps. Two large paneled doors marked the entrance of the villa. Before we had reached them, they swung open from the inside. Police had secured the entrance and a female police officer took the lead. She guided us through an atrium lit with baroque candelabra, and across a deep-pile red carpet rolled upon an ancient marble floor. From the moment I stepped inside, the history of this place felt palpable, as though one was being absorbed momentarily into a river of privilege and wealth that had flowed down the centuries. On the other side of the atrium, a grandiose stone entrance led into a short hallway from which a corridor ran both left and right. She turned right and we passed into a wide, stone passage lit by candles in sconces on both sides.

The corridor was labyrinthine. The policewoman continued smoothly until, around a corner, we encountered a very large and magnificently decorated door. Heraldic shields were carved into the massive timbers, embossed with rich colors. Baroque ornamentation and elaborate gilded frames left visitors in no doubt that they were about to enter a room of great distinction. On the other side of this door, I surmised, members of the *Accademia del Cimento* were gathered for their dinner.

The policewoman paused, her eyes meeting Marchetti's. He, in turn, looked significantly at the two large policemen accompanying us. They stepped to either side of the entrance, evidently taking up a pre-planned position. Then the police chief turned to me. He didn't say anything. Nor did he need to. The message in his eyes was unequivocal: I was to keep out of the way. Inconspicuous Close-mouthed. I was not to interfere in his operation.

Leaving behind the two officers, we followed the policewoman further along the corridor, then to one side where she drew open a curtain to reveal a narrow, circular staircase.

I followed them up several cycles of the circular steps. As we ascended, we heard a voice in the distance. One that grew louder as we reached a landing.

An open doorway in the landing led to a small viewing area, like a box or loge in a theatre. At the front of the box, facing into the room, stood guards in livery that featured the famous gold shield of the Medicis, with five red balls and a blue one. Arriving in the box, the voice of the speaker was louder still—we were now in the same room, only a short distance away. It was a voice I recognized from earlier in the afternoon.

The guards gave no indication that we were behind them, although they must have been aware of our arrival. Marchetti stepped closer to the front of the box, but stayed in the shadows and out of view behind the guards. Turning to me, with his chin he motioned that I may edge closer to the front too.

As I did, I found myself looking down on a long dinner table. Forty men and women in evening dress were gathered around it. The attention of them all was fixed on the individual who stood at one end of the table next to a candelabra. Along with his white tie and black coat, he was wearing an ornate burgundy waistcoat embroidered in gold with Tibetan syllables.

A short distance from where he stood, somewhat incongruously, was a workshop table – also bedecked in a white tablecloth – equipped with a metalworking vise. A hacksaw was placed at the ready.

# CHAPTER EIGHTEEN

'SINCE THE DAWN OF MANKIND, SCIENTISTS HAVE SET THEIR SIGHTS on a goal that has proved elusive,' Pascal Lascelles declaimed. Right hand tucked into his waistcoat, and left-hand gesturing expansively, he was relishing his audience. 'We have prevailed through many victories in our war against disease. But deep in our hearts each one of us knows there can be no stopping until we have won the final battle. Until we have found a genuine solution to the question of what causes cells to age. How to stop entropy.' He paused, theatrically.

'*Elixir vitae* was the dream of alchemists. The ancient Greeks had a vision of the philosopher's stone, which could turn base metal into gold.'

Reading from autocues placed to both sides of the table, Lascelles lectured *Academia* members on the advances of biology since Renaissance times, and how, despite all the progress, no permanent solution had been found to the problem of aging.

With his intelligent features, shoulder-length, silvering hair and European baritone, Lascelles had presence. He was the charismatic grandee in the role of arch rebel—in person, exactly as I had imagined, except for the sense of entitlement. Alice and I had been fully witness to it earlier. I would have thought he'd have the discernment to tone it down for a gathering such as tonight's. Despite being in the presence of Nobel prize-winning molecular biologists, astrophysicists, and organic chemists, he held the floor as though he were not simply their equal, but their superior.

Lascelles explained how scientists had been looking in the wrong place in their search for *elixir vitae*. Instead of biology and chemistry, it was pure physics that held the key. In particular, the impact of sound on cellular structures. Reading sentences he'd probably lifted wholesale from Alice's thesis, he had assumed her hypothesis as his own. No doubt he'd intended using her results as the triumphal centerpiece of tonight's performance. Only, things hadn't gone as planned. Instead of a significant, longitudinal study supported by the credibility of Trinity College, he confined himself to talking about population statistics in the Himalayas.

Specifically, he appeared to bring the audience into his confidence in explaining the Bhutan blip. How he had commissioned specific data, in conjunction with the World Health Organization, which had exposed compelling findings about longevity among the monastic population—slides appearing behind him with data and graphs. How one monastery in particular, Tiger's Nest, had revealed the most extraordinary data of all.

With the flair of an illusionist leading his audience, step by step, towards his most breathtaking trick, Lascelles explained what he believed to be the reason for this.

'A specific practice was introduced at Tiger's Nest monastery in the early 1960s. It is since that time that longevity has increased so dramatically. And only at Tiger's Nest—one of the most isolated monasteries in the world.

'This practice involves a specific mantra. One which has remained a closely-guarded secret—until tonight. It is a mantra thought to be transcribed by none other than the great Padmasambhava, the founding father of Buddhism in Tibet. Although known to only the very small group of practitioners – all of them living to a very advanced age – it has never been revealed more generally. Instead, for the past thousand years, until the time was right for it to be shared with all humanity, it has been kept sealed in this!'

From his pocket he produced the metal cannister which, until recently, had been hanging around my neck.

Around the table there was a mixed response to Lascelles's showmanship. Many *Accademia* members leaned forward in their seats, regarding the *terma* with curiosity. Others wore puzzled frowns: this was almost certainly not the usual approach to *Accademia* presentations. A few sat pressed back in their chairs, their arms folded. One large, bearded man close to where Lascelles stood, watched him with an expression of twinkling amusement.

Lascelles gestured towards a metalsmith in a dark blue apron, who had been standing in the shadows near the door, to step up to the workbench. Separately, a young Asian woman in traditional Tibetan clothing stepped towards a screen behind Lascelles on which was currently projected a close-up image of the vise. She appeared to be on hand to assist with translation.

With a flourish, Lascelles handed the *terma* to the metalsmith who, with all due reverence, received it in both hands. He then inserted it into the vise, closing the clamp on both sides, leaving only a short length protruding.

Picking up the hacksaw, the metalsmith leaned over the scroll, marking the surface with a few confident forward movements. It was a soft metal, brass or bronze. The seal at the end was self-evidently not the product of advanced engineering. In little time, the blade of the saw smoothly cut through the surface and the metalsmith stood aside to allow Lascelles to check that the contents of the *terma* wouldn't be damaged.

Only after receiving Lascelles's consent did he resume his work.

The expression on Lascelles's face was one of intense anticipation. Focused, single-pointedly, on the opening of the scroll, this was the moment to which his life had been heading for most of the past decade. It was his self-ordained purpose through all the years that Alice had been doing her research, and I had been in the Himalayas. Inserting himself as the mastermind, the presiding genius, this evening, right now, was the moment his dream of achieving scientific acclaim was about to be realized.

The metalsmith smoothly worked his way to the other side of the tube. With expert precision, he delivered a final stroke—and the *terma* seal fell to the bench. Putting down the hacksaw, he released the vise pressure, lifting the open metal tube, and offering it to Lascelles.

Lascelles took the tube and turned to the Tibetan woman who approached him. He held it at the level of his chest while, bending slightly, she reached into it with her index finger. All of this was being captured on camera and projected onto the screen behind them. The tremulousness of Lascelles's hands as he held the tube. The delicate poise of the Asian woman, as she withdrew her finger. Curled around its tip was yellowing paper.

With a nod from Lascelles she extracted the contents of the scroll. The paper was rolled and looked as though it may be brittle. Stepping to the bench where the metalsmith had been working, directly under the camera for the best possible exposure, she unfurled the paper. With great care she unrolled it until its contents became visible, not only to her, but on the large screen.

At this point, the silence in the room became deafening. Because what held everyone around the table, and Lascelles himself transfixed, was not some ancient handwriting of Padmasambhava, disclosing the secret formula of *elixir vitae*. It was a full-color line drawing of a book cover: 'Tintin in Tibet.'

For a few moments, no one knew what to do. Certainly not Lascelles who stood, staring at the screen, expression frozen. Most of his audience was similarly dumbfounded. Even those with arms folded or legs crossed had expected something different. At the very least, an extraordinary historical souvenir.

The weight of awkwardness deepened, moment by moment, as though the longer it went on, the less anyone knew what to do. Disbelief, mystification, and acute embarrassment weighed down on the whole gathering. It would have been easier if the earth itself had opened up and engulfed their presenter who, instead, stood paralyzed before them.

Eventually it was the bearded man at the table, who had seemed amused during Lascelles's presentation, who was the first to respond. Looking around at his fellow *Accademia* members, he clapped his large hands slowly, three times as he looked at their presenter with an expression of droll humor. 'Congratulations, Pascal!' he spoke with a booming, Italian-accented voice. 'Your florid presentation and melodrama is a lesson to us all. Humility. That is what you are here to teach us tonight, is it not?'

Turning to face the table, face ashen, Lascelles nodded, trying to compose himself.

'Nonsense!' Cried another voice. English accented. 'He's been banging on about *elixir vitae* for years. Is this the best you have to show us?'

'Hear, hear!' agreed someone else.

'Nothing wrong with humility. Or Tintin. But we're here to discuss science!' An American voice sounded.

'Fiasco!'

'Waste of time!'

'Total bullshit!' An Australian put it plainly.

'Getting all of us under one roof for an evening is a major logistical exercise,' a female voice cut through. 'What a missed opportunity this evening has been!'

There was general agreement and a rising hubbub before several of the eminent scientists began banging their heels on the wooden floor. Spontaneously, most of the others followed suit. A drum roll of humiliation quickly turned into a thunder. All the while focused on Lascelles, they began banging the table with the heels of their hands too.

Lascelles had no choice. The only way his ritual humiliation was going to come to an end was by leaving. Which he did. Shaking his head, flummoxed by the turn of events. Averting his gaze from the same people whose attention he had so commandingly held onto moments before. It was a retreat in disgrace through the hallowed chamber. Instead of crowning glory, he left amid a gathering tide of opprobrium.

The instant he moved, Marchetti had raised his police radio and pressed a button. About-turning, he headed back down the circular staircase, the policewoman immediately behind him. I followed in their wake. Down and round the spirals. Out from behind the curtain and along the candle-lit passageway.

Even before we reached the doors, we could hear what was happening. Lascelles insistently calling for staff members who weren't there. Protesting that the police had no grounds to stop him. In his bewilderment, he was associating their presence with the debacle that had just happened.

Then Marchetti appeared and his attitude suddenly changed to one of towering fury.

'You?! Call your dogs off!'

The police chief nodded towards one of his officers who, in a single fluid motion had Lascelles's arms behind him and locked cuffs around his wrists.

'I'll call your superiors!' his voice rose.

Moving rapidly as a group, police officers at front and back, Marchetti towered over the irate billionaire. 'I hope you enjoyed your night out, Signor Lascelles. It may be your last entertainment for a while. I am arresting you for unlawful detention of two persons. For conspiracy to murder. And for possession of stolen property.'

'What have you done with my chauffeur?'

'Assisting with police inquiries.'

'I want my lawyer!' demanded Lascelles.

'Certainly,' agreed Marchetti.

Reaching the entry hall of the Medici villa, we were returning across the red carpet towards the entrance. Directly outside, under the portico, the cobalt-blue Bentley Continental had gone. In its place was a dark blue Iveco truck with the words "Polizia Penitenziaria" emblazoned down the sides.

'First you will accompany us to the police station in Como. I have arranged transport.' Marchetti nodded towards the vehicle.

We watched Lascelles being led to the truck. Guided onto the step leading into the grim, steel-lined interior.

Directly behind the truck was a police Mercedes. With elaborate courtesy, Marchetti was opening the back door of it for me.

On my way, I paused briefly near the open doors of the truck, looking at where Lascelles hunched on a steel seat, arms behind him.

'I have to agree with you on one thing, Monsieur Lascelles,' I said. Tonight will definitely be an evening that everyone remembers for all the right reasons.'

Lascelles fixed me with a look of contempt. 'Imbecile!' he spat.

'Perhaps,' I agreed. 'But the dear, old lamas aren't as stupid as you thought, are they?'

I joined Marchetti in the back seat of the police car. As we watched his fellow police officers close the door on the fuming Lascelles, he turned to me. 'Hubris. Nemesis,' he said.

I nodded.

•••

The return journey to Como wasn't as fast paced as the trip up. We were traveling directly behind the prisoner transport truck. There were further police vehicles to the front and back.

Marchetti was making and receiving calls most of the time.

'The legal papers for the arrest have to be perfect,' he explained briefly, during a pause between calls. 'Men like Lascelles have lawyers who—'

'I know.' I had dealt with his kind in the past. I realized that Marchetti would be doing all he could to prevent Lascelles being granted bail.

'Can we find out about Alice?' I asked, at the first opportunity he was off the phone.

Marchetti called the hospital. After a brief conversation he turned to say, 'Still under observation. No change.'

I didn't know if "no change" was a good thing or a bad thing. Was it the case that the longer she lay there, the more the effect of the toxin was diluted? Or the more deeply it became entrenched? Without my own phone, I was unable to call friends who might be able to tell me.

Marchetti said I would be dropped at the hospital as soon as we were back in Como. In the meantime, driving through the night, leaning against the headrest, I tried to process the events of the tumultuous day.

Somewhere between Milan and Como, Marchetti turned and fixed me with a significant expression. 'Signor Dalberg. I said I would call him after the rescue.'

'It was him, wasn't it, who called you this afternoon?'

I had wondered how the emergency services had been tipped off to what was going on at Lascelles's villa. But as the police chief mentioned his name, something clicked into place. How Alice had sent photographs of several stolen items to Dalberg using her phone before returning it to her scarf. How Lascelles's security guards had emptied her bag, and frisked her body, while she was lying, face down on the floor—but failed to check her scarf.

I remembered her crying out in the dining room, "You can't do this! You can't lock us in handcuffs!" There had been something incongruous about her plea. Out of character. Now I knew why. Her words hadn't been intended for Lascelles's guards at all, but for the person at the other end of the phone.

Across the back seat, Marchetti nodded in confirmation. 'His call was the opportunity of a lifetime.'

Searching through his contacts, he found a number and pressed dial. When the phone was answered, he spoke in Italian. Given Dalberg's many years as an international dealer in antiquities, it should perhaps be no surprise that he was fluent in a variety of languages. But it did mean I could only guess at what was being said.

Marchetti seemed to be telling him about the police entry into the villa. The discovery of the Interpol-listed stolen items. Lascelles's arrest at the *Accademia* meeting. After some time, he handed the phone to me.

'Are you okay, Matt?' asked Dalberg, in that distinctive voice.

'I'm well. And thank you for calling the police when we were held hostage. If you hadn't, we would both be dead.'

'Just as well Alice had the presence of mind to press the "redial" button of her phone.'

'It's Alice I'm worried about.'

'Marchetti has updated me. You're about to visit her in the hospital?'

'Yes.'

'As the custodian of the Sangye Menla statue, you'll know exactly what practices to carry out for her benefit,' he observed. Then after a moment, 'I believe this evening didn't go too well for Lascelles at the *Accademia del Cimento?*'

'Total humiliation. Instead of revealing the contents of a *terma* written a thousand years ago by Padmasambhava, he came up with the cover image of *Tintin in Tibet*.'

At the other end, Dalberg chuckled. 'So the metal tube around your neck?'

'Was not the one from inside the Sangye Menla statue.'

It was a pause before he said, 'Well-played, Matt!' His tone was warm. 'The lamas would be proud of you for safeguarding the *terma* from an enemy as powerful and determined as Lascelles.'

'It was their idea,' I said. 'Specifically, Lama Tsering's. He sent me a message, via Geshe-la, reminding me of some particular advice. You know, one of his favorite phrases about the best place to hide the truth.'

'In plain sight?' responded Dalberg.

'Yes,' I agreed. 'That's the start of it.'

After a moment he admitted, 'I wouldn't know anything more than that,' he said.

In the back of the police car, the night-time country rushing by, I pondered for a while about how it seemed that I had learned at least one thing in the past seven years that Grayson Dalberg didn't also know.

•••

Arriving in Como, our car pulled away from behind the van transporting Lascelles, another police vehicle taking its place. We made a short drive to the hospital where Alice had been taken, pulling up directly at the entrance.

Marchetti escorted me into the building, spoke to the duty nurses and left me with one of them. 'She will take you to Miss Weisenstein,' he said, returning briskly to his car.

I was led along a corridor with an antiseptic smell, and patient wards off either side. It was nearly midnight and the place was in semi-darkness. The nurse who led me was young and spoke no English. I asked her about Alice's condition, but she just shrugged.

Finally, we paused outside the door to a ward on the left. The nurse pointed to a hand sanitizer dispenser, waiting for me to cleanse my hands, before opening the door.

Alice had her own, small room and was lying with arms outside the bedclothes, right arm intubated. The only light in the room came from where a streetlight turned the curtain into a glowing white panel, making her appear pallid and bloodless, her hair unfamiliarly bedraggled on the pillow.

There was a chair under the window. I pointed towards it and the nurse nodded once before stepping back into the corridor and returning to her desk.

It was just Alice and me in the quiet of the sleeping hospital. It had been the longest of days, but the events of this evening had made me paradoxically energized. In some undefined way I knew I'd reached a turning point.

Dalberg had correctly guessed what I had planned. His comment about practices revealed an insight that made me wonder if he understood the real significance of what was written in the Sangye Menla *terma.*

For the moment, however, I let go of all such reflections. I fetched the chair from under the window and placed it at Alice's side. I sat upright, a straight spine being the only absolute element of the meditation posture. For a few moments I was simply present to this moment, here and now. To the unfamiliar traffic sounds from outside the building, vehicles coming out of nowhere, their sound levels rising as they sped along the road past the hospital, rising to a crescendo before fading into the distance. There were electronic bleeps and humming arising from inside the hospital, some of them rhythmic, others not. The occasional exchange of nurses speaking in Italian, echoing down the corridor.

I let the sounds come and go, without thinking about them, or commenting to myself about them. Just as I let the odors of hand sanitizer and other disinfectants, chemical and other smells come and go.

As outside, so within. Thoughts arose, quite naturally, and I treated them the same as sounds or smells. As always, they would arise, abide, and pass. If I didn't engage with them, there was nowhere for them to remain—they had no power to do so on their own.

Once settled, I recollected my bodhichitta motivation: *By this practice, may I quickly, quickly achieve enlightenment in order to lead all other living beings – wherever in the universe they abide, equally and without exception – to complete and perfect enlightenment.*

For a while, I focused on the nine-round breath meditation, to settle, re-balance, and allow clarity.

I recollected Lama Tsering's instructions from one Himalayan morning, sitting in the hermitage garden.

'The purpose of becoming familiar with this practice, the visualization, the colors, their meaning, and so on, is not only for one's own benefit.' As our eyes met, I was drawn into the timeless energy of his gaze. 'Through this extraordinary practice we can also help others.

'If there is some being you wish to help, human or animal – especially a being with whom you share a strong, karmic connection – this is a very powerful practice.'

I was following him intently.

'Visualize lights and nectars streaming from the Buddha's body and from his bowl of healing nectars. You know the colors and what they symbolize, yes?'

I had nodded.

'Imagine that they come from where the Buddha is sitting just above you, and pervade the body of the being you wish to benefit as well as yourself. They infuse every cell of the body. They provide all the qualities needed to ward off poisons and infections, imbalance and disease. They purify, energize, rebalance, and restore. This is very powerful practice, Matt. And of course, while doing the visualizations, repeat the healing mantra. This is an energetic practice. A profound one.'

He had recited the mantra several times. Just as he had when he'd first transmitted it to me, and in every subsequent session we'd ever had. I had sometimes wondered why he did this. It wasn't a difficult mantra to learn. But I had come to be very thankful for it. Now, every time I recited the mantra on my own, I thought of Lama Tsering. Without any effort, it was like I heard his voice. Repeating these special syllables had become like an invocation, a means of bringing his presence into the moment. This had been a recognition I'd first made when at Tiger's Nest, whenever I was meditating on my own. It was a recognition made all the more poignant after his death.

'Do you believe that enlightenment is possible?' Lama Tsering had asked me, that same day in my garden.

I had, by then, become quite used to his conversational ambushes. With my guru, you never knew what he was going to say or do next. He liked to keep me on my toes. Even in his nineties he wouldn't tolerate a lazy answer.

'Of course,' I had nodded.

'Why?' he demanded.

'Because if suffering has causes, we can eliminate its causes,' I referred directly to the teachings. 'And if enlightenment has causes, we can cultivate those. Our texts set out how to do so. It's a path that has been followed by others. Some have followed it already and attained realizations—even enlightenment itself.' I gestured the hermitage around us where there were several monks regarded as extraordinary. Not least of them, Lama Tsering himself.

'Very good answer,' he replied with a twinkle. He was commending me on my text-based response, but I had the sense he wanted to take me somewhere else. 'If you call out "Lama Khensur!"' he gestured to one of the monks across the garden, widely regarded as a fully enlightened master, 'Or "Lama Chodak!"' he nodded towards another renowned for his clairvoyance. 'Will they pay attention to you?'

The question seemed so easy to answer, I wondered if there was a trick in it. I considered my answer carefully before I said, 'Yes.'

'And what happens to the minds of such beings when they die?' he asked.

'They continue,' I replied.

'They continue,' he repeated. 'Not bound by their body. Do you think if you call out "Lama Khensur!" or "Lama Chodak!" after they have died they will still pay attention to you?'

I realized now why he'd asked the question the first time.

'I suppose' I said tentatively.

'*Definitely!*' he corrected me. 'When you become enlightened for the benefit of all living beings and you hear someone in difficulty calling out "Buddha Matt! Buddha Matt—please help!" are you just going to do this?' Lama Tsering folded his arms, drumming the fingers of his right hand against his left arm while looking round and pretending to whistle.

'I suppose not,' I chuckled.

Lama Tsering gave up his make-believe and leaned towards me.

'To the extent that you are able to help, you will help. Never forget! A Buddha cannot take away your negative karma—only you can do this. A Buddha cannot give you virtue—again, this is up to you. But if a Buddha can help you then, of course! Immediately! The Buddha will be there. And do you know the best way to call a particular Buddha?'

I was shaking my head.

'You say the mantra of that Buddha. You repeat it, again and again using your mala,' he held up the string of beads he kept in his pocket at all times. 'It's like this ..." he gestured using a phone.

'Speed dial?'

'Exactly,' he nodded. 'Repeating a mantra is like calling that Buddha on speed dial.'

•••

IN ALICE'S HOSPITAL WARD I TOOK OUT THE STRING OF MALA BEADS I kept in my left pocket at all times. The same mala that Abbot Lhamo had given me, which had belonged to Lama Tsering himself. Having recollected my bodhichitta motivation and settled my mind with the nine round breathing cycle, I imagined my Guru with his lapis-blue body appearing, like a rainbow above us, at once brilliantly present, and at the same time, utterly ethereal. I recollected what he'd told me that day in the hermitage as if he'd intended me to remember it at precisely this moment. The consciousness of Lama Tsering on speed-dial. And I began to recite the mantra he had taught me:

*Tayata Om Bekadze Bekadze*
*Maha Bekadze Bekadze*
*Radza Samungate Soha.*
*Om Bekadze Bekadze*
*Maha Bekadze Bekadze*
*Radza Samungate Soha.*
*Om Bekadze Bekadze*
*Maha Bekadze Bekadze*
*Radza Samungate Soha.*

Colored lights and nectars emanating from his whole, vibrant being, for one round of the mala, as I repeated the mantra, I visualized the while light of purification cascading into Alice's body, cleansing her of all sedative and toxins, permeating her whole being to achieve complete purification.

With the second round I visualized the archetypal blue of healing, instantly removing all pain, damage, and hindrances to complete and immediate recovery. In the third round, it was vibrant red energy I imagined streaming into her form, powering her capabilities to bounce back, to renew, to return to us in vigorous good health. Next was green, the restoration of harmony and reconnection to herself and to her purpose. And finally, gold, the color of radiant good health, abundance in all things material and spiritual.

It was a comprehensive practice, drawing on mantra and visualization, on intention and concentration—and on the Buddhas themselves. It evoked whatever healing energies I possessed within my own energetic field. And, if some part of Alice's consciousness was able to perceive and resonate with the powerful vibrational energies, on her too. I continued for many rounds of the mala, as much as possible becoming one with the process itself, leaving behind all sense of meditator, meditation, and result of meditative absorption and instead simply becoming non-dual with the flow. Sometime during the night, fatigue got the better of me and I fell asleep in the chair.

Next thing I was aware of, there was a movement on the bed. In the grey light of dawn I opened my eyes. Alice was lying, staring at me.

Our eyes meeting, she reached her arm out towards me. 'Mattie,' she whispered.

# Chapter Nineteen

*Two days later*
Dublin

Alice had been discharged from hospital in the morning. Our afternoon flight would get us to Dublin by mid-afternoon. During the past two days since she woke, she had experienced some nausea, but nothing worse. The speed with which she'd first received treatment, after the dangerous dose of barbiturate, meant that she'd been able to avoid the worst impact of the drug while having it flushed out of her system. She would suffer no permanent damage.

I'd spent most of the past two days by her bedside. During that time, Marchetti had visited to return my phone, which had been retrieved from Lascelles's security guards. They had been imprisoned in cells next to their former boss. Bail had not been granted to Lascelles. The public prosecutor was confident that the case against him would keep him behind bars for many years.

In the meantime, through Interpol, the Government of Bhutan had been contacted so that plans could be made to return statues and wall-hangings to their rightful owners. Officials from Thimphu would soon be on their way to Milan to take custody of the precious items.

The Sangye Menla statue had not been on the Interpol list. But I had given Marchetti the abbot's contact details, and a brief exchange he confirmed that I was the nominated courier to return the statue to Tiger's Nest Monastery. In the overhead compartment of our plane, wrapped by a Como-based antique dealer, who was used to shipping fragile items, the Sangye Menla Buddha was finally on his way home.

As soon as Alice had woken fully, the first thing she'd done was to call Josh. I got up from my chair and left the room so she'd had privacy to talk to him—as well as to Michael, with whom he was still staying. A plan had developed that I'd see her home as soon as we reached Dublin. At the hospital, she'd been told to continue resting for several days, and to avoid anything physically strenuous.

I'd had plenty of time to ponder things, while sitting beside her hospital bed. This included the journey home, as well as what would happen once we reached our destination.

The intensity of all we'd been through together during the past week had been like a fire burning everything away. All that we'd held to be so important. Our grandest hopes and wishes. The preoccupations in which our lives had become so inextricably bound during the past several years.

Somehow we had survived the ordeal. Pulled through. And what we'd found, even after all the loss, was that we were still us, Alice and me. And we had emerged from it together.

Yesterday afternoon, doctors had deemed Alice well enough to take a short walk by the lake. Eager to get out of hospital, if only temporarily, we had made our way to the lakeside, walking slowly under the trees of a park, absorbed by the idyllic tranquility of this special place. It was just the lake and the trees and the freshness of the breeze blowing off the water. There was no talk of scientific research or secret *termas*. No pressure to do anything except abide in this moment.

In that time and space, I had felt all the barriers drop. All the tension and defenses from Alice's side. All my own expectation. We had held hands as we walked, savoring the beauty. Connected to each other as well as to the sun and the sky and the earth. It had been simple and perfect, just the two of us. I had no doubt that Alice had sensed it too.

In a way, I had wanted to leave things right there. But of course, I must accompany her back to Dublin. See her into a cab at Shannon airport which would take her home to Josh and Michael. She had spoken to them both, several times in the hospital. From the warmth of her voice, I knew how deeply she cared for them, and how much she wanted to be back with them. They were her family, and for my own sake I had let go of whatever fancies I may have had about something happening between Alice and me. For that reason it was best that we leave things like this: peaceful and easy and ready to slip back into our separate worlds.

But as we were sitting in Milan Malpensa airport, waiting to board, Alice had a call from Josh saying that Jack Bradshaw had phoned, wanting to speak to her. He, too, had been discharged from hospital. And he didn't have her new phone number.

Alice had sent Bradshaw a text. Moments later he'd messaged her back. He had asked to see her, and she had agreed to meet at his office at 4 p.m.

She wanted me to come with her.

•••

Trinity College campus was abuzz with activity when our taxi arrived at the building accommodating the Institute of Information Medicine. After signing me in, we headed directly to Alice's office, where we safely stowed the bag containing the Sangye Menla statue. Then we made our way along the corridor to Bradshaw's office.

He looked normal enough from the window into his office. Sitting upright and side-on in his office chair, his tall, spare frame gave no clue to what he had so recently had to endure. But after Alice knocked on his door, which was ajar, and stepped into his office, he swiveled around in his seat. The whole left side of his face was black with bruising. Scars formed welts from his cheek all the way up to his temple. His left eye blinked from a deep, purple mark.

'Jack!' gasped Alice.

'Uh,' he raised his eyebrows in acknowledgement. 'Walked into a cupboard door.'

She wasn't buying his ironic humor. 'It looks—!'

'Worse than it feels. Fortunately.' He rose to his feet and silently extended his hand in my direction.

'Good to meet you, properly,' I said.

He gestured for us to sit.

'So, you've had your own adventures?' he asked Alice.

She told him briefly about how we'd been pursued by the same men who had attacked him. How events had taken us to a mansion on Lake Como, and the diabolical scheme that had rebounded on Lascelles, who was now in jail facing serious charges.

Bradshaw took all this in, wearing an expression of bleak satisfaction. After Alice had finished he said, 'We may, or may not want to add to those charges. I've had battles of my own with Lascelles. I tried to protect you from them and leave you to manage the research. It's my role, as clinical supervisor, to ensure rigor both in the integrity of the research, as well as in the management of the findings. Most funding organizations understand the protocols to be followed. I explained this to Lascelles, but he wouldn't listen.'

We both listened attentively.

'Things got worse and worse,' Bradshaw was contrite. 'I'm sorry I proved so unreliable in recent weeks. I was trying to keep you at arm's length from what was going on.'

Alice nodded.

'In the end, I felt I had no choice but to tell you what was happening. The last time we spoke, I hinted at it. We were going to meet, and I planned to bring you into the picture. Only, Lascelles's thugs got to me first.'

Alice grimaced.

'In the weeks leading up to that, he'd put me under immense pressure to delay publication of your findings. And to reveal them to him before you'd seen them yourself.'

'He wanted to claim them as his own,' said Alice. 'He was hoping they'd validate his theory. A few days ago he had this presentation at—'

'The *Accademia del Cimento.* I worked that out,' said Bradshaw. 'I came to realize I was up against forces I couldn't resist. Which left me with only one option.'

'To speak to me,' nodded Alice.

'Methodologically,' his response was dry.

She looked puzzled. 'The program methodology was agreed years ago.'

'Sure,' he countered. 'But the way I saw it, if I couldn't stop Lascelles from hijacking research to which he was not entitled, my only option was to invalidate the research itself.'

'Invalidate?' Alice glanced at me, wide-eyed.

'That's why I was burning the midnight oil,' Bradshaw leaned forward in his seat. 'After I had the double-blind removed and stored copies of true findings off-site, I went through the entire report manually and sample switched.'

'You mean—'

'Test Sample 1 became Test Sample 2.'

Unable to contain herself, Alice leapt to her feet. 'So the research proved that mantras—?!'

Bradshaw smiled, his delight self-evident despite his ghoulish appearance. 'A massive endorsement!' he told her.

Alice raised her hands to her face as she welled up with emotion.

'Probably—,' continued Bradshaw, '—the most significant set of results I've seen in my career!'

Alice was hugging Bradshaw, who stood to reciprocate, before she turned to hold onto me. I felt her heart pounding, her breath on my cheek.

'I just can't believe ...!' she kept repeating. 'Oh Mattie! I just can't believe!'

After all that she'd endured, especially having scrutinized what she had thought to be her own, apparently failed, results. Having been on the receiving end of Lascelles's blistering lecture on her inadequacies. Now, as we stood there, holding onto one another, the events of the past week felt only the more surreal.

♦♦♦

We left Bradshaw's office a short while later. After an announcement like that, there was little point discussing anything else. Bradshaw said he wanted to talk about conferences and presentations and what journals to approach for publication. But that was for another day. For the moment, it was all Alice could do to cope with the flood of relief and joy, of astonishment and deep-down validation. Feelings that resonated deeply with me, given how closely her purpose was joined to mine.

It felt like we were floating as we returned along the passage. We retrieved the statue and our belongings from her office and headed down the stairwell and across the foyer. Entering the building, just as we were about to leave, was none other than Stan Sutton, cradling a bunch of fresh-cut roses in his arm.

'You two!' He greeted us. 'Everything okay?' he asked, utterly uninterested in our response. Instead he lifted up the floral display for our admiration. '"Heritage" roses. Fresh from the garden. Beauties, aren't they?'

Then after we'd made appreciative noises, he stepped closer, lowering his voice. 'Reported the Bradshaw incident to the police. They may want to talk. And I ran a comprehensive IT check. You can be assured the integrity of our system is intact. No hacks, break-ins, or anything else to worry about. We remain impenetrable!' He tossed his head as he headed towards the stairs.

Alice and I were snorting as we got to the doors.

'Except to schoolkids!' murmured Alice under breath.

Both of us burst out laughing.

•••

On the pavement outside she put her hand on my arm, eyes bright with excitement. 'You *are* coming home to celebrate? You must come and meet Josh and Michael.'

It was as though all the anguish of the past few weeks had blown over, and the sky, once thick with storm clouds, had cleared, leaving only dazzling, blue radiance. The *joie de vivre* of the Alice who had inhabited my Tiger's Nest dreams.

Being the focus of such dazzling attention, it was hard to say no. I really was thrilled for Alice. The revelation that her program had been an outstanding success was truly wonderful. Not only for her. For both of us. Her work was part of a broader purpose devised by Lama Tsering. I didn't understand the full significance of it. But I had no doubt that it would be revealed.

But rather than encounter the reality of Alice's domestic life with Josh and Michael, I preferred to leave it as an abstraction. It wasn't a world I could ever be a part of, so best to leave it well alone. Did I really want to see, close up, all that I was missing out on? To create bittersweet memories for the future?

'I'm heading back to the hotel,' I told her.

She frowned, confused.

'My stuff is still there,' I offered a ladder for her to climb down.

'I thought you'd asked them to put your things in storage?'

'I did.'

'We can swing by on the way and pick them up.'

'You've been away. I know you'll want to spend time with the family. You won't want me in the way—'

'Nonsense!' She brushed aside my objection. 'This is a champagne occasion! How often do we get to say that, Mattie?' There was joy in her eyes, and, it seemed, the intimation of our special connection. The same special connection that had been the underlying subtext of all our correspondence during the years I'd been away. I recognized that I must be misreading her.

She took in my perplexity before saying, 'Did you take the vow to abandon intoxicants?'

I shook my head. 'Not that I've had much opportunity.'

'I can't think of a better opportunity than this.'

'Is this you, as my Dharma teacher talking?' I asked, wryly, reminding her of the circumstances in which we'd first met.

She tugged me towards her so that her eyes were bearing directly into mine. 'This is me talking, Mattie. I won't let you sit by yourself in a hotel room on a night like this! Come home with me.' She kissed me, firmly on the lips, hooked her arm under mine, and led me along the pavement to a nearby taxi rank.

♦♦♦

BEHIND THE DARK RED FRONT DOOR, ALICE'S FLAT WAS BEAUTIFULLY similar to the way I remembered her apartment in Los Angeles. Off the short hallway was a spacious sitting room where comfortable sofas and chairs were decorated with Himalayan-design throws in rich, natural colors. There were bookshelves crowded with a huge variety of titles, intriguing paintings of ancient Indian palaces. And, as I looked around, I noticed a pair of exquisite lamps supported by ornate, carved elephants.

'The lamps!' I said, gesturing towards them. 'You had these in California.'

'Good memory,' she smiled, watching me with a smile of quiet amusement as I glanced around the room, taking it all in.

'And frangipani!' I recognized the delicate, five-petal stars at the centerpiece of a gorgeous bouquet in a vase, the fragrance instantly transporting me to another time and place. They used to grow in perfumed profusion outside the center where we'd met. 'Just like West Hollywood!'

'That's why I like them so much' she said. 'They're not easily available around here, but I found this specialist florist who gets them in for me.' She nodded. 'Memories ... '

Further back into the flat was a brightly lit, open plan kitchen, leading onto a dining table and, beyond that, a conservatory overlooking a small garden.

On the way here, we'd not only stopped to collect my luggage from the hotel. I had also bought a bottle of Taittinger, which Alice placed on the kitchen bench.

'You can leave your things here,' she headed upstairs. Several doors led off a corridor and she showed me the way to the front of the house, pushing open a bedroom door and pointing to where I could leave my stuff.

Back downstairs, she looked through a cupboard for champagne glasses as I fetched the bottle of champagne. Alice had called Josh and Michael with her news from the taxi. They'd been thrilled—and promised to meet us back home.

I would soon have to face the reality of Alice's personal life. Specifically of Michael. It was something I continued to have mixed feelings about. It wasn't so much a matter of jealousy—I had no claim to Alice. I never had. It was just that through all those years in the Himalayas I'd nurtured a small flame of hope. Attachment, the lamas would have called it. And just like they said, in the end, attachment was always a cause of pain because at some point we would lose whatever it was we were attached to. Even if that was only hope.

Time to recollect the Dharma, I told myself, and to practice non-attachment. If love was the wish for others' happiness, and pure love was such a wish, free of expecting anything in return, then this was my chance to practice pure love.

'Shall we wait till Josh and Michael get here to open this?' I asked, waving the bottle.

'Josh is still a bit young. Doesn't have the taste for it,' she was clinking glasses as she reached to the back of a cupboard. 'And Michael hardly ever drinks.'

As I took off the gold foil wrapper, I told Alice about my experience at Barchetta. How, on my first opportunity in five years for a glass of wine, I'd taken a sip of Tempranillo—and had instantly felt a stabbing twinge in my jaw.

'I kept thinking about the Chief Disciplinarian at Tiger's Nest Chogyam Bhuti,' I said. '"Abandon intoxicants!" I also had this strong intuition that I needed to stay alert.'

Retrieving two champagne glasses, she brought them to the bench.

'I hope you're okay with the champagne,' she said, sympathetically.

'I will be.' I was untwisting the muselet from around the cork. 'I'm pretty sure it was the tannin that caused the twinge. And we don't have to keep looking over our shoulders anymore.'

Having removed the wire, I had the bottle on the counter. 'Soft and sophisticated,' I looked at her impishly, easing my thumbs under the cork. 'Or loud and messy?'

'Loud and messy!' She laughed.

Moments later came the celebratory pop as the cork blasted out, hitting the ceiling. I was soon pouring out two foaming flutes of champagne.

'Congratulations!' I chimed my glass against hers, looking deep into her eyes. 'The most wonderful validation of the power of mantra ever researched in the West! And, let's not forget, the most significant set of results in Jack Bradshaw's career! The lamas, Buddhas, and bodhisattvas will all be so glad with what you've achieved.'

'You too!' she clinked my glass. 'What were the chances of getting back what Lascelles stole? Stopping him in his tracks?'

'It's not quite over yet,' I said. 'But thanks.'

We raised the glasses to our mouths, taking in the orchard-like aroma, while bubbles exploded against the tips of our noses. As we took our first swig, I felt effervescence bursting in my mouth. The lively taste of fresh fruit and honey, along with the matured crispness. Alice was studying me solicitously as I swallowed.

'No twinge?' she asked, eyebrows raised.

'None at all.'

She put Karen Souza on the sound system, and went to the fridge to fetch some dips. As she was doing this, I stepped over to browse the framed photographs on her wall. My first surprise was to find a photograph of her, Geshe-la, and me, taken outside the West Hollywood Buddhist center where we'd met. It was an enlarged image and prominently displayed.

'I've never seen this photo!' I exclaimed.

'Which photo?' She was placing wafers around a bowl of hummus.

'The one with Geshe-la and us. I don't even remember it being taken.' Leaning forward, I looked at our faces. It seemed like a different time and place.

Last time I'd seen Josh, he had been a ten-year-old kid. The teenager featured in some of the photographs was a handsome, young man.

'Josh has grown into a very good-looking young guy,' I observed.

'He's a very special person. I know mothers say that about their sons. But just about everyone else says it too. It's like he's got this presence about him. This energy.'

'Where did he get that from?' I raised my eyebrows.

'Not me,' she was shaking her head. 'Nature. Nurture. I get it. But there's also karma, and he landed on this earth with particular dispositions, conditioning, whatever, which I don't see as having anything to do with genes or upbringing. Sometimes I wonder if it's even karma,' she sipped her champagne.

I regarded her closely. 'Are you saying ...?'

'Absence of karma?' she shrugged. 'I don't know. It's like he's somehow beyond it. He's very musical you know. He sings and plays keyboard. Writes his own stuff. He has this enormous online following. Hundreds of thousands of people around the world. Does it all from his bedroom.'

Surprised as I was by the revelation of Josh's digital audience, I was even more astonished by what Alice was suggesting about him being free of karma. Alice was a serious-minded Dharma student. Was she really suggesting her own son was a bodhisattva?

Looking at more of the photographs, I found a couple of pictures I had sent from the Himalayas. One of the view from Kopan Monastery, with its sweeping vista overlooking Kathmandu. Another of simple, but beautifully painted mani stones, of the kind found throughout the countryside in Bhutan. Devout practitioners would carve or paint the syllables of Chenrezig or Avalokiteshvara's mantra on stones – *Om mani padme hum* – and place these on the side of mountain paths and waterfalls, a constant reminder of the Buddhas' presence.

There were a several photographs of Alice with Dharma groups. A couple of these were interfaith gatherings, featuring men and women in a variety of ecclesiastical garments along with Hindu Siddhus, Jewish Rabbis, Sufi dervishes, and African shaman.

'Any photos of Michael?' I asked.

'There's a couple of him somewhere.' Pouring pistachio nuts into bowls, she was distracted.

'He lives just along the street, you said?'

'Yes. It's really wonderful, him being nearby, especially as he and Josh have this amazing connection.'

'Has he been, like, a father figure?' I hazarded.

'You'd think so,' said Alice. 'And there may be some of that. But it's kind of different. Michael is devoted to Josh. It's like, he's his number one fan.'

•••

AT THAT MOMENT THERE CAME THE THUD OF THE FRONT DOOR OPENing, and the jangle of keys.

'You home, Mom?'

'In the kitchen!'

There came the sounds of footsteps in the hall. A deep, belly-laugh, rolling along the corridor.

Josh appeared, long, dark hair falling about his shoulders and his mother's piercing blue eyes. He certainly possessed an arresting quality that went beyond youthful good looks. He emanated a charismatic power, but at the same time, a boyish gentleness.

'So good to have you home,' he hugged his mother. 'And fantastic news! Congratulations!' Before drawing back, 'What happened to your jaw?' he was looking at the bruise that remained.

'Long story,' Alice gestured dismissively. 'For another day. You remember Matt?'

He was already heading across the room. I'd been about to offer my hand, but he threw his arms around me for a hug.

'So pleased you're here. Mom's always talking about you.'

'She is?'

I'd barely had time to take this in when, behind Josh, there was a flurry of whiteness. Josh stepped aside and suddenly, there was Michael. A large man with long, grey hair, it wasn't so much his age that struck me first, as what he was wearing: the white robes of a Benedictine monk.

After congratulating Alice warmly, he, too, was turning in my direction.

'Matt, this is Michael, *Father* Michael McIntyre, to give him his correct title—'

'No, no, no, just Michael,' Father Michael was already approaching me. Tall, portly, and saintly in appearance – perhaps on account of the robes – he was shaking my hand with surprising vigor.

'I know lots of Buddhist monks,' I told him. 'But never—'

'Camaldolese Benedictine,' he spoke with a gentle Irish accent.

'That's exactly what I said when we first met!' Alice looked over, eyes sparkling.

'At the Interfaith gathering,' confirmed Michael. 'Years ago. All these contemplatives coming together, and it turns out that Alice and I lived a few doors away from each other. What are the chances? I suppose you could call it divine planning,' he looked from Alice to me, merrily provocative.

'Could you?' queried Josh, mock-innocent. 'I thought it was kismet?'

•••

THE EVENING CONTINUED IN CELEBRATORY STYLE, WITH A LOT OF PLAY-ful banter. After our drinks – Michael permitting himself a glass "only so as not to dampen the atmosphere" – we headed out for dinner to Chinta, a delightfully Indonesian-themed restaurant where we found a snug corner among the palm trees and colored lanterns, Josh and Michael sitting on one side of the table, Alice and me on the other.

Conversation flowed effortlessly from subject to subject, at some point in the evening Michael explaining how Saint Benedict was considered a master of monastic living, and Saint Romauld expressed the Camoldolese way according to what was known as The Threefold Good: a synthesis of living together with fellow monastics, regular retreats for periods of silence, and devotion to others more than oneself.

He quoted the words of Saint Romauld, "Sit in your cell as in paradise; put the whole world behind you and forget it; like a skilled angler on the lookout for a catch, keep a careful eye on your thoughts."

A similar message, I thought, to what the Chief Disciplinarian at Tiger's Nest Monastery might say.

Graham and Robyn, who ran Chinta, were the epitome of Bali-chic and hospitality, with an uncanny knack for predicting exactly what their customers wanted, producing dish after delicious dish of food without our even prompting.

I asked Josh about his music and he spoke excitedly about how much he enjoyed composing, and with digital channels so easily available, how his songs were a medium for the messages he wanted to share. He communicated such passion and authenticity it was easy to see how he had acquired such a large following.

Beneath the swell and ebb of words, as I leaned back against the seat, I could scarcely believe how things had turned around. How badly I had got it wrong about Michael and Alice. While they were deeply fond of one another, there was nothing, whatsoever, romantic between them. The two of them and Josh made a cozy unit. Drawn together by common values, genuine affection, and history over the past several years, there was more familial love between them than I'd felt in many households.

Several times during the evening, as I looked over at Alice and our eyes met, there was a feeling of such closeness, and normality about our closeness, that I wondered why I had ever doubted.

I thought about my photographs that she'd kept on display at home. About "Mum's always talking about you." About that moment, tied to our chairs in Lascelles's dining room, when wordless communication had opened up through space and time, and I'd known her heart just as she knew mine. There had been no need for words then. And as I took her hand under the table, and she interlaced her fingers in mine, there was no need now.

After our dinner, in the highest of spirits, we walked home. The apartment Michael told me he shared with two other monks came first. Seeing him to his front door, it was less than two minutes' walk before we reached Alice's. There, Josh headed directly upstairs, before reappearing minutes later with a rucksack over his shoulder: a volunteer at a local youth counselling helpline, he was on the overnight shift.

We said our goodbyes in the living room and waved from the bay window as he headed down the road. After he'd disappeared from view, I walked over to the light switch and turned it off. The room was in darkness except for the yellow glow of streetlight filtering through the wooden shutters, casting golden bars on the carpet. Scented ribbons of frangipani, subtle and delicate, filled the night, an evocation of the time and place where we had first met.

I turned to Alice and there felt like something rapturously inevitable about this moment, her eyes holding fast to mine as I drew her to me. It was as if we had been drawn to this point by a thousand strands of invisible causality, reaching a moment foreshadowed through the warp and weft of numberless events. And here we were, together at last. In one sense, already deeply knowing and intimate beyond words. In a different, thrilling way, only just starting.

# Chapter Twenty

Two weeks later

It was a pristine Himalayan morning as we neared the last part of our journey. Sangay had collected us earlier that day from our hotel in Paro. From the drop-off point, it was a three-hour climb to our final destination.

This was Alice's first visit to Bhutan. And even though she'd had a framed photograph of the monastery on her kitchen wall for years, not even her familiarity with the image had prepared her for the jaw-dropping reality.

Reaching that bend near the summit where the mountain curved sharply away, as always, Sangay paused, gazing directly ahead, waiting for the two of us to catch up. There, revealed only a hundred yards ahead of us, was Tiger's Nest on its impossibly narrow ledge. The towering buildings and gold pagoda roofs, the glinting ephemera, magical and other-worldly, on the other side of a chasm which fell all the way to the valley floor.

I gazed at Alice, delighted by her expression of awe-struck enchantment. Staring ahead of her, after a while she was shaking her head. 'There are no words,' she said.

We took in the multiple strings of prayer flags, fluttering across the chasm.

'So this is where the legendary Padmasambhava flew, on the back of a tiger?' she confirmed.

'So legend has it.'

'Only a cave back then.'

'And what you see now,' I whispered, 'is one of the most improbable of illusions.'

She looked at me questioningly.

'Remember what I told you about Lama Tsering's message for me, the one he told Geshe-la after he died?'

'The best place to hide something?'

'In plain sight,' I confirmed. To which he also used to add the words, 'There it can also be the greatest distraction.'

She studied the ornately decorated buildings, with their burgundy highlights and gold auspicious ornaments, and window casements that were elaborately painted. The whole place was like an intricate ornament, something that might have been conjured up by a jeweler like the great Fabergé.

'You're saying all this is a distraction?' she asked.

I nodded.

'From what?'

Meeting her clear blue eyes, I smiled. 'Best you see for yourself.'

•••

A short while later, having followed Sangay along the final, precipitous jack-knife around the cliff, we flopped onto the lawn in front of the monastery gates. While Sangay went to ring the bell, we shrugged our backpacks off beside us.

Despite our wearying climb, Alice's eyes were shining with anticipation. Reaching over, she pressed my shirt at my chest, feeling the outline of the metal tube I was wearing around my neck. Before touching my backpack, feeling the edges of the box that was still unopened since we'd left Como, which contained the statue of Sangye Menla.

'Just checking,'

I smiled.

We held each other's gaze, aglow with new-found intimacy.

I had never considered it even a possibility that Alice would be joining me on my return to Tiger's Nest. It was a monastery, after all. Any woman who ascended the mountain had only ever been a visitor, leaving within hours that she had arrived.

After I had emailed Abbot Lhamo with the news that, with Dalberg's assistance, I had been able to retrieve both the statue and the *terma* it had contained, he had proposed a return date: the full moon in June. 'Then, in the hermitage, it will be time,' he had said.

I had set about making travel plans, contacting the house in Paro where I'd meet up with Sangay for the journey up the mountain. It was during that exchange of text messages that I'd received the extraordinary invitation: 'The abbot requests that you bring Alice with you. He is making a special dispensation for her visit. This is the first time, since the monastery was established, that a woman has been invited into the hermitage.'

When I'd read the line out loud to Alice, she'd been deeply moved.

'I can't believe he's doing this for me!' emotion tugged at her lips.

Holding her to me, I also felt overwhelmed. 'It's because of your research,' I told her. 'How it validates everything that goes on in the hermitage. As you'll find out.'

There was a movement at the monastery gate. It opened to reveal Kelsang, the abbot's assistant. He stepped forward, palms together at his heart, bowing. Despite our protestations, he and Sangay collected up our backpacks and led us inside.

Across a short courtyard was the flight of steps up to the entrance hall. Once inside, the monastery was a maze of passageways and chambers, some brightly lit by the sun shining through the windows, others, created from caves in the mountainside, in near-total darkness. I remembered the mix of bewilderment and anticipation I'd felt when first shown through this mystical labyrinth. Looking ahead at where Alice was stepping between Kelsang and me, I could see it was the same for her too.

As we made our way along a winding corridor and up two flights of stairs, at right angles to one another, I realized that Kelsang wasn't leading us where I'd thought.

'Aren't we going to see the abbot?' I asked.

'The abbot is looking forward to seeing you,' Kelsang returned. 'First, he asked me to take you somewhere else.'

We were heading in the direction of Lama Tsering's old room, which I hadn't visited since before my retreat. The staircase leading up to it, with its irregular landings and even more erratic windows, was a path with which I had become deeply familiar through the years. Instinctively I knew every curve and narrowing, where to bend and where to find the best footholds to get leverage. As I watched Alice ahead of me, working this out for the first time, I could still hardly believe what was happening: the two of us, together, at Tiger's Nest! Returning with the statue of Sangye Menla and the *terma* it had contained—a likelihood that had seemed impossible when I'd left here.

Sure enough, Kelsang was taking us to Lama Tsering's former room. We were heading along the final, narrow corridor now, right to the end, until reaching a wooden door. Ajar.

Kelsang bowed, before gesturing towards the door and stepping back from it.

Exchanging a puzzled look with Alice, I reached over and knocked three times.

'Matt?' came a familiar voice from within. 'Alice?'

We stepped inside to be warmly greeted by Geshe-la.

'I had no idea you'd be here!' I beamed, as he rose from where he'd been sitting and came to give me a hug.

Alice's eyes were glistening as he held her to him too. 'It's been over five years!' she managed, eventually, with a choked voice.

'But always ...?' he touched his heart.

As we nodded, a teardrop spilled down her cheek.

Geshe-la turned to sit in the same place that Lama Tsering previously occupied. Curled up in the shadows beside him, I noticed a familiar form.

For a long while we just sat, the joy of our reunion requiring no words to be spoken. Like my very first encounter with Lama Tsering, in this same room, the silence seemed to intensify the radiant glow of reunion that enveloped us. So much so that it couldn't possibly be contained within this small room. It felt as though it was emanating beyond where we were sitting, a radiant benevolence spreading across the whole mountainside, filling the vast space of the Paro Valley and far beyond.

After a while there was a tap at the door. A monk appeared with tea—something that only ever happened on very special occasions. Three cups and saucers, a teapot in a cozy, a pewter jug of milk, and an extra saucer were set on a tray. Plus, a battered tin I knew would contain biscuits, its dark green color embossed in gold with the trademark 'Harrods'.

We thanked the monk as he retreated, then Geshe-la began pouring out first the milk, then tea into the cups. Right on cue there was a movement beside him, and from the shadows, two large, golden eyes blinked open. Zorro got up from where he had been sleeping, placing both paws in front of him, and performed a sun salutation to stretch. He was languorously stepping off the side of the daybed, and onto the floor beside the tray.

I'd told Alice about Zorro in my letters, and she watched, transfixed, as he made his way towards her, placing both front paws on her leg, and stretching up to touch her nose with his own.

'Zorro!' she whispered under breath, taking in his masked face and luxuriant coat.

He walked across her lap and sidled behind me, sweeping my back with his tail in acknowledgement, before making his way to where Geshe-la was pouring milk into his saucer. He was soon lapping it noisily as the three of us watched, smiling.

Having not had any direct contact with Geshe-la since India, before anything else happened there was something I needed to say. 'Geshe-la, I feel really bad about doubting the abbot over Dalberg.'

Geshe-la nodded. 'Guru yoga is difficult. Especially for Westerners.'

'Another thing,' I might as well get it all out, here and now. 'That final retreat when I was preparing myself to receive the *terma*, I chose a solitary retreat, in a cave down the mountain. Lama Tsering said perhaps it would be better to stay here. I wanted to prove to him that I could do it. That I was self-sufficient. Only later I discovered that, in drawing attention to myself, I may have started this whole thing: the Khampas coming here, stealing the statue, and killing Lama Tsering. Has this all been down to me? The result of the bad karma I created because I didn't do as my teachers asked?'

'That is another thing about Westerners,' Geshe-la regarded me closely. 'Good at beating themselves up.'

His shoulders began shaking, before he chuckled out loud, dispelling the gravity of the moment.

'Did Lama Tsering say that you must stay at Tiger's Nest?' he asked.

I shook my head.

'Then you didn't disobey. Did the abbot tell you not to use your own judgment, your discretion?'

Again, I shook my head.

'Then you didn't disobey.' Geshe-la paused, allowing this to sink in. Before he continued, 'As for karma, this is a very complex subject. And in matters like this one, revealing a precious *terma* for the benefit of all living beings, it is most certainly not only about you and your karma.'

The moment he pointed it out, the truth of it seemed self-evident. Without realizing, I had created a melodrama with myself at the center of it and convinced myself that it was all about me. Self-grasping had, as so often, snuck up without me even recognizing it.

Geshe-la gazed into the mid-distance for a while before suggesting, 'I think, perhaps, the timing wasn't quite right.'

'Timing?'

'For the *terma* to be revealed.'

'But Lama Tsering said I should come back at the time of the full moon in May.'

'Timing is not always certain,' he nodded. Turning to Alice he said, 'The results of your work. Should they have been ready by May?'

'Definitely,' she said.

'But they were not?'

'We had trouble with Lascelles.'

'They are ready now?'

'Of course!' she beamed.

I recalled the meeting with Bradshaw just before leaving Dublin. He'd prepared a long list of journals to which he wanted Alice to submit articles. Conferences and other forums she could address. He was even preparing a media release.

'You see,' Geshe-la looked at me, gesturing towards Alice. 'There were also other factors for the delay. When engaging in an activity that involves or affects others, especially if it may affect *many* others,' he looked from

Alice to me significantly, 'our own karma is only one factor. We may be willing to give, but what if others lack the karma to receive? We may see what is of extraordinary benefit to them, but what if they are blind to it?'

For a while we sat in silence, absorbing what he had just said. Then Alice said, 'Geshe-la, Matt and I are only students, but we are sincere. We try. We make efforts to purify negativity and to accumulate virtue. But in the past few weeks, we've been physically attacked. All our goals have been threatened even though they are virtuous. There've been times we thought we'd lost everything.' She looked over at me, poignantly. 'When we are trying so much to do the right thing, why are we experiencing such pain?'

Geshe-la's face was filled with compassion. Reaching over the tea tray, he took her hands between his. 'The Buddha answered this question directly. In the Diamond Cutter Sutra he said: "Bodhisattvas practicing transcendent wisdom will be tormented – indeed, they will be greatly tormented – by past actions that would have brought suffering in future lives, but have ripened in this life instead."'

Allowing her hands to fall, he leaned back in his seat. 'In this lifetime we may try our best,' he nodded. 'But our mind streams have existed since beginning-less time. Through numberless lifetimes, in so many different realms, we have created the causes for future suffering. We have killed. We have stolen. We have caused others pain. These are definite causes for lower rebirth.' He gazed at us significantly. 'Now that we recognized the truth of our situation, we know we possess Buddha nature. Our primordial minds are pure. But the karma we have created in the past doesn't just disappear. When causes meet conditions, they still create effects.

'When we practice the Dharma, especially when we study transcendent wisdom, we are conducting the most powerful purification. If we had created the cause, say, for a future lifetime filled with sickness and suffering, we may experience only a headache. Being attacked, physically, is bad—but much better than a life in a war zone, watching our family being slaughtered, before being shot dead ourselves.

'The latencies still exist. But they ripen in ways that we can manage. And then, we have dealt with them. Purified.'

Alice and I were following him.

'Is that the only way we can deal with negative karmas we've created in the past?' asked Alice.

Geshe-la held up two fingers. 'There are two ways,' he said. 'One way is to minimize, as I described, or sometimes our purification can also be postponed. We may keep putting off negative effects. Kick the can down the road. The permanent way, the ultimate way,' he nodded meaningfully, 'is to realize *shunyata*. To understand one's own true nature, and the nature of all things in a state of deep, meditative equipoise. At that point we let go of the experience of a self which can be afflicted by karma or delusion.'

He had given us much to reflect on. As we considered what he'd said, Zorro hopped up on the mattress, licked his paw, and began washing his face.

Looking over at him, we all smiled.

'This one doesn't have such bad karma for an animal rebirth,' observed Alice.

Geshe-la nodded. 'True. There are some at Tiger's Nest who doubt he is an animal at all.' Then meeting her raised eyebrows, 'They say, perhaps, he is the manifestation of a bodhisattva who keeps us company when we meditate.'

'Lama Zorro?' inquired Alice.

Zorro instantly stopped his face-washing, and looked up at her, his paw mid-air.

We all laughed.

•••

After tea with Geshe-la, we were escorted by Kelsang, who had been personally directed by the abbot to take care of us. I guessed this was as much to ensure that Alice's presence wasn't too disruptive to the monks, as for our own benefit. Kelsang was careful to avoid the busier passageways as he led us to some of the monastery's most impressive look-out points, and through its most ancient chambers, offering a commentary on all the meditators and mysteries associated with this ancient place.

After lunch in a private chamber, I suggested taking Alice onto the mountain. Kelsang was, I think, relieved to be free of his caretaking duties for a while. He had already delivered my backpack, containing the Sangye Menla statue, to the abbot, saying it needed to be cleaned and prepared before being returned to the temple.

Heading along a narrow path cut into the rocks, Alice and I emerged into a clearing where a flat expanse overlooked the Paro valley. In the center of it, a tall, lone pine.

'This is where you used to read my letters?' she confirmed as we stood under the tree, surveying the panoramic vista. The valley spread as far as the eye could see and, to one side of it, successive ranges of the Himalayas, deep blue in the afternoon light. More than anything, up here there was the wide-open feeling of space. No roof, no walls, nothing below as you looked down into the valley.

Alice looked out for a while in captivated silence. 'At a place like this,' she said, 'I can see you don't have to try to meditate so hard. The meditation comes to you.'

I put my arm around her.

'That's why this has always been my favorite place to meditate at Tiger's Nest.'

We took in the open spaciousness, the radiant, light-filled clarity, stretching from horizon to horizon. It conveyed not only an abiding peace but also, as an invisible, pine-scented breeze riffled across the clearing, the sense of boundless potentiality.

We meditated for a while, that afternoon, under the pine tree. It was too good an opportunity to miss. Like Alice said, meditation seemed to come to *you* when you sat here, something about the landscape helping release all one's usual preoccupations. Inner reflected outer with an effortlessness that was delightful and uplifting as you sat in the midst of everything.

•••

TIME SLIPPED BY. JUST HOW MUCH TIME WE ONLY REALIZED WHEN Kelsang appeared, calling over. The sun had slipped close to the horizon and he was shielding his eyes from the late afternoon rays.

We followed him back into the monastery and towards the abbot's office. As we did, we tugged at the white *khatas* we had brought in anticipation of being received by him, expecting to follow convention.

Shown into his office, however, it was evident that this was no normal occasion. In the middle of his office, several monks were gathered around the upside-down Sangye Menla statue, the base of which had been removed. They were carefully placing items inside, under the supervision of Chogyam Bhuti, Chief Disciplinarian. At his desk, the abbot was studying an illustration of an empty statue, marked with directions.

As we appeared, he rose from his desk, luminous intelligence seeming to emanate from his face as he bent to receive our *khatas*, and, with great reverence, place them back around our necks. He offered especially warm words to Alice, telling her it was an honor for the monastery to welcome a student who had devoted such important scientific study to Medicine Buddha.

Turning he gestured towards where the monks were working on the statue. 'As you know, the statue was ransacked in Kathmandu.'

We nodded.

'Before we return it to the temple, we must replace certain items, and re-consecrate it. Of course,' he leaned closer to us, 'Not every item.'

I touched my chest.

'This evening, we welcome the Supreme Healer home.' As twilight filled his room with a golden glow he continued, 'It is very rarely that one has the chance to take part in preparing and consecrating a statue. Such activity is considered most auspicious. Given that you both have such a strong connection to the Medicine Buddha, I thought you would like to take part in what we are doing.'

I glanced over at Alice—she had never looked so radiant.

For the next hour we joined the monks on the ornate, threadbare carpet of the abbot's room, taking part in the process of preparing Sangye Menla. Thousands of mantras, previously written in Sanskrit on strips of paper, and secured like rolls of tape, were to be placed inside the empty statue. At each of the statue's chakras, symbolizing different qualities of body, speech, and mind, precious jewels donated by sponsors were precisely packed into place. Holy texts were also used, including sadhanas, or practice instructions, specific to Medicine Buddha. Never had I truly understood how every Buddha statue was not simply a work of symbolic and artistic expression, but also a repository of all the elements required for its purpose to become manifest.

As each of us took it in turns to add sacred items to the statue, a lama and great scholar who had been living at Tiger's Nest for over forty years, recited the twelve vows that Medicine Buddha had made upon attaining enlightenment. These included vows to help all those who are physically disabled or sick to be blessed with good health, both physically and mentally. The vow to relieve all pain and poverty of the very sick and poor. The vow to help women who are undergoing suffering and deprivation. The vow to help free beings from evil thoughts. The vow to shine beams of brilliant light throughout the universe, empowering all beings to attain complete and perfect enlightenment.

It was only after this process was completed to the satisfaction of the Chief Disciplinarian, that the base was sealed and the statue carefully turned the right way up. Sangye Menla was ready to resume his place in the temple of Tiger's Nest.

•••

THAT EVENING, WE TOOK PART IN A PRIVATE CEREMONY OF THE DEEPEST personal significance to Alice and me. Those of us who had worked on the statue in the abbot's rooms, joined by several others including Geshe-la, gathered in the small monastery temple. Through the windows, directly facing the Paro Valley, the light of the full moon streamed into the small, misshapen room, the ethereal silver offering a perfect counterpoint to the flickering gold of the butter lamps, reflected in a hundred brass offering bowls.

Led by Chogyam Bhuti acting as chant master, we recited refuge and bodhichitta prayers, the short mandala offering prayers to the lineage gurus. Then as we watched, up the stairs on a palanquin carried by two monks came the statue of Sangye Menla. The abbot with the assistance of Geshe-la, lifted the statue and placed it back onto position on the altar, from which it had been removed.

Then we all recited the sadhana of Medicine Buddha, Sangye Menla, the Supreme Healer. This included mantras said for the benefit of all those suffering from sickness and pain, physical or mental. We visualized immeasurable rays of light and nectars, touching the hearts and minds of all those who needed them, throughout universal space.

There was such power in the practice, especially in the presence of the bodhisattvas with whom we were sitting, beings whose outward appearances may be those of ordinary monks, but who, in reality, had long left behind all notion of mundane reality, and abided in a state of transcendental bliss.

It may be true that Buddhas could not give us their insights or attainments, but in that small room I was uplifted in a way for which there were no words, absorbed into a dimension where, while still fully aware of what was going on at a conventional level, time ceased to have meaning and the most overwhelming feeling was a profound knowingness that all is well.

•••

AFTERWARDS, ALICE AND I WALKED WITH GESHE-LA TOWARDS OUR rooms. After our experience in the temple, words were superfluous. Reaching a landing where Geshe-la needed to turn, he paused.

'Tomorrow, we open the *terma*.'

Alice and I nodded.

'"*In the time that the iron bird flies,*
*And horses run on wheels,*
*The Tibetan people will be scattered*
*across the face of the earth like ants,*
*And the Dharma will come to*
*the land of the red-faced people.*"'

He recited Padmasambhava's most famous prophecy, in so doing, confirming that the *terma* did, indeed, contain the words of the 8th century master.

But how did he know for sure?

I thought about the abbot's message: 'in the hermitage, it will be time.' Imagining the hermitage, I wondered what the weather would be like tomorrow.

As Alice and I bade Geshe-la goodnight, we headed in the opposite direction from him.

'A sunny day is forecast' he called out, chuckling.

◆◆◆

We had been allocated what had been my old room, and this was the first time Alice had seen it. At the end of a narrowing passage, it was small—not much longer than a mattress in length, and about four yards wide. In recognition of her visit, a second, single mattress had been laid out beside the one I'd used. There was the small, wooden trunk which had contained my belongings. The wardrobe was a peg on the back of the slanting door—to which, I noticed, had been added a single clothes hanger, presumably for Alice's use. Heating consisted of two rubber hot water bottles.

'My home for the past five years,' I murmured.

Alice glanced around, eyes gleaming. She knew that most of the monks slept in dormitories. 'Your own room at Tiger's Nest!'

'Very spoiled.'

She stepped inside, sinking onto one of the mattresses to take in the view a low window that overlooked the valley. Closing the door, I sat beside her.

The moon had already lifted over the brink of the far valley wall. Being full, it had already begun its ascent through the vaulted sky, improbably large and close, and so brilliantly radiant we could even see the colors of the pine forests on the distant mountains—numinous, green shadows in the silent night.

Moonlight transformed every element of the shimmering landscape. The ice-capped Himalayas, successive ranges of them, rose to glistening transcendence on the far horizon. Waterfalls foamed over distant cliffs, plunging into white veils that dissolved in mid-space. Down the sheer sides of the valley, rivers shimmered like silver ribbons.

Alice turned to me. 'I have never felt so wildly, improbably, crazily lucky as I feel right now!' she said.

I put my arm around her shoulders, and we flopped back on the mattresses.

'Me neither.'

•••

In the darkest hour of the night, just before dawn, I awoke to some kind of vibration. On the mattress next to me, I felt Alice stir. We opened our eyes at the same moment and looked at each other. The movement hadn't been frightening—but something was happening. The aroma of sandalwood was filling the room.

We both propped ourselves up on our mattresses and turned. Lama Tsering was sitting with his back to the door in a meditation posture, floating about four feet from the ground. His body was a radiant lapis-blue and light-natured. Wearing beautifully ornate monk's robes, in his right hand he held a small branch of cherry plum, with exquisite white flowers and ripe, red fruit. At his naval, on his left hand, a bowl of dazzling multicolored healing nectars. He looked down at us both with an expression of such indescribable love that as I met his eyes a surge of bliss ran through me, from the crown of my head to the bottom of my spine. I knew it must be the same for Alice, too, just as I knew she needed no explanation about who he was. Lama Tsering, and in the form of Medicine Buddha, Sangye Menla, the Supreme Healer.

'I am so happy to see you both here,' he spoke.

We folded our palms to our hearts and bowed slowly.

'Yours is a historic purpose. Padmasambhava wrote his instructions over one thousand five hundred years ago. He placed them in a *terma* to be revealed only when world was ready for them. And he meant, the whole world.

'There has been an understanding for some time in the East about the nature of reality. How illness can become the pathway to personal transformation. We needed to allow time for the West to complement this subjective science, with objective science.'

We were nodding.

'I think you both know what you will find in the *terma* tomorrow.'

Alice and I looked at each other, swallowing.

'When I found the *terma* and brought it from Tibet in 1959, I knew what it contained. I understood that for the revelations to be of greatest benefit, I needed to establish the power of their embodiment. This is why I taught the practices to the monks in the hermitage. They are living long. And why I taught the practices to you,' he looked at me. 'So that you could develop personal experience. Also why we asked you to undertake your scientific study,' his eyes met Alice's—in the darkness they were incandescently blue.

'Know that I will be there with you later, and always, along with all the Buddhas and bodhisattvas, because we arise from the same mind. We are of the same taste.'

Again, I felt an inexplicable, whole-of-body, wave of rapture as if, for a moment, I was able to resonate in some way with his transcendental bliss. It was a feeling so wonderful I didn't want it to stop, or for him to go. From what he said, he seemed to be signaling that he was about to go. But it would be with us yearning for more of this feeling, this energy he was able to communicate.

As I'd found so often in the past with Lama Tsering, he was merely preparing the ground for what he was about to say. The real reason he had appeared to us.

'Do you remember the definition of a blessing?' he asked.

'A blessing is the power to change,' I replied.

Nodding in acknowledgement, Lama Tsering said, 'Whenever you wish to invoke this power, and to invoke the healing qualities of Medicine Buddha, remember this blessing.'

For a moment I wondered what blessing he meant. Was it the image of him, as Medicine Buddha, floating at crown height a short distance in front of us? Was it his radiant, light-natured form, which had the same quality as a rainbow—both indescribably brilliant at the same time as being utterly ephemeral?

But I didn't wonder for long because I realized that something about him was changing. He was demonstrating the blessing here and now. Right in front of us, he was shrinking in size, little by little, all the while keeping perfectly in proportion. At the same time as shrinking, the radiance of his form wasn't diminishing. If anything, it was increasing. The smaller he became, the more dazzling. Radiant, lapis-blue light radiated from his every pore. The brilliant, multi-colored lights and nectars in his bowl were dynamic with energy, and all-pervasive, moving and glowing and transforming whatever they touched.

My guru, in the form of Medicine Buddha, was also coming towards us. Having diminished to the size of an apple, somewhere between the door and where we sat, he effortlessly became two. One, ever-shrinking and ever-radiant, floating towards the top of my head and the other towards Alice's. At the same time, he was gently turning in mid-air, coming to face the same direction as each one of us, all the while sending out, all-pervasive, rainbow lights.

By the time he reached our foreheads, he had shrunk to the size of a thumbnail. Perfectly formed, intensely brilliant, for a few moments he remained poised above the crowns of our heads. Then he dissolved into us.

If felt like an inner explosion of joy as his light-natured form entered us at the crown, in an instant transforming every element of our bodies with healing lights and nectars. An ecstatic thrill of luminosity just like when he'd first looked at us—except this time it was coming from within.

For moments we sat there, absorbing the pervasive bliss. Before I noticed that he hadn't stopped moving. I could feel his presence, a tangible, energetic force, descending smoothly and steadily from crown towards the throat. As soon as he reached that place, there was Ir explosion of lights and nectars like an inner atomic happening. This time I intuitively knew his presence was purifying anything negative I'd ever said, while at the same time empowering useful speech, virtuous words, insight, and wisdom that could help others.

Continuing on his smooth and constant glide downwards, after a while he reached my heart. Which was where he stopped. And the charge of energy this time was greatest of all, seeming to dazzle outwards, way beyond the confines of my body, this room, even the monastery itself. An energetic event of universal magnitude, blazing lights and nectars to the ten directions of space which, in that moment, I knew to be the size of my own consciousness. All negativity of mind was purified, and virtue was empowered. Whoever and whatever I might have once imagined myself to be was, in that moment of blinding truth, revealed to be merely temporary, contingent. Instead, the ultimate reality was a boundless clarity and bliss. Not a bag of bones with an ego attached, but a numinous intelligence that was omniscient, a compassionate energy so oceanic that it was without limits. Pure, great love that pervaded all things.

How could it be any different? For a moment, in a room, on a cliff, my mind and the mind of my kind root guru, who was Medicine Buddha, had become one.

Alice's too.

# Chapter Twenty-One

Kelsang came to our door the next morning. We had washed and dressed in readiness for what was to follow. And gratefully eaten the breakfast delivered to our room.

We had spoken very little about our experience of a few hours before. It had been so unexpected, and such a profound blessing – in the true sense of the word – that it would probably be a while before we were able to make sense of it. But it had, unambiguously, been a source of joy. I felt as though it was a different version of me who was waking that morning. A lighter, less burdened, freer being. One who had, if only momentarily, caught a glimpse of what might be my own, primordial nature.

'You are ready?' asked Kelsang, glancing from me to Alice.

I reached to touch my chest. For what would be the last time, I realized, I felt the heft of the ancient, metal tube pressed my skin.

We nodded.

I had wondered if it would be just the two of us, or if someone would meet us, to show Alice through to the hermitage for what would be her very first time. As it happened, Geshe-la was there, on a landing. Accompanied by Zorro.

'Slept well?' he asked us, eyes twinkling.

There was no need to reply. We all just chuckled. I didn't doubt for a moment that Geshe-la had been witness to the whole thing.

Kelsang continued for a short distance, leading us along the main corridor towards the temple. There was a flight of stairs upwards, to the right and against the mountainside, leading off the main passage to an alcove a few yards above it. It was a nook I had explored during my very earliest days at Tiger's Nest. A hollow in the mountain had been turned into a library of sorts. Two large, sturdy bookshelves were filled with esoteric books in a number of European and Asian languages. These weren't the standard texts, studied by monks, but commentaries by a variety of authors. I guessed that the books had accumulated at the monastery over a period of time. None of them had been of particular interest, so I'd never spent much at the shelves. Which, I suppose, was the point.

Kelsang pushed back a few books on a shelf midway down the right-hand bookshelf and slipped his hand into a recess, turning a handle. There came the soft but deliberate click of a bolt sliding open.

Checking the passage below to ensure there was no one else around, he pushed against the bookshelf, which revealed itself to be a door. Ushering us urgently, we were soon on the other side and he was closing it shut.

We were suddenly in very deep gloom, the only light coming from a low wattage electric light on the wall. We headed along a corridor directly towards the center of the mountain. Looking over I met Alice's eyes and caught the glint of excitement. The same anticipation I'd felt, not only the very first time I'd stepped in here, but on every subsequent visit.

In spite of the darkness, this was no dripping underground dugout. The corridor was dry, and the floor surface carpeted. I watched Alice glance around, just as I had initially, working out that this was a substantial cave leading who knew where. Was the hermitage she'd heard something about – and which I was forbidden to talk about – a vast cavern in the middle of the mountain? Was it a labyrinth of caves and tunnels like a Himalayan version of the Derinkuyu complex in Turkey?

Kelsang led the way forward. At our feet, Zorro padded along, right behind Kelsang. This was a familiar path for him. We didn't have long to walk before we paused again. Another door. Kelsang was reaching for a handle. Turning a lock. As he drew it towards us, it was to reveal a large rectangle of blinding luminescence.

It was taking a while for our eyes to adjust after the darkness. We were following him, light-dazed, through the door and into a covered walk formed out of mountain rock. As we made our way forward our eyes were adjusting to what lay directly ahead. A sight as dazzling as it was utterly unexpected.

'Where are we?' Alice turned towards me, her expression beatific—but confused. 'Did we somehow walk through the mountain?'

We continued, following Kelsang onto an emerald-green lawn where he paused, allowing us a while to take everything in.

Surrounding us were luxuriant gardens the size of a football pitch. Immediately in front of us, terraced lawns were bordered by flower beds, lush with rhododendrons in vivid reds, pinks, and whites. The air was fragrant with alpine flowers—clematis, daphne, and primroses. At the center of the lawns was a fountain, with the heads of water dragons facing each of the cardinal directions. From their mouths, water plumed in white arcs against the azure morning sky.

Stately oak trees grew along the sides of the garden, and as Alice looked up at one, a flock of plum-headed parakeets swooped, screeching from its branches. A short distance away from us, a few monks were enjoying the sun beside a rose garden, prolific with blossoms—including many varieties of David Austen.

'We're not on the other side of the mountain,' I replied to her question after a pause. 'We're inside it.'

She looked at Geshe-la and me with such child-like glee that we all laughed.

'So *this* is the hermitage?' she confirmed.

We nodded.

'A whole ... ecosystem!' she exclaimed. She was looking at where the lip of the mountain surrounded the entire garden, the equivalent of two to three stories high. This protection, as she had observed, meant that the micro-climate in the mountain-top crater was quite different from elsewhere. Winters were very much milder. In summer, warmth was retained. Like a nature-made greenhouse, on the far side of the gardens, orchards bore more than enough fruit for the whole of the monastery, while the vegetable gardens were abundant through long stretches of the year.

Centuries ago an elaborate irrigation system had been devised, leading water from melting ice on the mountain tops, via a channel with a shallow gradient, all the way around the circumference of the protective, moss-covered walls and down into the gardens. A soothing ripple of water played constantly in the background amid the lush, green ferns which grew up the garden sides.

Marveling at this all, Alice was scanning the cloisters which ran around the perimeter of the garden. Zorro was making his way along one, towards where a monk was greeting him as a much-loved friend.

'Remember you were wondering how 150 monks could live on the side of a cliff?' I reminded her.

Alice was shaking her head, smiling. 'I'm guessing this is where the Bhutan blip resides.' As we took in the ambrosial scents of that warm morning, she added, 'It's like a pure land! I'm surprised they can ever bring themselves to leave.'

'There are some who've been here nearly forty years,' I told her. 'They came at retirement age.'

Glancing around at the monks who were present, Alice's incredulity was obvious: were these relaxed and health-looking monks really in their 90s? After a while she said, 'I also remember you telling me what Lama Tsering said about the best place to hide something is in plain sight.' Looking from me to Geshe-la she added significantly, '*And* it can be the best distraction. Tiger's Nest sure is some distraction. Never in a thousand years would you guess that it conceals all this!'

Geshe-la cleared his throat, 'You told Alice Lama Tsering's message to you, after he died?' he asked.

'Yes, Geshe-la.'

'A most useful message, no?'

I nodded. Yesterday, during our reunion with Alice, we hadn't referred to Lama Tsering's message, or how critical it had been in all that had followed. Alice still wasn't aware why the *terma*, stolen from around my neck in Ireland, had turned out to contain nothing more significant than an image of 'Tintin in Tibet.' Nor what had become of the real *terma* I'd retrieved from Rakesh Sharma in Kathmandu.

'When you first told me the message, I didn't see how it could be relevant,' I admitted to Geshe-la now. 'But you said to keep it in mind. That its meaning would become obvious. The very next day, outside a bus terminus in Kathmandu, I came across these stalls selling Tibetan Buddhist items. The usual bells and incense holders and prayer wheels. Among them I saw a scroll, almost identical to the real *terma* from the statue.'

'An imitation scroll?' Alice looked surprised.

I nodded.

'They are not common,' said Geshe-la.

'Suddenly, I was recalling Lama Tsering's message,' I continued. 'About hiding things in plain sight. I didn't figure it out immediately. But I bought the scroll for a few dollars and put it in my pocket. Then, the first chance I got, I swapped the *termas*, putting the fake one round my neck.'

'In case you were cornered?' confirmed Alice.

'Exactly. The greatest distraction. I hid the real one in my luggage. Then,' holding Alice's eyes, 'I transferred it to a safety deposit box at the bank near my hotel in Dublin. I kept wearing the other one. It had become like a kind of talisman to me. I felt almost protected by it.'

'Turned out you were,' she said.

I shook my head. 'It wasn't till Galway that I worked out who those two thugs were after. Though I still hadn't realized why.'

There was a pause while Alice took this all in. Before she observed, 'It was a distraction that could have saved our lives.'

I nodded. 'And our purpose.'

•••

SOON, ABBOT LHAMO APPEARED, WITH A SMALL ENTOURAGE OF MONKS. We all folded our hands at our hearts and bowed in greeting.

'Welcome to the hermitage,' he greeted Alice with especial warmth.

'Thank you so much for letting me visit!' She met his eyes. 'It's the most beautiful place I've ever seen.'

The abbot, accompanied by Kelsang, led us to where a flat-topped rock protruded a couple of feet above the lawn. Gesturing us to step closer, he said, 'When Padmasambhava first discovered Tiger's Nest, over one thousand, five hundred years ago, he would meditate in the gardens and caves. And it is said that he used this,' he leaned down to touch the rock, 'for his desk.' Looking from Geshe-la to Alice to me he said, 'Perhaps it may be appropriate to reveal the words that he wrote for our benefit, at the very same place he wrote them.'

He was reminding us of the magnitude of what we were about to do. And also, how natural and right it felt to be doing it here and now.

'We are receiving the blessing of Lama Tsering?' he asked, more as a confirmation than a question.

We were all nodding.

'Matt. You are ready?'

Bowing my head, I touched my chest.

The abbot gestured to Geshe-la as he always did, when deferring to a lama. Geshe-la brought his palms to his heart. Together we recited verses of refuge and bodhichitta. Geshe-la intoned the names of lineage gurus, asking for their blessings. As he did, I was aware of a shift in what was happening behind and around us. Monks from the hermitage were joining us too, sitting in meditation on the lawns. Emerging from the cloisters. Walking across the lawns. Actively engaging in what was happening. I was reminded of Lama Tsering's teaching in this very place.

*'If you call out "Lama Khensur!"' he had demanded, 'or "Lama Chodak!" Will they pay attention to you? And what about after they have died— will they still pay attention to you?'*

*'I suppose' I had answered.*

*'Definitely!' he had corrected me.*

Was it possible that all the lineage lamas from the past fifteen hundred years were gathering here and now? Whether in human form, or at a more subtle, energetic level? It certainly felt like it. Amid the pristine scents and intense colors of this enchanted garden it was as though we were standing at a gathering vortex of benevolent energy.

At Geshe-la's instruction, we visualized all things dissolving into their primordial nature, and it was as though we were dissolved into a light of perfect clarity, the presence of Buddhas and bodhisattvas suffusing all with radiant bliss.

I met the abbot's eyes and he nodded towards me. Without him needing to say anything, I removed the *terma* from around my neck.

At the same time, Kelsang was drawing a small hacksaw from his robes. He gave it to me, before kneeling by the rock, to help me steady the *terma*, which I placed on its smooth surface.

I marked the end of the *terma* with a few, forward sweeps.

Before this moment had arrived, I had wondered how the process would unfold. Would my hands be shaky with the attention of others on me? Would I have difficulty cutting the metal?

Now, having reached the moment, it was as if I was taking part in an event which was progressing of its own volition. Merely acting out my part in an effortless drama. The fine-toothed saw was marking, then cutting through the metal with smooth fluidity. Not too fast, to avoid creating excessive heat that might damage the precious paper within.

In a short time I had cut almost all the way through. Just a few, final sweeps and the end of the *terma* was all but separated, pushed away from the rest. Raising the tube to eye level, I looked inside. Thick, yellowing paper was rolled within. Using the tip of my little finger, I eased it very gently, little by little, checking that the paper wasn't so brittle or decomposed that it was at risk of cracking or turning to dust.

It was surprisingly robust for a parchment that had been manufactured over one and a half millennia ago. When enough of it was protruding from the tube, I was able to slide the rest out quite easily. Unroll it slowly. And, discovering that it was doubled over, unfold it with the greatest of care.

Bold Tibetan handwriting covered the piece of paper, which had opened to the size of a large postcard. I was about to give it to Geshe-la to read and translate when I glanced up. Around us, at least a hundred monks from the hermitage were sitting on the lawn in meditation posture, not so much spectators to what was happening, but in some way participants. Their bodies seemed to have transformed into more subtle, diaphanous versions of their former selves, their presence not only physical but also energetic. Looking over at Alice, when I met her eyes, instead of their usual clarity, they were reflecting something completely different. Turning to look up, I saw that a rainbow had formed above us across the full sweep of the sky. Dazzling against the clear, bright-blue, at that moment there seemed nothing more improbable or propitious.

With a bow, I handed the paper to Geshe-la who, in a clear voice, read it out to everyone in its original Tibetan, before saying, 'I can confirm this is the mark, the signature, of Padmasambhava, Guru Rinpoche.' Then translating the *terma*, for our benefit he read:

*When men speak aloud to the invisible*
*And are killed by their own thoughts and actions*
*By this mantra the wise will be healed of*
*the true causes of sickness, pain, and untimely death.*
*These words form the perfect ring by which*
*the Buddhas hook all beings to enduring bliss.*

Just as with his most famous of prophecies, in the first two lines Padmasambhava was speaking to the time that the *terma* was to be revealed. When he referred to men speaking aloud to the invisible, I immediately saw people walking along city streets, using earpieces for their phones, talking intently to someone who wasn't, physically there.

Being "killed by their own thoughts and actions": was it not the case that stress, anxiety, and suicide accounted for dramatically more deaths in our time, than at any time before?

Geshe-la was reciting the mantra of Medicine Buddha. The mantra Lama Tsering had taught me in anticipation of this moment. That Alice had studied. The mantra that all of the monks around us were joining in and repeating in a group chant.

Padmasambhava's lyrical line about the perfect ring reminded me, once again, of Lama Tsering's insistence, 'If you call out "Lama Khensur!"' he had demanded, 'or "Lama Chodak!" Will they pay attention to you?'

'I suppose.'

'Definitely!'

The Buddhas, those who had gone before us, wanted to help. To hook us out of samsara to a state of enduring bliss. But first we needed to be able to be helped. 'The perfect ring' was the practice through which we were enabled to embody Medicine Buddha, just as our precious teacher had demonstrated last night. When we did, when we recognized that there was no self and other – nor had there ever been – but only one, non-dual experience of reality, and that this reality was a state of oceanic clarity and abiding wellbeing, *then* we healed the true causes of sickness and aging.

As our chanting rose from the hermitage gardens, a scatter of rain descended from the cloudless sky. Looking up, each falling drop reflected the dazzling colors above, so that it was as though rainbow-colored lights and nectars showered down upon us. Was it prana, Qi, or a flood of electrons that descended at that moment? Who knew or cared? Surrounded by enlightened beings, how could we not resonate with their loving kindness, their benevolent intention? I held hands with Alice on one side and Geshe-la on the other, absorbed in every moment of this transcendent bliss.

*'Tayata Om Bekadze Bekadze*
*Maha Bekadze Bekadze*
*Radza Samungate Soha.*
*Om Bekadze Bekadze*
*Maha Bekadze Bekadze*
*Radza Samungate Soha.*
*Om Bekadze Bekadze*
*Maha Bekadze Bekadze*
*Radza Samungate Soha.'*

•••

# Author's Note

*The Secret Mantra* is a work of fiction. If the characters, stories, and themes in this book have the feeling of authenticity to them, it is because I have woven elements of reality into this tale from experience as well as from my imagination.

It is important for you to know that there is nothing fictitious about the practice of Medicine Buddha. Part of the Kriya Tantra tradition, Medicine Buddha is both rare and precious, and can greatly empower our meditation, especially when we focus on healing ourselves or others. These practices have been of profound benefit to many generations of meditators.

The mantra of Sangye Menla, or Medicine Buddha, has been recited for hundreds of years, exactly as described. It is my heartfelt wish that, through writing this novel, many more people may wish to learn about the transformational qualities of this extraordinary practice.

To find out more, download my non-fiction, introductory booklet to Medicine Buddha available on the 'Free Stuff' section of my website. It's called: *Healing: Unlock the Power and Purpose of Your Mind through Medicine Buddha.*

**www.davidmichie.com**

*May all beings have happiness and the causes of happiness.*
*May all beings be free from suffering and the causes of suffering.*
*May all beings never be parted from the happiness that is without suffering, great nirvana liberation.*
*May all beings abide in peace and equanimity, their minds free from attachment and aversion and free from indifference.*

# ABOUT THE AUTHOR

DAVID MICHIE IS THE INTERNATIONALLY BEST-SELLING AUTHOR OF *THE Magician of Lhasa*, *The Dalai Lama's Cat* series, as well as the non-fiction titles *Buddhism for Busy People*, *Buddhism for Pet Lovers*, *Mindfulness is Better than Chocolate* and *Hurry Up and Meditate*.

In 2015 he established Mindful Safaris to Africa, combining wildlife viewing and meditation sessions in journeys to unexplored places, outer and inner.

For more about his work go to: davidmichie.com

*Read the Prologue and First Chapter of The Magician of Lhasa*

# Prologue

## *Tenzin Dorje*

(pronounced Ten-zin Door-jay)

***Zheng-po Monastery—Tibet***
**March 1959**

I AM ALONE IN THE SACRED STILLNESS OF THE TEMPLE, LIGHTING BUTter lamps at the Buddha's feet, when I first realize that something is very wrong.

"Tenzin Dorje!" Startled, I turn to glimpse the spare frame of my teacher, silhouetted briefly at the far door. "My room. Immediately!"

For a moment I am faced with a dilemma. Making offerings to the Buddha is considered a special privilege, and as a sixteen-year-old novice monk I take this duty seriously. Not only is there a particular order in which the candles must be lit, each new flame should be visualized as representing a precious gift—such as incense, music and flowers—to be offered for the sake of all living beings.

I know that nothing should prevent me from completing this important rite, but is obedience to my kind and holy teacher not more important? Besides, I can't remember the last time that Lama Tsering used the word "immediately." Nor can I remember a time when anyone shouted an order in the temple. Especially not Zheng-po's highest-ranking lama.

Even though I am only half-way through lighting the candles, I quickly snuff out the taper. Bowing briefly to the Buddha, I hurry outside.

In the twilight, disruption is spreading through Zheng-po monastery like ripples from a stone thrown into a tranquil lake. Monks are knocking loudly on each other's doors. People are rushing across the courtyard with unusual haste. Villagers have gathered outside the abbot's office and are talking in alarmed voices and gesturing down the valley.

Slipping into my sandals, I gather my robe above my knees and, abandoning the usual monastic code, break into a run.

Lama Tsering's room is at the furthermost end, across the courtyard and past almost all the monks' rooms, in the very last building. Even though his status would accord him a spacious and comfortable room directly overlooking the courtyard, he insists on living next to his novices in a small cell on the edge of Zheng-po.

When I get to the room, his door is thrown open and his floor, usually swept clean, is scattered with ropes and packages I've never seen. His lamp is turned to full flame, making him look even taller and more disproportionate than ever as his shadow leaps about the walls and ceiling with unfamiliar urgency.

I've no sooner got there than I turn to find Paldon Wangpo hurrying towards me. The pair of us are Lama Tsering's two novices but we have an even stronger karmic connection: Paldon Wangpo is my brother, two years older than I.

We knock on our teacher's door.

Lama Tsering beckons us inside, telling us to close the door behind us. Although the whole of Zheng-po is in turmoil, his face shows no sign of panic. But there is no disguising the gravity of his expression.

"This is the day we have feared ever since the Year of the Metal Tiger," he looks from one to the other of us with a seriousness we only usually see before an important examination. "Messengers have just arrived at the village with news that the Red Army has marched on Lhasa. His Holiness, the Dalai Lama, has been forced into exile. A division of the Red Army is traveling here, to Jangtang province. At this moment they are only half a day's travel from Zheng-po."

Paldon Wangpo and I can't resist exchanging glances. In just a few sentences, Lama Tsering has told us that everything about our world has been turned upside down. If His Holiness has been forced to flee from the Potala Palace, what hope is there for the rest of Tibet?

"We must assume that the Red Army is coming directly towards Zheng-po," Lama Tsering continues quickly. From outside we hear one of the women villagers wailing. "If they travel through the night, they could arrive by tomorrow morning. *Definitely*, they could get here within a day. In other parts of our country, the army is destroying monasteries, looting their treasures, burning their sacred texts, torturing and murdering the monks. There's little doubt they have the same intentions for Zheng-po. For this reason, the abbot is asking us to evacuate."

"Evacuate?" I can't contain myself. "Why don't we stay and resist?"

"Tenzin Dorje, I have shown you the map of our neighbor China," he explains. "For every soldier they have sent to Tibet, there are ten thousand more soldiers ready to take their place. Even if we wanted to, this is not a struggle we can win."

"But—"

Paldon Wangpo reaches out, putting his hand over my mouth.

"Fortunately, our abbot and the senior lamas have been preparing for this possibility. Each of the monks has a choice. You can return to your village and continue to practice the Dharma in secret. Or you can join the senior lamas in exile."

He holds up his hand, gesturing we shouldn't yet reply. "Before you say you want to join us in exile, you must realize this is not some great adventure. Traveling to the border will be dangerous—the Red Army will shoot dead any monks trying to leave. Then we must try to cross the mountains on foot. For three weeks we will have to travel very long distances, living only off the food we can carry. We will have to endure much hardship and pain. Even if we finally arrive in India, we don't know if the government will allow us to stay, or send us back over the border."

"But if we return to our villages and continue to wear our robes," interjects Paldon Wangpo, "the Chinese will find us anyway, and punish our families for keeping us."

Lama Tsering nods briefly.

"If we disrobe, we would be breaking our vows." Paldon Wangpo has always been a sharp debater. "Either way, we would lose you as our teacher."

"What you say is true," Lama Tsering agrees. "This is a difficult decision even for a lama, and you are novice monks. But it is important that you choose, and do so quickly. Whatever decision you make," he regards each of us in turn, "you will have my blessing."

From outside comes the pounding of feet as people hurry past. There can be no doubting the crisis we're facing.

"I am getting older," Lama Tsering tells us, kneeling down to continue packing a leather bag, which is lying on the floor. "If I had only myself to think about, I might go into hiding and take my chances with the Chinese—"

"No, Lama!" I exclaim.

Next to me, Paldon Wangpo looks sheepish. He has always been embarrassed by my impetuousness.

"But the abbot has asked me to play an important part in the evacuation."

"I want to come with you!" I can't hold back any longer, no matter what Paldon Wangpo thinks.

"Perhaps you like me as a teacher," Lama Tsering is cautioning. "But as a fellow traveler it will be very different. You are young and strong, but I may become a liability. What happens if I fall and hurt myself?"

"Then we will carry you across the mountains," I declare.

Beside me Paldon Wangpo is nodding.

Lama Tsering looks up at us, an intensity in his dark eyes I have seen only on rare occasions.

"Very well," he tells us finally. "You can come. But there is one very important condition I have to tell you about."

•••

Moments later we are leaving his room for our own, having promised to return very quickly. As I make my way through the turmoil in the corridor outside I can hardly believe the condition that Lama Tsering has just related. This is, without question, the worst day in the existence of Zheng-po, but paradoxically for me it is the day I have found my true purpose. My vocation. The reason I have been drawn to the Dharma.

Opening my door, I look around the small room that has been my world for the past ten years: the wooden meditation box, three feet square; the straw mattress on the baked-earth floor; my change of robes and toiletry bag, the two belongings monks are allowed at Zheng-po.

It is hard to believe that I will never again sit in this meditation box, never again sleep on this bed. It is even more incredible that I, Tenzin Dorje, a humble novice monk from the village of Ling, have been accorded one of the rarest privileges of Zheng-po and of our entire lineage. For together with Paldon Wangpo, and under the guidance of my kind and holy teacher, we are to undertake the highest and most sacred mission of the evacuation. It means that our flight from Tibet will be much more critical, and more dangerous.

But for the first time ever, at sixteen years of age, I feel in my heart that I have a special part to play.

My time has come.

# Chapter One

## *Matt Lester*

***Imperial Science Institute—London***
April 2007

I'M SITTING IN THE CRAMPED CUBBY-HOLE THAT PASSES FOR MY OFFICE, late on an overcast Friday afternoon, when my whole world changes.

"Harry wants to see you in his office," Pauline Drake, tall, angular and not-to-be-messed with, appears around the door frame two feet away. She looks pointedly at the telephone, which I've taken off its cradle, before meeting my eyes with a look of droll disapproval. "Right away."

I glance over the paperwork strewn across my desk. It's the last Friday of the month, which means that all timesheets have to be in by five. As research manager for Nanobot, it's my job to collate team activities, and I take pride in the fact that I've never missed a deadline.

But it's unusual for Harry to dispatch his formidable secretary down from the third floor. Something must be up.

A short while later I'm getting out from behind my desk. It's not a straightforward maneuver. You have to rise from the chair at forty-five degrees to avoid hitting the shelves directly above, before squeezing, one leg at a time, through the narrow gap between desk and filing cabinet. Then there's the walk through a rabbit's warren of corridors and up four flights of a narrow, wooden staircase with its unyielding aroma of industrial disinfectant and wet dog hair.

As I make my way across the open plan section of the third floor, I'm aware of people staring and talking under their breath. When I make eye contact with a couple of the HR people they glance away, embarrassed.

Something's definitely up.

To get to the corner office, I first have to pass through the anteroom where Pauline has returned to work noiselessly at her computer. She nods towards Harry's door. Unusually, it is closed. Even more unusually, an unfamiliar hush has descended on his office, instead of the usual orchestral blast.

When I arrive, it's to find Harry standing, staring out the window at his less-than-impressive view over the tangled gray sprawl of railway lines converging on King's Cross station. Arms folded and strangely withdrawn, I get the impression he's been waiting especially for me.

As I appear he gestures, silently, to a chair across from his desk.

Harry Saddler is the very model of the mad professor, with a few non-standard eccentricities thrown in for good measure. Mid-fifties, bespectacled, with a shock of spiky, gray hair, in his time he's been an award-winning researcher. More recent circumstances have also forced him to become an expert in the area of public-private partnerships. It was he who saved the centuries-old institute, and all our jobs, by completing a deal with Acellerate, a Los Angeles-based biotech incubator, just over a year ago.

"A short while ago I had a call from L.A. with the news I've been half-expecting for the past twelve months," he tells me, his expression unusually serious. "Acellerate has finished their review of our research projects. They like Nanobot," he brushes fallen cigarette ash off his lapel. "They *really* like Nanobot. So much that they want to move the whole kit and caboodle to California. And as the program originator and research manager, they want you there, too."

The news takes me completely by surprise. Sure, there've been visitors from the States during the past year and earnest talk of information exchange, but I never expected the deal with Acellerate to have such direct, personal impact. Or to be so sudden.

"They're moving very quickly on this," continues Harry. "They want you there in six weeks ideally. Definitely eight. Blakely is taking a personal interest in the program."

"Eight weeks?" I'm finding this overwhelming. "Why do I have to move to California at all? Can't they invest in what we're doing over here?"

Harry shakes his head in weary resignation. "You've seen the new shareholder structure," he says. "As much as Acellerate talks about respecting our independence, the reality is that they hold a controlling interest. They call the shots. They can strip what they like out of the institute and there's really not a lot we can do to stop them."

I'm not thinking about Acellerate. I'm thinking about my fiancée, Isabella.

Harry mistakes the cause of my concern. "If you look at what's happened to the other research programs Acellerate has taken to L.A.," he reassures me, "they've gone stratospheric." Pausing, he regards me more closely for a long while before querying in a low voice, "Isabella?"

"Exactly."

"She'll go with you!"

"It's not that simple. She's only just been promoted. And you know how close she is to her family." I glance away from him to the where a commuter train is chugging slowly into the station.

Harry and I go way back and he knows a lot about Isabella and me—he's been there since the beginning. But the main problem with Isabella leaving London is something that's only happened very recently. Something I haven't told him about. The truth is, Isabella and I are still getting to grips with the enormity of the news ourselves.

"A girl like her," Harry has met her at institute functions over the years, "she'll get a job like that in Los Angeles," he snaps his fingers. "And you'll be giving her family a good excuse to visit Disneyland."

As always, Harry is trying to focus on the positive. I understand, and I'm all the more appreciative because I know how hard this must be for him. Nanobot has always been one of his favorites. It was Harry who brought me into the institute when he discovered the subject of my master's thesis. Harry nurtured the program through its early stages. He and I enjoy a close relationship—more than my boss, he's also my mentor and confidant. Now, just as the program's starting to get interesting, he's having it taken off him. What's more, who's to say it will end with Nanobot? It seems that Acellerate can cherry-pick whatever they like from the institute and leave Harry with all the leftovers. Small wonder he's in no mood for the Three Tenors.

"Try to see this as the opportunity that it is," he tells me. "With Acellerate behind you, you can ramp up the program way beyond what we can afford here. You could get to prototype stage in two to three years instead of seven or eight. The sky really is the limit."

I'm watching the fingers of his right hand rapping the desk.

"You'll be working at the heart of nanotech development for one of the best-funded scientific institutes on earth. Plus you can catch a suntan."

I look up, eyebrows raised. Tanning is not a subject in which I've ever had an interest. As Harry well knows.

"Think of it as a great adventure!"

His phone rings, and we hear Pauline answering it outside. Evidently Harry has told her we aren't to be disturbed—something he's never done before.

There's another pause before I finally say, "I guess whatever way you package it, I don't have much choice do I? I mean, Acellerate isn't going to leave the program in London just because of Isabella and me."

Harry regards me significantly, "Of all the programs we're running, yours is the most likely to make the most revolutionary impact. You're the first cab off the rank, Matt. It's flattering that Acellerate is so keen to take you off us."

"It's a bit sudden, that's all," I'm nodding. "I mean, ten minutes ago, my main concern was getting the time sheets in."

Harry regards me with a look of benevolent expectation.

"I'll have to get used to the idea."

"Good."

"*And* speak to Isabella."

"Of course." Harry reaches into a desk drawer, takes out a large white envelope which he hands me across the desk.

"Before you make up your mind, you might like to study the terms and conditions," he says.

A short while later I'm heading back to my office in a daze. Not only is Harry's announcement life-changing, the conditions of my appointment are way beyond anything I could have imagined. Almost too much to believe.

As I return through HR, I'm so preoccupied I don't notice anyone. Even the reek of the stairs passes me by. I'm trying to get my head around the paradox that this is terrible news for the Imperial Science Institute, but an amazing opportunity for me. It's even more confounding that Isabella is about to be upset by what is an opportunity for me beyond my wildest dreams.

I have to speak to Isabella.

CPSIA information can be obtained
at www.ICGtesting.com
Printed in the USA
LVHW042302131020
668666LV00004B/288

9 780648 866527